DOVECOTE

ANNE BRITTING OLESON

DOVECOTE

BInk *Bink Books*
Bedazzled Ink Publishing Company • Fairfield, California

978-1-945805-38-7 paperback

Cover Design
by

DESIGNS

F
Oleson

Bink Books
a division of
Bedazzled Ink Publishing, LLC
Fairfield, California
http://www.bedazzledink.com

2018/01 Am

For Julia Hawkes-Moore, who sees ghosts, and possibly the future.

Special thanks to the Hewnoaks Artist Colony for the residency which enabled me to work on this novel.

Part I
Blue Door

1

GWYNNETH APPROACHED THE blue door, key in hand. On the stoop before it, a small earthenware pot was tipped on its side, the dry friable soil spilling out onto the stone, the unrecognizable plant dead and spindly. A sudden shiver wracked her, and she glanced around hurriedly. A dead plant on the step of a dead woman's house. Why hadn't it been cleaned off, taken care of? In her exhausted state, she was petty. Peevish.

A cold pelt of rain had her ducking forward on the tiny stone terrace, shoving the key into the lock. At least this had been oiled recently. The key turned easily, and with one last look down into Eyewell Lane, where the cab had disappeared, she put her shoulder to the door and bumped her suitcase inside.

Inside, she found the front entryway, this late in the afternoon, to be dark and cold. Unwelcoming. She shook herself. *Don't be stupid. It's just a house.* A faint scent of beeswax and lavender floated on the air. She left the suitcase behind, moving warily, a hand to the wall. To the left, a door leading into a room that ran the length of the cottage. Her footsteps were hushed on the worn carpet. She explored the wall for a moment before she realized there was no switch. The fading light falling from the single window to the front of the room didn't reach far inside, but was enough to show her the lamp on the table beneath it. Other lamps, beside two chairs at the opposite side of the room. In the center, a dining table surrounded by four carved-back chairs. She moved and was startled until she realized that the motion on the far side of the room was only her reflection in a heavy-framed mirror. Slowly she backed out and turned to the right hand doorway.

Here was the sitting room. Two more arm chairs, one of them wing-backed, faced a Queen Anne sofa. To her left, a bookshelf, atop which a steadily ticking clock reposed. A wood-burning stove in a low stone arch took up the far wall. Kitty-corner to that, the door, which should lead to the kitchen—or so she surmised, anyway—and Gwynn made her way around the sofa toward it. The carpet here was less worn, and her footsteps made no sound. The kitchen door was closed, and she put a hand to it, suddenly cautious again, suddenly nervous. She pushed the door open. No one was there. *Of course there was no one there.* The appliances stared back at her blindly. This room had a small window to the front, but this late in the day, this late in the season, very little light came in anyway. A wall switch to her right gave life to an overhead light, and the room sprang up, bright, newly scrubbed.

A tea tray stood near the polished stove top, an electric kettle, flex cord wound loosely, next to it. Gwynn crossed the tiled floor for a closer look. All set save the milk. She opened the refrigerator to find an unopened pint, and a pan of what revealed itself to be, when she lifted the cover, lasagna.

A welcome of sorts. Gwynn closed the refrigerator, then unwound the cord and plugged it in. She wondered whether she had her great-aunt's solicitor to thank for this. Or the cleaning lady—also her great-aunt's—he'd kept on to make the cottage presentable for her.

Either way, when the kettle clicked off, she made the tea and carried the tray back into the sitting room to have a cup, and to consider her next steps.

THE SOLICITOR'S FIRM. Simms and Son. The particular Mr. Simms she had spoken to earlier today in his office had to be the son, as he couldn't have been much older than she; and any son *he* had couldn't have been old enough to have been called to the bar—couldn't have been old enough to get into a bar, come to think of it. Sitting across from him, she had smirked to herself, watching his long-fingered hands sift through a sheaf of papers as he had spoken.

"Mrs. Chelton was adamant," he had said, shaking his head, his tone mournful as he mouthed her great-aunt's name. "You were to be the heir."

"But there are others," she had protested once again. Some distant cousins: she knew of them, though she did not know them. She didn't even think she knew their names. *Your English cousins,* her mother had always called them in passing, when anyone had mentioned them.

"You were to be the heir," the solicitor had repeated. He had held out first one page for her to sign, then another. His glasses pushed up unto the bridge of his nose, he had peered at her. "Perhaps she thought you might be the one relative who would live in the house. The one who wouldn't sell up. At least not immediately."

It might have been a question.

"We'll have to see," she had said cautiously.

When they had finished the formalities, she had risen, clutching the folder of documents to her chest. Mr. Simms had stood as well, had come around his great ark of a desk to hold out his hand. "You are still intent upon staying at the cottage this evening, at least?"

Gwynn had nodded. "For a few days, yes."

A nod in answer. "So you had said." He had turned back, jotted something on a square of paper, then handed it to her. "This is the telephone number of Mary Tennant, whom I asked to clean after we spoke last week. She was formerly Mrs. Chelton's housekeeper, and can answer many of your questions about the cottage, I expect."

Mary Tennant. Gwynn now dug the paper from the inner pocket of her purse. She'd give the housekeeper a call in the morning.

FOR NOW SHE uncovered the lasagna pan and slipped it into the oven, then hit the switch to heat the water for more tea. While she waited, she climbed the stairs to investigate the bedrooms. To the left of the narrow landing, the bigger bedroom had the flowered duvet turned down and the pillows plumped; Mary Tennant again, she assumed—that woman must have decided that the new mistress of Gull Cottage should sleep in the master bedroom. Gwynn left the bedside lamp on, then looked in at the smaller bedroom and the bath. Both were tidy and ready. She had dragged the suitcase upstairs behind her to the landing, and now she shoved it into the room she guessed she'd be occupying until she herself decided otherwise.

Downstairs the tea water was boiling. She rinsed the teapot, remembering that, if she was going to be a good English person like her grandmother Lucy, she needed to dump that and fill the pot again. She had done it wrong the first time. *Warming the pot,* she vaguely remembered her grandmother saying, suiting action to words. Gwynn wished now that she'd paid more attention to the old woman, who had died when Gwynn was barely in her teens. Carefully she made another pot of tea, then refilled the creamer, and returned to the sitting room.

Gwynn seated herself again in the chintz-covered wing-backed chair to pour the steaming tea and realized how chilly it was. She threw a glance at the wood-burning stove, remarkably clean and black. Next to it, a basket for logs: empty. Something the charwoman had forgotten.

There was a woodshed at the side of the cottage, she remembered the solicitor saying; but the night had fallen rather quickly, and she didn't think she could bring herself to explore further, even in search of wood and possible heat. Tomorrow would be good enough for that; for tonight, she would have some dinner, then crawl under the thick duvet upstairs.

Decision made, she returned to the kitchen at the summons of the timer. As she bent to pull the warmed pan from the oven, she heard the front door. Just a snick, as though someone were closing it gently. She straightened quickly, listening. Nothing further. She shook her head: she was just unused to the cottage. *Imagining things.* She reached into the cupboard for a plate, then searched until she found silver. As she was closing the drawer, she heard the steps on the stairs.

THERE WAS NO one else in the house. No one upstairs, no one in any of the other rooms. The front door was locked, and she checked the kitchen door as well, just to be certain. Also locked. She left all the lights on, looking over her shoulder frequently as she ate her dinner at the coffee table before the sofa. There was a television in the corner— surprisingly new, considering the previous owner—and she turned it on. She flipped through channels until she stumbled upon a replay of *Qi* on Dave, letting Stephen Fry keep her company. There was no one in the cottage with her; of course there was no one else there. She was just tired—overtired—having come all this way out of London by train this morning, having met for the better part of the afternoon with the solicitor. *Just imagining things.* Like she had done all those years ago, after Richard's death.

When the credits rolled, she brought the dirty dishes to the sink for the morning and took herself upstairs to bed. After checking the doors one more time.

2

THE TELEPHONE RANG promptly at nine the next morning, just as the mantle clock was chiming that last note—almost as though the caller had been watching that clock, or one synchronized to it, carefully. Gwynn staggered down the stairs, clutching the rail with one hand while wiping her eyes with the other; she felt drugged, and thought she might have had bad dreams, but they were all confused and incoherent. *Jet lag,* she told herself, following the sound of the ringing into the sitting room, to the book shelf at the side wall. The phone sat in its charging base on a hand-stitched runner.

"Mrs. Forest?" The voice was business-like, no-nonsense. "Mary Tennant here. I was Mrs. Chelton's char?"

"Yes. Yes, hello." Gwynn stifled a yawn. "I'm sorry. I'm still not quite with it this morning. I've got you to thank for the spotless house and the wonderful dinner last night, haven't I?"

"Yes. Was it all right, then?" Without waiting for an answer, Mary Tennant continued. "Mrs. Forest, I've still got the key Mr. Simms gave me, the key to your cottage. I wonder if I might drop it by later this morning, if that would be convenient?"

"Of course. And—" The decision seemed already to be made, as though she'd dreamed of it in the night. "I'd like to discuss the possibility of hiring you for a few mornings a week, when you come by. Would that be all right?"

Mary Tennant's brisk voice softened over the line, but only barely. "That will be fine. Would ten suit?"

That gave Gwynn an hour to shower and dress and clean up the mess she'd made in the kitchen; one could hardly present oneself or one's house to a prospective cleaning lady at anything less than spotless. Judging from the precise timing of the call, Mary Tennant's knock on the door would no doubt come at precisely ten by the ringing of the clock on the book case. Gwynn rushed upstairs, rifled the contents of her suitcase in search of clean clothes, and hurried into the bath. She came downstairs some half an hour later, hair wet but combed, and turned her focus to washing up the dirty dishes she'd left in the sink.

The weak morning sun dappled the kitchen tiles through the starched curtains. After putting the last of the tea things away, Gwynn unlocked the rear door to look out into the garden and get a breath of air. She stepped out onto the stoop and the mess of overgrowth surprised her.

The brambles had grown up in the rear garden, encroaching on the small square of scruffy grass. Gwynn froze at the kitchen door, feeling the malevolence, branches creeping ever closer, bearing their small sharp knives. A garden whose mistress must have lost hope in the end, must have given up the fight. She recognized the feeling. Above, the thick sky was pressing down, bruisy dark clouds fending off the sun: all in league with the thorny growth. If she had any thought to escape the claustrophobia of the cottage by stepping outside, she had been sorely mistaken. This garden was a jungle, angry and aggressive.

Yet she could see, some yards away, a gate in the high stone wall which surrounded the garden, the heavy planks weathered and mossy. She was drawn to it. The brambles caught at her jeans as she forced her way through; she wished, as thorns tore at the skin of her hands, that she had gloves. An iron latch, rusty and black, held the gate closed. She pushed forward, grasped it: nothing. The latch refused to open, the gate standing fast, guarding the exit through the crumbling wall. She leaned back, looked upward. Ivy crept over the stones, displacing the mortar in spots. The tree branches beyond, skeletal and bare, whispered and dripped. She pulled at the latch again. Again, nothing.

From the open door, the faint chimes of the mantle clock came to her. She turned quickly back to the house.

"IS THIS YOUR plant?" The woman held the pot, with its dead contents, gingerly, eying it with distaste. "No, of course it isn't." She frowned, set the pot at the edge of the terrace. "I don't know how such a thing came to be here."

Mary Tennant might have been forty-five, might have been sixty-five. Her face was stern but unlined, her hair gray but held back by an Alice band. She wore a short black coat over a flowered dress, and this coat she deigned to unbutton before she sat on the sofa, her square bag firmly on her lap. She looked uncomfortable sitting, and her eyes darted back and forth, as though listing things she needed to be doing instead of lazing about. Gwynn felt guilty, looking around the room as well, searching out things she might have disturbed since the char's last going-over.

Mrs. Tennant had a small notebook out now, and with a blue pen, she tapped a page. "I used to give Mrs. Charlton two hours, three mornings a week."

Gwynn nodded. "I'd appreciate your doing the same for me while I'm here."

"You'll be living here?"

Gwynn looked out the front window at the roofline of the pub across the way. A single seagull stood at attention on the ridgepole. "I don't know. I've just come to see about the place; I don't have any firm long-term plans as of yet."

The pen scratched on the rough paper of the little notebook. Mrs. Tennant wrote, squinted fiercely at what she had written, wrote some more. Wearing reading glasses was apparently something simply not done. "I've written you in, then, for eight to ten, Monday, Wednesday, and Friday." She looked up. "I'll keep the key, if you don't mind. Now— what about cooking? Will you need me to do any of that? Mrs. Chelton didn't require that, though I would have been willing." For a moment a shadow crossed the stern features, but then was gone. Gwynn wondered if perhaps she had imagined it.

"I'll cook for myself, thanks," Gwynn said. "But perhaps you could tell me where the nearest market is? The one you use yourself. I'll need to stock up on the staples."

Mrs. Tennant nodded. "I've got to go myself later this afternoon. Perhaps I could call for you and we could go together."

For a moment Gwynn felt as though she were in the presence of a particularly demanding schoolteacher, one who would show her the correct way to do things before allowing her to try on her own.

"Thank you," she said meekly. "I would like that."

Mrs. Tennant got to her feet, snapping her black bag shut on the little scheduling notebook. "Then I'll see you this afternoon, about three, after I get done with the Condons'." Her smile was stiff, as though she didn't bring it out all that often. "And I'll see you again tomorrow morning at eight."

Gwynn, too, stood, and walked her out to the front door.

Hand on knob, Mrs. Tennant turned back. "Is there anything else I can help with in the meantime? You have enough lasagna left for lunch, I expect."

Probably for the next three lunches. People of Mary Tennant's acquaintance obviously ate heartily.

"I do," Gwynn said. "Thank you. It's delicious. But—" She glanced back into the sitting room at the empty basket near the wood stove. "Firewood?"

"Ah." The door was open on the gray morning. "Of course. "I'll make sure you have some by this afternoon as well." Mrs. Tennant looked up at the sky. "Cold's drawing on." She shook her head. "It always does." Then she was clicking down to the street in her sensible shoes, bearing the dead plant away.

3

FIGHTING DOWN A quick stab of anxiety, Gwynn opened the door to a stranger, who had, having knocked, turned away to look down into Eyewell Lane, beyond the pub to the empty call box at the corner. "Yes?"

"Forest? Mrs. Forest?" he asked, turning back slowly. His grey gaze was startling, steady.

"Yes?" she repeated.

He jerked a thumb over his shoulder. "Wood."

Down in the street, a battered work truck idled, pulled halfway off the road. The bed was laden with firewood, a barrow strapped to the top of the load.

"That was quick," she said, surprised. "I just mentioned to Mrs. Tennant about getting some in this morning." She frowned, her eyes flitting from the truck to the tall man on the stoop. "But somehow I thought—her husband—"

He shrugged. "Bert's too old for that sort of thing." His voice was low, unapologetic, as he delivered this doom upon the absent Mr. Tennant. "Moore. Colin. I used to do wood for Mrs. Chelton."

"My great-aunt," Gwynn said, and then didn't know why she felt the sudden compulsion to justify her presence in the cottage to this stranger.

"Your great-aunt," he repeated, as though fully cognizant of her defensiveness. "You'll want the shed filled, then? It's just about empty."

Fleetingly, she wondered what had happened to the last of the wood. Surely her great-aunt had not used it all up, planning her death that carefully? A morbid thought, that, unbidden and ugly. Once more her eyes went to the full-laden work truck. "Yes. Thank you." Then, remembering herself, "Can I give you a cup of coffee before you start?"

He shook his head. His dark hair, she saw, was graying at the temples. "I'd best just get it done. I've a few more deliveries before dark." He took a step away, pulling on a pair of heavy work gloves, then turned. "Maybe after, then?"

She nodded.

GWYNN HAD NEVER used a French press, and now stood looking at it in perplexity.

She had found the coffee and the grinder, but had no idea where to go from there. She set the tray, then again cursed herself at not having the solicitor make sure there was Internet laid on; she could have at least then looked up the process. She'd have to call and get that taken care of. Hands on hips, she glared at the press. The sound of Colin Moore's barrow wheeling around the side of the cottage grew stronger, only to be replaced by a measured series of thunks as he emptied the wood into the shed. She'd offered the man coffee and now couldn't make it. What kind of failure was she?

There was no help for it. When he next wheeled a load up the drive from the street, she called out to him from the front doorway. "Can we do tea instead?"

He set the barrow down, lifted a piece of wood in each hand. "You don't have coffee? Leah down at the shops has some, next time you're down in the village."

She felt her face warm. "I have the coffee. I just don't know how to use the press."

Colin stepped out of view into the shed and just as quickly emerged empty-handed. He tripped off the gloves and handed them to her at the door. "Let me must wash my hands and I'll start it for you."

Feeling somewhat stupid, she pulled the gloves onto her own hands—they were way too big—and approached the barrow. The wood was small, cut and split as if expressly for the stove in the sitting room; it was so dry that its light color was fading to gray. She grabbed a couple of pieces, took them into the low shed, returned for more. After a moment Colin reappeared, letting the front door swing shut behind him.

"Coffee's brewing now," he said.

She nodded, carrying another armload into the shed. There was something zen in the movement, something soothing.

He watched for only a moment before he loaded up his own arms, waiting for her to emerge before he entered. He had to duck.

"You want your gloves back?" she asked.

Colin Moore shook his head, his gray gaze even on her face. "No. You wear them."

When the shed was filled, Colin lifted the barrow back onto the remainder of the truckload and tied it down. Gwynn handed him his work gloves, and he tossed them through the open window into the cab.

"If you want to pour the coffee, I'll get the money," she offered.

Over lunch, she had decided to make the dining room her studio office. Now, when she returned from it with the notes, she found he had carried the tray through from the kitchen to set it on the low table before the sitting room sofa. Then he bent to the stove, laying paper, kindling, and a small bit of firewood. In a moment the crackling of the hungry flames and the ticking of the warming stove pipe filled the room.

"Milk?" Gwynn asked. "Sugar?"

"Both," he said, straightening. "For you, too, most likely—I forgot the coffee while we were stacking the wood, and it's brewed probably until it's Turkish."

She handed him a mug, then fixed one for herself. Colin was right—the coffee was strong, and bitter, but hot and fortifying. She took the wing-backed chair across from the sofa, her own mug cradled in both hands. Like Mary, he sat, but on the edge of the sofa cushion, as if prepared for flight. Gwynn wasn't sure why she thought that; it wasn't that he seemed nervous—far from it. Rather, he seemed impatient, as though he had somewhere to get to, something else to take care of. There was an energy that felt held in check. Well, he did have the rest of the firewood in the back of the work truck; he had told her, too, that he had another delivery to make.

They drank in silence for a few moments.

"You haven't changed anything here," he said finally.

Gwynn shrugged. "I've been here one day. I came with a suitcase."

He nodded.

They drank.

Gwynn felt uncomfortable in the silence, but she felt incapable of witty conversation. At last she said, "You knew my great-aunt." It was a statement, not a question. He'd delivered wood to the old woman. He'd known where the kitchen was. He was familiar enough with the furnishings that he would recognize change, apparently.

Still, Colin took a moment to answer. "As well as anyone could, I suppose." He took a long drink from his mug. "She didn't like people."

This assessment surprised her in its baldness. She stared across the table at him, but he was examining his coffee as though the world depended upon it.

"She liked you," Gwynn objected.

He shook his head. "No. But I didn't pay much attention to that." His smile was more of a grimace. "She was old. I delivered the wood. She paid me. After a while, when I saw something needing doing, I did it. She didn't like it. But she could hardly argue, because she couldn't do some things herself."

Gwen's eyes traveled around the sitting room; she wondered what other *things* he might have done for her great-aunt. In an older cottage like this, it might have been anything. Everything.

"I was surprised," she said slowly, watching him, "that she willed me this house."

He looked up, raised a questioning eyebrow.

"We never met," she explained. "Never spoke on the telephone. Never exchanged Christmas cards."

"Odd."

Gwynn poured more coffee into her mug for something to do, took a sip. Quickly she reached for the milk. "It does. I knew she existed— my grandmother used to talk about her sometimes when I was a kid— but I figured, like everyone else in my family, that she had probably died long ago."

Her hand shook, and the hot coffee spilled onto her lap. She swore, set the cup down quickly, grabbed a napkin.

Colin had not moved. "All right?" he asked after she threw the crumpled cloth onto the table.

He was the most still person she thought she had ever met. Few words, few motions, much consideration. His eyes, though, were watchful, weighing—something.

She felt herself flush. "Sorry." But she wasn't sure for what she was sorry. The shaking hands, the spill, the swearing. "What do you know about her?" she asked, the words coming fast to cover up her discomfort. "My great-aunt? Surely there are other relations she might have chosen to leave the house to." She considered picking up the coffee mug again, but decided against it, and clasped her hands together between her knees instead. "I feel sort of guilty about this."

Another admission she had not meant to make. Damn. It had to be the stillness which forced her to let these things escape. Which made her say these things to a perfect stranger. She didn't make small talk with people, hadn't for years. Easier that way.

Colin considered. "There were others. Paul Stokes, publican across at The Stolen Child—he's one. Grandson of her older brother. No one any closer than you. She didn't have children."

"No?"

"Husband died young. She never married again."

Still he was watching her.

Gwynn shivered. Cold? She got up quickly, moved to the stove to check the fire. It was still burning well, but she put another log into the firebox anyway.

Her husband died young. And her name was Gwynneth.

And I'm living in your house, Gwynn thought.

She held her shaking hands out to the fire, trying to warm them.

Behind her, Colin was collecting the coffee things; without speaking, he took the tray back through the kitchen. When he returned, he cast her a single glance.

"I've got to get this wood over to the Flynns'," he said.

He let himself out.

4

"MRS. TENNANT—" GWYNN was hesitant.

"Mary, now. I've told you that, Mrs. Forest."

"Gwynn, then."

They were walking side-by-side along the pavement to the Co-op, to pick up staples for the house, Mary with an old-fashioned string bag over her arm, fat and swinging with her black purse. She wore her short black coat over her twinset—having changed out of her work dress—and sensible shoes.

"What is it, then, Gwynn?" she asked, sounding uncomfortable but determined.

Even with the prodding, Gwynn was unsure how to ask. "First, thanks for getting Colin Moore for me."

Mary nodded. "He's a good man. Brought the firewood right over, I expect."

"He did." They rounded the corner and headed up toward the B-road. "It made all the difference in the world this afternoon. The whole cottage is so much more comfortable with the fire in the stove."

Mary looked her, her dark head cocked to the side. "But—? There's something else. Speak your mind." Her brows were knitted, as though she expected some criticism. Of Colin Moore? Why, if he was such a good man?

A pillar box appeared on their right. Mary stopped, snapped open her purse, and withdrew two envelopes, which she dropped through the slot before continuing.

"He said—Colin Moore said—that my great-aunt didn't like anyone."

Mary visibly relaxed. Her grimace was very much like Colin's had been earlier. "Oh, I don't know. He's more than likely right about that."

"He said she had no children, never married again after her husband died."

They had reached the Co-op lot. "Get us a trolley, if you like," Mary said, pointing to the serried rows in a rack to the side. "Put a pound in the slot."

Inside, they strolled down the aisle examining the vegetables. Gwynn frowned at the metrics. Mary shook her head sadly at the state of the produce.

"Get a few things," she advised. "Wait for the rest until market on Thursday."

She examined the beetroot, selected a bunch. Gwynn did as well, and then chose a couple of potatoes. When she paused beside the peas, Mary again shook her head; and Gwynn withdrew her hand.

"You seem to have got quite a lot out of Colin," Mary finally said, turning into the next aisle. "A man of few words, that one."

No more than he got out of me, Gwynn wanted to say, but didn't. "You know him well?"

"Oh, heavens, yes. Cousin to my husband, he is." Mary reached purposefully for a package on the shelf, then changed her mind and chose a different brand.

Gwynn pushed the trolley slowly; it had a recalcitrant wheel. Even in another country, she managed to choose the cart with the wheel that didn't turn properly.

"More like son of my husband's cousin." Mary shrugged. "All related one way or another around here. More than likely you're some sort of cousin to us, too, if we went far enough back up the family tree."

They'd have to climb back up to her grandmother, who'd run off with a pilot once the war was over, straight across the Atlantic Ocean, never to return. And her grandmother's older sister, and in turn, their older brother. The all had parents, aunts, uncles, cousins. No doubt Mary Tennant was right. No doubt the village of strangers she'd found herself in was actually a village of family. The thought shook Gwynn again, another shock in a series. Maybe she really wasn't alone in the world. Maybe there were others. Maybe this was a place where she could fit in.

"You look as though someone'd walked over your grave," Mary said, placing a package of Bird's custard mix in the trolley.

"No," Gwynn replied slowly. "No, I'm not dead yet."

She didn't know why she said that.

UPON THEIR RETURN to the cottage, Mary stiffly accepted the offer of a cup of tea.

"Tell me more about my great-aunt," Gwynn said, leaning against the door frame of the sitting room; Mary was again seated uncomfortably on the sofa, back straight, hands crossed over the handle of her purse. "Gwynn." The name, her name—their name—tasted odd in her mouth. "Colin Moore said she didn't like anyone. Not even him."

Mary did not look up, seeming to find great interest in the dying afternoon outside the window. "Oh, there's plenty don't care for Colin, I'm afraid. Find him stand-offish."

"That's not what I asked."

Mary sighed, and now her gaze dropped to her hands playing with the catch on her purse. She frowned and twined her fingers together. The silence between them grew and lengthened. Gwynn fought the urge to prod further, in an attempt to emulate Colin Moore: he needed only wait to have someone spill the beans. She found herself half-smiling at the thought. No doubt people here would find her stand-offish as well. But she could wait out Mary. She was willing to wait for the answer about her great-aunt, because that answer seemed suddenly very important.

Behind her the tea water was boiling. Gwynn turned to fix the tray—what a civilized thing it was, the tea tray—then brought it out to the low table.

"Mary," she said. "Relax. Take off your coat."

Mary reluctantly undid three buttons, but stopped there. She looked poised—not for flight, but for cleaning. Had Mary ever been invited to sit down by Gwynn Chelton? *She didn't like anybody.* Somehow Gwynn didn't think her great-aunt had.

"I can't stay long," Mary protested weakly. "I've got to get home to make Mr. Tennant's tea." She pursed her lips. "We spent more time at the Co-op than I'd intended."

Gwynn shrugged, implacable. "I'll pay you extra."

Mary's eyes flashed, a spark of anger momentarily animating her expression. Gwynn kept her own face still, watching. She poured a cup of tea and handed it to Mary, who immediately looked reproachful and reached for the milk and sugar.

"You poured the tea the wrong way," she said. Another dodge.

"My great-aunt," Gwynn repeated.

"She was an angry old woman," Mary said suddenly, setting the creamer back on the tray with a decided click. "Col was right. She didn't like him. She didn't like me. If she could have done without either of us, she would have."

It was a bald statement, like Colin's, one that obviously made Mary uncomfortable. She glared across the table at Gwynn as though to challenge her.

"But you both worked for her anyway."

The look Mary cast at her now had something of the Colin-ish in it. "She paid." Then she backed down. "She always paid. She paid Colin extra when he did other things around the cottage for her—general handyman things he did in passing, when he delivered the wood." She sipped her tea cautiously. "It was as though she wanted to make sure we kept a proper distance. She didn't want our friendship. She didn't want our kindness."

"She sounds sad." Gwynn was suddenly awash with an unfamiliar kind of sorrow for the old woman she had not known, but who had left her home to someone as far away as possible without leaving it out of the family. *Never met her, never spoke to her on the telephone, never wrote.* Her great-aunt had been the stuff of myth when she had been growing up. Gwynn did not even remember her grandmother speaking of her older sister without a kind of *I wonder what she's doing now* tone of voice. As though it were impossible to find out. The sadness in her chest suddenly steeled, morphing into a hard, angry loneliness, and Gwynn caught her breath at the foreignness of the feeling. She lifted her eyes to find Mary staring at her speculatively.

"She sounds lonely," Gwynn said quickly.

Mary lowered her gaze and began to inspect the shortbread laid out on the china plate. She slowly reached a hand to take one not-quite-perfectly round cookie and bit into it, as if suspicious of some further shortcoming.

"That's how I always thought. That's why I really kept coming back, and Col, too. I lied to you when I said it was for the money. It wasn't really. Of course, Mrs. Chelton would never have admitted to any such feeling. But you can be lonely without admitting it to anyone, can't you?" Mary cocked her head, thinking through this radical thought. "Without even admitting it to yourself."

Yes, you could. You could live that way until you died.

The voice in her head didn't even sound like her own. For a moment Gwynn felt tears threatening behind her eyelids, and she squeezed her eyes shut.

5

GWYNN SPENT THE rest of the evening restlessly rearranging the dining room, trying to make it conform to her idea of a makeshift studio. Without a desk, the dining table, heavy and dark, would have to do; she pulled it out of the center of the room and closer to the front window, choosing the armed dining chair from the head of the table for her own. The other dining chairs she ranged along the wall until she could figure out what to do with them. She should have asked Mary; perhaps there was someone who would need the set? The ornately carved legs, foursquare and stocky, were enough to put her off. The room, with only the single window, was gloomy enough without the dining set's heaviness to drag it down further.

The two occasional chairs and small coffee table found their way to the rear of the room. The arrangement was highly unsatisfactory from an aesthetic point of view. Gwynn wiped her hands down her jeans and frowned. It was a workspace, that was all, until she could figure out what to do with the cottage. She'd never had a studio. All those years working in the office, all those years after art school when she'd followed Richard's star and not her own—even with the unsatisfactory lighting, this room pleased a tiny hidden place in her. A studio. To see if she could do it, come up with the whimsical drawings Belinda had requested for her book. To see if she could at least make a start as an illustrator.

Now she considered, looking down at her empty palms. She should have asked Colin Moore's help in shifting the furniture earlier. Yet he had been the one to remark upon her not changing anything in the house—in the first twenty-four hours. Would he approve? Even if he didn't, she had a feeling he wouldn't speak his thoughts. She slid into the chair at the table, where she could look out on Eyewell Lane, and wondered whether she'd moved things around now just to spite his judgment. An old boxy Volvo passed, laboring its way up the hill away from the village. A man in a red windcheater and tweed hat was walking downhill opposite; he turned into the pub doorway and let himself in. A customer? Gwynn put her chin in her hand and imagined he was her cousin. Grandson of her great-uncle, actually. Second cousin? Something like that. She wished she'd asked the solicitor for more details about other relations.

The gloomy day had segued into a gloomy evening, and she could see a vague reflection in the window glass. Her hand, her chin, her frown. If that were indeed her second cousin, she should probably make her way to the pub soon and introduce herself. *Except.* What if he felt cheated at not having inherited? Here he was, working—living? There appeared to be a flat above the pub—just across the street from the great-aunt they shared, while she had lived three-thousand-five-hundred miles away; and their great-aunt had chosen her over him. It was telling, she supposed, that he had yet to come across Eyewell Lane to introduce himself. Of course, he had a business to run, so he might just have been busy.

Somehow she didn't think so.

Gwynn stared down at the pub door, painted red and with a big gold handle, a light on either side. It was unnerving to think a cousin might be behind that door. That there were others, too—Colin Moore had used the plural—who were related to her. Once Richard had died, Gwynn had slowly grown used to the idea of being on her own, an only child of only children, the last in her family living anywhere near what had always been her home, the last one there standing. That's what had made it so easy to fly over and claim this windfall: there was no one left in Southport to hold her back, once she had learned of the cottage and her inheritance. There had been no one for years, really.

The tears surprised her. Gwynn hadn't cried out of loneliness for a long time. She hadn't cried for Richard in years. Slowly she lowered her face into her arms on the table and let the tears come, just for a minute. It hurt, she was surprised to realize; it was raw. Still. After all this time. *Just for a minute,* she told herself, because she might be lonely, but wasn't she independent? Hadn't she come to a point where she could sell the company she and Richard had started together? Hadn't she come to the point where she could start looking for something to do with her own life that she enjoyed? *Hadn't she?* But in this minute, dislocated and disjointed, she found herself staring down a dark tunnel of empty years leading to the future. At the loneliness of knowing there was no one else who cared. Much as, she suddenly knew, her great-aunt had felt.

Gwynn let herself cry just a little bit longer, then ordered herself back to practicality. She lifted her head, hoping no one in the street below the window had witnessed her brief breakdown. She looked to the glass, wiping her eyes quickly when she thought she was seeing double: two vague reflections. Her own, white-faced, teary-eyed—and the other standing behind her, white-haired, a shimmering image of an old woman who lifted a hand, then was gone.

6

THE BELL OVER the shop door tinkled as she entered. Behind the counter, the proprietress—Leah, Colin Moore had called her—looked up and smiled. It seemed the first real smile Gwynn had seen in days. Her own face felt stiff when she smiled in return.

"What do you need, love?"

Leah looked like someone's mother—or at least, how one would hope a mother would look. Her dark hair was held back from her round face with clips; her cheeks were flushed. Yet she couldn't have been all that much older than Gwynn.

"I've got a gate latch that's rusted shut," Gwynn said. "I don't know if you've got some penetrating oil or something that would loosen it up."

Leah frowned for a moment in thought, then pushed back her stool from the counter and stood. "I think out here." She was wearing a flowered bib apron, but Gwynn saw when she stood that she was wearing jeans. Still, she absolutely *bustled* around the counter and toward the back. Gwynn followed through a room with racks of towels and hangers of aprons very much like the one the woman wore. Another room held shelves of light bulbs and fixtures. There seemed no logical order, and yet the woman seemed to know exactly where she was headed, along the narrow passage, deeper and deeper into the building. Finally she ducked through a low doorway and stopped so quickly Gwynn nearly ran into her. "Here." She reached up onto a shelf to the left and pulled down a small can. "You're in luck. I think this is the only one left. I'll have to have Harvard order some more." Again the smile. "Would there be anything else today?"

Gwynn shook her head. "I don't think so."

"You're in Gull Cottage over on Eyewell Lane now, aren't you?" Leah asked over her shoulder as they returned through the labyrinth to the front counter. "Gwynneth Chelton's old place? How're you finding it?"

"Yes," Gwynn answered, suddenly wary. "It's—interesting."

Leah shot back an openly curious look. "You're on your own?"

They reached the counter. Leah, surprisingly, wrote out a receipt by hand on a block. She made change from a drawer under the bench, then dropped the can of oil into a small paper bag. She seemed not to notice how long Gwynn took to answer, so intent was she upon the sale, a tiny frown between her dark brows. "Harvard just mentioned he'd seen all the lights on, upstairs and down, the other night. Thought you might be throwing a party." She laughed, handing Gwynn the bag, though there was more than a hint of question in her tone.

Gwynn's smile was again tight, making her feel her face was not her own. "No, it's just me."

Leah shrugged, still cheerful, still curious. It was like playing chess. "Well, if you need anything more, you stop in." She waved her hands at the wild array around her. "We've got some of everything."

GWYNN STUFFED THE paper bag and receipt into the cold stove on the way through to the back garden. The dead leaves whispered wetly underfoot as she forced her way through the brambles, and the closer she came to the wall, the darker the day seemed to grow. She shivered, wishing she'd worn a heavier jacket, wondering if the sun ever fell at the rear of the cottage. Those brambles she had shoved aside on her previous trip had sprung back as though insulted that she would wish to tame them. Determined, she pushed her way to the gate, still black and stubborn; she ignored the scratching at her legs and arms.

Apply liberally. Allow to work into rusted metal.

Gwynn opened the nozzle, made a test squirt, and then worked the point down into the innards of the latch. The rusted metal darkened with the spread of the oil. After a moment's consideration, she squirted some into the gate's two equally rusted hinges as well. From somewhere beyond the high wall came a sudden rustle of wings, a chorus of cooing. Doves? She wasn't sure. The air was still and cold and wet; with her free hand, she rubbed her arm, trying vainly to warm herself. It was no use: the dampness which had rusted the metal had worked its way into her bones.

She waited impatiently for a few minutes, then grasped the latch and pulled it. Nothing. It did not move. She shoved the flat can into her back pocket and used both hands. Still nothing.

This was getting ridiculous. Gwynn jerked the can out again and squirted the remainder of the oil all over and into the latch, cursing it for the foul thing it was. The smell of the oil worked its way into her nose, overlaying the scent of wet leaves and mold and old, wet wood. Probably she would have to leave it overnight, and the thought of having to be that much more patient infuriated her.

The sound of the doves grew louder, as though an entire flock roosted just on the other side of the wall. She looked up at the ivy, wishing it were possible to see over. One more glance at the latch—she wouldn't touch it this time, in case she jinxed the efficacy of the oil— and she turned away, disgusted, resisting the urge to haul off and kick the damn thing.

Gwynn shoved her way back through the brambles and heard, above the crying of the doves, a soft human sobbing. She turned and gazed intently at the closed gate, to the high wall.

"Is—anyone out there?" she called after a moment.

But there was only the low cooing of birds. Nothing else. She must have imagined it.

7

GWYNN WAS UNSETTLED all afternoon at her drawing, and when the light, never strong to begin with, began to fail, she set the pencils aside and pushed back from the table. Still she remained sitting in the chair before the window, watching the streetlights bloom in the lane. The hulking stone facade of the pub across the way grew darker, the gold handle on the red door sparked by the lamps beside it. The afternoon was still gloomy, but now the daylight had bled away. All day, each time she'd looked up, it had looked like a rainy scene—but without the rain. Two men emerged from the pub's door and stood huddled under the overhang between the glowing bow windows on either side. One shook a cigarette out of a packet and offered it to the other, who waved it away. The first man lit a match and bent over it, cupping the flame in his hand. After a moment, he leaned back, pulled the cigarette from his lips, and blew a long cloud into the air, where it hung over their heads.

She watched the two take their leave from one another, one man heading up the hill, the second down toward the village.

It would be companionable, she thought wistfully, to spend an hour in the local with a friend. Talking football or the EU, perhaps. She could imagine the low murmur of voices punctuated by the occasional laugh, the clink of glass against glass. All romanticizing: she had yet to set foot inside the pub. She felt hesitant, knowing what she knew about the proprietor. A cousin. More than likely, a resentful one. She sighed.

The clock in the sitting room struck the hour.

There really was no way around it. She plucked her coat from the tree by the front door, checked to be sure she had her keys and cash, and let herself out.

THE PUB WAS very much as she had imagined it, though dingier, not quite as firelit, not quite as noisy. It was early yet, and there were only a handful of people scattered about the low heavy tables, and a couple more at the fruit machine to the right. The man she had seen the other day, *sans* cap and red jacket, had his shirtsleeves rolled up as he wiped down the bar, his backward twin in the speckled mirror behind him. He looked up as she entered and nodded shortly, as though they were acquaintances. Which, after a fashion, they were.

"What'll you have, Mrs. Forest?" he asked, tossing the bar towel aside. He was wearing reading glasses, and he dipped his head to look over them at her. His voice was not hostile, nor was it overly friendly. Just neutral. On guard.

She looked at the taps; they all advertised Bowman Ales. "What do you recommend, Mr. Stokes?" Two could play this game, she supposed—as long as she hadn't made a grievous error in guessing his identity.

Again he nodded. Acknowledgement of points to both sides.

"I'd suggest a Swift One."

"A pint, then. And have something yourself." She laid her money down and watched his large hands upend a glass and pull the tap handle.

The ale gushed out a warm light amber. Almost the color of her hair, she thought, catching a glimpse of herself in the back bar mirror. Almost the color of his, too.

"You know who I am, then," she said as he slid the pint glass across the buffed wood of the bar.

He nodded again, his eyes narrowed above the glasses. "Not hard. You've been in the village—what? Two days now? Three?"

Something told her he knew exactly how long she'd been in the village, in the cottage, down to the minute. She nodded. She recognized the beginning of a dog fight, the two of them circling warily, getting a sense of one another.

"And you know who I am." He drew himself a half, took a long drink, then wiped his sandy moustache with the back of his wrist.

"Cousins," Gwynn said. "Of a sort. I didn't even know I had any cousins until James Simms the solicitor told me I did."

"So you thought you'd just slip across and say hello."

"I did."

"You want to gloat?"

The anger burst out so swiftly and unexpectedly—violently, even—that it was like being slapped. Gwynn reeled back, staring at Paul Stokes.

"No," she gasped, catching her breath.

He tossed back the rest of his half as though it were water, then set the glass on the bar so sharply Gwynn thought it would break. She too took a long sip from her pint, rolled it around on her tongue, buying time. Perhaps she had imagined the anger. Perhaps she was just paranoid. She blinked, letting the world right itself.

"This is good," she offered weakly after a moment.

Stokes sneered at the inanity. "If that's all you can come up with." Leaning with both hands against the bar, he watched her with those narrowed eyes. They were dark, deep-set.

She willed herself to hold his gaze. Not so paranoid after all.

"Stokes. What Gwynn's having," Colin said.

Gwynn had not seen him come in; perhaps he'd been in the pub all along.

Stokes started, though, more so than she thought he might have at the request. A moment passed before she realized that Colin had used her given name; he had not once called her by it the previous afternoon, maintaining a formal distance. The name had jarred her cousin: Gwynn. The given name of their mutual great-aunt.

"If Sarah's around, come join us and sit for a minute." Colin's suggestion was firm, saying more than the words. He paid for his pint, nodded in the direction of an empty table in the rear corner. Gwynn followed him through the gauntlet of customers, the pub filling now; he heard Paul Stokes shout "Sarah!" over his shoulder before skirting the bar to join them.

Perhaps later in the evening someone would touch a match to the already-laid fire on the broad hearth beyond their corner table. Perhaps Stokes would, after he'd calmed down. Right now, though, he was too angry to do much of anything save yank the chair out and throw himself heavily into it. Gwynn felt the waves of fury rolling off him as though heat from a furnace. No fire needed. She recoiled, inching her chair a bit further away from him.

"Why are you here?" Stokes demanded. He'd abandoned his half-pint glass for a full one.

Gwynn reminded herself that she had expected the antagonism. Whether her cousin owned this pub or simply managed it, having lived with expectations of inheritance for so long and then having those expectations dashed must have been gall in his mouth.

"I told you," she said. "To meet you. I didn't know I had any relations left in the world until Mr. Simms told me about you."

"Didn't know you were taking from me, then?" Stokes didn't sound convinced. He held his glass between both hands. The dim light glinted on the sandy hair on his thick arms.

"Our great-aunt made that choice," Gwynn protested. "I had nothing to do with it. We never spoke about it." *Nor about anything else,* she thought, but that was beside the point.

"You could have refused the bequest. But you didn't."

She hated being made to feel defensive. She had always hated it. She knew, from experience, that someone who worked to make her feel that was immune to reason, so there was no point in attempting to defend herself anyway. The hole would only get deeper.

"No. I didn't." She sighed, took a sip of ale. "I'm not here to gloat." She set her glass down in the wet circle on the scuffed table.

"No? Well, I'm guessing you're not here to turn the house over to me, either." Stokes nearly spat the words. He'd taken off the reading glasses, and now turned the wire frames in his beefy hands as though he might crush them.

"Tell me why I should give you Gull Cottage." The words sounded more of a challenge than she had intended; she'd have to moderate her tone if she expected this conversation to go anywhere.

Stokes leaned toward her. "Because you were nothing to Gwynn Chelton. *Nothing.* You didn't even know her."

"But Mrs. Chelton obviously knew about *Gwynn,*" Colin said, laying heavy emphasis on the given name.

"Stay out of this, Moore," Stokes said. "It's none of your business. This is a family matter, between Mrs. Forest and me."

His voice, though low, sounded clear over the clink of glassware, the shouts of the men at the fruit machine. The rage was loud and obvious.

"You weren't here, Not when the old woman needed you. Not like I was. You're not the one who grew up here. You're not the one who looked in on the old woman, who took care of things for her when she wasn't able. You did sod all for her, and she left the entire bag to you in her will? Why's that, then? Because you two shared a name? That's just not on. You don't deserve the house. You're an incomer, taking what isn't yours—what you have no right to." Again Stokes leaned closer, so close the smell of cigarette smoke on his clothes was acrid in Gwynn's nostrils. "If you had half a shred of decency in you, you'd refuse the bequest, and let it go to relations who were closer. Relations who are deserving. Relations who were *here.*"

Again Gwynn felt the fury like a slap, and again she recoiled. It was black, powerful, and frightening. Was it right, though? Perfectly legal, the solicitor had reassured her, but was her inheritance morally right? She shook her head.

"What did you do for her?" she asked.

Gwynn thought Stokes' face grew redder at the question, but in the dim lighting she couldn't be sure.

"I was *here*. Here for her. Unlike you." He slapped a beefy hand on the worn table. "And I am contesting that will, you can be sure of it." He stood up, kicked the chair aside. "You'll be hearing from my solicitor. So don't get too comfortable over there, because you'll be out on your ear. It's only a matter of time."

With that, he wheeled away from the table, knocking over the remainder of his pint. By the time Gwynn had jerked away from the beer flooding across the wood and looked up, he had disappeared through the swinging door beside the hearth. The woman who had taken his place at the taps met her eyes for just a moment, then looked away again, quickly.

"I'LL JUST SEE you across the way," Colin said, letting the pub door close behind them on a wave of raucous laughter.

"No need."

He apparently felt no need to answer. Across the road and up the path, the front window glowed softly with lamplight. Had she left the light on? Gwynn couldn't remember. She turned abruptly to the right and headed downhill.

"What is it?" Colin asked. Hands thrust into the pockets of his heavy coat, he shortened his steps to hers.

"I need to walk that off." *Had she left the light on?* She refused to look back over her shoulder.

At the foot of the hill, the intersection. They crossed the road, followed the footpath to the estuary. The tide was just below high; the darkness smelled of brine. She leaned against the low wall, breathing deeply. Colin stood a few feet away, looking down at the water, hands still in pockets.

"That went well," she said at last.

Colin's laugh was short, sharp. "Line's drawn."

Somewhere on the other side of the estuary, a gull cried.

"I had to try." She felt close to tears. "I haven't felt that kind of anger in years. That kind of *hatred.*"

"Strong word," Colin said slowly. "It's not personal. He'd feel the same way about anyone else who had inherited." He sighed. "But you had to try."

"You knew how it was going to turn out." Biting her lip, Gwynn turned her back on the water. Back down at the intersection, the street lamp near the call box flickered.

"Known the man all my life." Colin shrugged. "People stay true."

For some reason Gwynn resisted this indictment. "But is he right? Have I taken away from someone who's more deserving? He might have had a point. I'm an interloper. He spent his life with her, as he said. Helping—"

"No. Mrs. Chelton didn't want his help any more than she wanted it from the rest of us."

"But you kept coming back—"

"And he didn't." Colin still gazed down at the tide below. Tides which remained as true as the people of his acquaintance. "Don't be fooled."

"What are you saying?"

His profile was in shadow. He tipped his head, considering. "If there's anyone more deserving, it wouldn't be him. In all the years I did work for Mrs. Chelton, I never once saw him cross the road for her. Never heard of him doing it, either." He fell silent for a moment. "If Mrs. Chelton had left the property to the one who cared for her, she would have left it to Mary Tennant, is all. If there is anyone more deserving, it's Mary. The things she did for Mrs. Chelton, without question, without thanks—she'd be the one."

Mary Tennant would be the first to say Colin Moore had been the one, Gwynn knew instinctively. Above them wisps of cloud against the night sky obscured the stars. She stared upward anyway, hoping for a glimpse of a familiar constellation. She always navigated by the stars, and right now, standing in a strange village in a strange country, she was lost.

"So Paul Stokes hasn't a case?"

Colin shook his head. "I don't think he does." *Which doesn't mean he won't try.* The words hung silently between them. Gwynn sighed and pushed away from the wall.

"I'll walk you up," Colin said.

"No need."

He laughed.

Through the intersection, up the hill, up the path to the tiny stone terrace. On the stoop before the door lay a dead dove, its eye staring blankly upwards.

8

SHE SLEPT LATE.

The morning was reaching in through the windows with long gray fingers as she turned over under the flowered duvet to see the time. She heard again the sound of the wood stove door—the sound which she knew had awakened her—and for a moment felt her breath catch. Then she remembered: Colin, his jaw hard and his eyes adamant, insisting that he would sleep on the couch.

"I don't need protecting," she had protested.

"The dove," he had said. "It's not right."

It wasn't. She had had trouble falling asleep herself, tangled up in the duvet, trying to get comfortable first on one side and then the other. And now, having slept in, well past nine in the morning, she heard her guest—her protector?—moving about downstairs. She scrambled to her feet, found her slippers, and pounded down the stairs.

It wasn't Colin; it was Mary. The extra blankets Gwynn had brought down for him were folded carefully at the end of the sofa. The fire burned warmly, extra wood in the basket beside it. Mary had set her a breakfast tray on the coffee table.

"Tea or coffee?" Mary now asked, glancing sideways at Gwynn's sweatshirt and flannel sleep pants, and her tousled hair.

Gwynn flushed, sinking down on the sofa. "Tea, I guess," she mumbled. The pillow lay on top of the pile of blankets; she picked it up and crushed it against her chest. "Thanks."

Mary bustled out and back in again; she must have had the water boiling already.

"It's not what you think," Gwynn said, letting her hair fall across her face to hide her warm cheeks as she took a sip from her teacup.

"I don't have to think anything," Mary replied tartly, gathering up the spare blankets and holding out a hand for the pillow. "He was still sleeping when I let myself in this morning. On the sofa. Downstairs. In the sitting room." She crossed to the foot of the stairs. "Fully clothed." She sounded disapproving.

AFTER SHE WASHED and dressed, Gwynn began the task of cleaning out the upstairs. Master bedroom first, with Mary's help. She opened the wardrobe upon the hangers full of dresses, dark shoes lined up in neat rows beneath them.

"Can we donate?" she asked Mary. "Is there someplace that can take these things?"

Mary nodded. "Oxfam. We can have Colin come by for them this afternoon if you like." Her look might have been arch.

She had brought boxes with her this morning, which were quickly filled. She had also carried a bin bag upstairs, and what they deemed unusable to others they tossed into it. It was warm dusty work, despite the general gloominess of the day. Mary sniffed frequently as they cleared away the remnants of Gwynn Chelton's life, though whether from the dust or mournfulness over the gradual eradication of her former employer, it was difficult to tell. Easier not to ask.

By ten, Mary had completed a vicious and thorough hoovering of the carpet, and the corners, and had taken down the curtains to bring them to the cleaners.

"Mind you stay away from the front window tonight in your nightdress. Don't give them anything more to talk about over to the Child." She nodded in the direction of the pub, and let out what might have been construed as a chuckle.

"You know about that?" Gwynn asked, mortified.

"Oh, everybody does." Mary waved it away. On the way by with the vacuum cleaner, she paused to pat Gwynn on the shoulder, much as one would a child or a puppy. "Don't even worry about it. The lines are drawn, but you're on the side of the angels." She thumped away down the stairs.

The lines are drawn. Those had been Colin's words. Shortly before they'd found the dead dove.

Gwynn's neck prickled.

IN THE AFTERNOON, she called the taxi company and asked for a ride into town. There she bought new sheets, a duvet, and cover, and some curtains—all in a lighter, colorful pattern.

She would not be that other Gwynn. She would lighten the place up.

Maybe she would take a lover.

The thought made her almost laugh aloud, handing her bank card to the sales associate.

AFTER SHE HAD made the bed, she sat on its edge and looked across the room at the empty wardrobe, the empty dresser. Even the top of the dresser had been cleaned off, divested of combs, hairpins, a hand mirror with a broken handle. Gwynn had chosen to keep the small greet metal music box, which tinkled a tune she did not recognize when she lifted the cover; it was empty, save for a single gold wedding band. She left that in there.

There had been no photographs: none in small frames or tucked into the edge of the mirror. Not even hidden away in a drawer with nightdresses and underthings. Nothing. No husband, no parents, no picture of her great-aunt as a younger woman. No wedding photo. Gwynn hadn't really thought about it as they worked, so intent had she been on the task she shared with Mary. Now, considering, it seemed odd. When there were no photographs, it was almost as though there had been no life. Again Gwynn was struck by the feeling of emptiness, of desolation.

Almost idly, she opened the drawer of the nightstand next to her. They hadn't thought to clear this out—perhaps it was the singleness of the drawer, the smallness of it. Nestled inside was a pair of reading glasses, plastic-framed. Underneath them, a folded sheet of paper with her—and her great-aunt's—name written on it. For only a moment she was jolted: but the ink was old, faded, and the hand that had incised the name was spiky and unfamiliar.

With a finger, she nudged the glasses aside to look more closely at the single word. *Gwynn.* Her hand was shaking as she lifted the paper; it felt brittle, and the crease was so worn as to make her nervous just opening it up.

Dovecote. T

Just the one word and the initial. She flipped back to the name. Both words written on the yellowed page with such force that they seemed carved.

A message. But of what? And from whom? Obviously it was of such importance that her great-aunt had kept it when she seemed to have kept so little else. Gwynn held the paper gingerly in her fingers, trying to make sense of it. But the two words and the letter gave no further clue.

DOVECOTE. SHE HAD heard the doves the other day, out in the garden.

There had been a dead dove on the step.

"Is there a dovecote around here anywhere?" she asked Mary when she next appeared for her morning work.

Mary frowned. "A dovecote?"

"Does anyone around here keep doves?"

The thing that she had noticed about Mary was that she didn't dismiss a question out of hand, but gave it careful consideration. Of course, her answers were often guarded, as though she were playing some sort of verbal hide-and-seek. "Now, I can't think of anyone who does. Why would you ask?"

Gwynn suddenly didn't want to mention the note she had found; her great-aunt had kept it, and kept it secret, all that time, and it seemed wrong to bring it out into the open this morning. Instead she said, "I just thought I heard doves. The other afternoon. When I was oiling the gate in the back garden."

The back garden. The rusted gate. Damn it. Caught up in working on the illustrations, she hadn't thought to go check; she wondered how long it took for penetrating oil to evaporate.

Mary was busy with her broom, brow still knitted together. Today she wore a flowered bib apron—very much like those from the shops— over her dress, her hair pulled back into a tight braided bun at the back of her head.

"I don't think anyone keeps them around here," Mary replied slowly, without looking up. "Not anymore."

An opening. A test, to see whether Gwynn would rise to the bait.

"But someone used to."

Mary nodded, still not raising her head. Her hands tightened on the broom handle. "I'd heard Mrs. Chelton's husband used to." Her voice held that suspicious tone that was beginning to become a familiar part of their conversation. "Out back. Beyond the wall."

Gwynn pondered the information. "He's been dead for years."

Again the single nod. "More than fifty, I would say."

Gwynn poured herself a cup of coffee from the press—thank God Mary had shown her how to use it properly—and gathered the mail to take it into the dining room. Once there she tossed it onto the table, uninterested, and sat, looking out the front window at the grey sky. Neither did she pick up a pencil. Gwynn Chelton's husband had been dead for more than fifty years; those doves she had heard were not his. Could not have been his.

Out back, beyond the wall. Beyond the gate which would not open. Beyond the brambles which reasserted themselves as soon as she fought them back.

Gwynn. Dovecote. T

"Mary?" she called after a few minutes.

There was an answer, though she could not make out the words. Probably Mary was cleaning the oven, or the refrigerator, or under the sink.

"What was my great-aunt's husband's name?"

There was a muffled clatter, and an equally muffled exclamation. Then footsteps as Mary looked through from the sitting room.

"I'm sorry. What was that?"

"Mr. Chelton. What was his given name?"

Mary appeared to be thinking hard, trying to remember.

"Thomas, I think," she said finally. "Thomas. But they called him Tommy."

THAT EXPLAINED THE *T.*

In a way, she thought later, once again drawn to take the faded note out of the drawer, that took a bit of romance out of it. She had to admit that, for the few hours between discovery and information, she had dreamed up a number of scenarios. A note, kept in a bedside drawer for years, the bedside drawer of a woman long widowed: perhaps she had, after all, taken a lover. Perhaps this was a note slipped under a door, through a mail slot, left in a hymnal at church—to arrange a tryst.

Gwynn smiled ruefully to herself. A lover's tryst, outside the walls of the garden. The fantasy had all sorts of Edenic overtones. There was deep romance to it.

All for nought. The note was obviously from the other Gwynn's husband. *T—Thomas—Tommy.* Now Gwynn turned the paper over in her hand, gingerly, not wanting to tear it where it had grown thin along the fold. Nothing else was written on it. So what had it meant? Tommy had kept doves. Somewhere. Outside the garden wall, as there was no room for, nor any evidence of, a dovecote within. But the note wouldn't be an invitation to a lover's tryst when the pair of them were married, living under the same roof. He wouldn't have had to make an appointment with his own wife.

Gwynn folded the paper back over, so her own name, in that pointed script, stared back up at her. The downward strokes were so strong they nearly scarred the paper. Perhaps Tom had left the note on the table, to let his wife know where he was when she returned from some errand in the village. Yet that didn't seem a suitable explanation, either. Not with the name carved into the front, and the rest of the message hidden until the paper was unfolded.

No. There was an intent here she didn't understand. *Dovecote.* It struck Gwynn as more of a command. There was nothing of the *I'm up there if you want me* about it.

There was something stronger.

Something nastier.

Gwynn thought of the crying of the doves she had heard out back. Then she remembered—even heard it again in her imagination—the very human sobbing.

The paper suddenly felt hot in her hands, as though it were burning. Gwynn gasped and dropped it to the floor.

The gate in the rear garden still refused to open. The brambles had grown up again.

9

"I NEED YOUR help," she said to Colin over the phone.

"Okay." He was waiting. Perhaps it was a genetic trait, she thought, the inability to make small talk. He had it. Mary had it. But then, they were only related by marriage. Son of her husband's cousin, or something like that.

"There's a gate in the back garden."

"I've seen it."

"I can't get it open." Gwynn realized that her palm, wrapped around the telephone, was sweating. "I've tried penetrating oil, but it didn't help. The thing's rusted shut."

"Maybe you're not meant to go through it."

It took her a moment to realize he was serious.

"Can you help me get it open, or not?" she demanded.

There was a long pause.

"Likely I could," he said finally. "If you really think we should."

"Great," she said, trying to keep the peevishness from her voice. "When would that work for you?"

"I've got a couple of small jobs to tend to this afternoon. I could probably stop by before the gig. Three-ish?"

"I'll be waiting."

She hung up the phone, and heard a muffled crash from upstairs.

GWYNN COULDN'T STICK to her drawing all afternoon. Her mind kept wandering, and her eyes did, too, looking out at Eyewell Lane, down the hill to the intersection where the red call box stood sentinel, under its dying streetlight. The afternoon was still gloomy—this had been the gloomiest week in October that she could remember, but then again, she had never spent a week in October *here*. She had not even known *here* existed until the unexpected arrival of the registered letter from the solicitor.

Discouraged, she threw down her pencil, which skittered across the tabletop and fell to the floor. She'd simply have to finish the miniature another time, because it wasn't happening right now. She pulled her desk diary toward her, more for something to do than to really look at it: she already knew what it said about when Belinda wanted the preliminary pen-and-ink drawings. At this rate, she'd never meet the deadline, and her second career would be finished before it had even begun.

She was still staring at the diary, unseeing, when the movement of the truck outside the window, as it slid to the curb, caught her eye. Almost at the same time, the clock in the dining room chimed a quarter. The door of the cab opened, and Colin Moore slid out, his eyes scanning the front of the cottage. When he saw her in the window, he raised a hand in greeting, then he stopped, his expression clouding slightly. He reached into the bed of the truck to pull out a toolbox and headed up the path toward the tiny terrace.

She opened the door to him, and his glance flickered immediately over her shoulder, back into the room from which she'd come.

"Sorry I'm late," he said. "You have company?"

She, too, glanced back into the dining room. "No. Why?"

He only shook his head. "Nothing."

She saw now that on top of the tools in his box lay a short-handled pry-bar.

"Not much time," he said. "Let's go."

Gwynn opened the kitchen door to the jungle of brambles, which seemed to lunge at them threateningly. Even the ones she'd fought back previously seemed to have grown up with a vengeance; she couldn't tell where she'd stomped them down and shoved them aside. Colin stepped out, switching the pry bar to either side, beating the brambles back. Still the thorns sprang out and dragged at her clothes. Irrationally, she felt as though they didn't want them anywhere near the rotten door. A shiver traveled down her spine; she shook her head, trying to rid herself of the thought. A thorn caught at her wrist, drawing a ragged bracelet of blood. She put it quickly to her mouth.

"I've been out here several times," she said. "I keep fighting this stuff back, but it's like it's the thorn around Sleeping Beauty's castle—it grows up stronger, thicker."

"Brambles grow up, gate won't open." Colin's tone rose slightly. A question.

"What?" she demanded.

He didn't answer.

At the gate she paused, listening. There was no sound from the other side.

"I poured nearly an entire can of penetrating oil into the latch and the hinges," she told him, stomping back more brambles so there was room for them to stand side by side at the high stone wall. "Left it for twenty-four hours—more—as per instructions. Nothing."

Colin held his head to the side, evaluating. The wooden gate was aged and black, punky with damp. He ran an exploratory hand over the metal and the wood, tracing the line where they met. "It looks as though I could put my hand through it, it's in such bad shape."

"But you can't."

Colin shook his head. "I can't." He bent closer, examining the lock, and then the hinges. The metal, oil notwithstanding, had moved far beyond rusty red to pitted black. Again he ran his hand over the fittings, then held up his fingers, stained as though with old blood. He tried the latch, which did not turn. He pulled it with a sudden jerk; there was no result. He didn't seem surprised.

He stepped back, looked down. "Why do you want to open this?"

Gwynn was determined. "I want to see what's out there." She raised her chin.

Colin met her gaze, his own unreadable. "Why's that important?"

She didn't know. She couldn't tell him. But it *was*. "It's the only gate. The only way out. Or in."

After a moment, he shrugged and set down his tool box. "If we open this, we might not be able to close it again."

It wasn't reluctance in his voice. It was a warning.

Gwynn said nothing.

"Some doors aren't meant to be opened."

"Let's do it," she said. Firmly.

Now he bent over the tool box, rattling things around until he withdrew a long-bladed screwdriver. With the tip he scraped away at the rust filling the screw heads on the latch. He tried to turn them, leaning into the handle with his full weight, but the door resisted him again.

The screws were rusted solid. But she had known that.

Carefully Colin returned the screwdriver to the tool box and picked up the crowbar.

Suddenly the air around them was filled with the crying of the doves.

SCRAPS OF ROTTED wood lay at their feet from the now-scarred door. Colin had pried the latch apart, the tongue mechanism now hanging lopsidedly from the planks. He inserted the tapered end of the crowbar into the gap between the door and frame and pulled back; the door edged toward him a few inches, scraping and sticking in the ragged grass at its base. He handed the bar to Gwynn, grasped the wood, and dragged inward inch by inch.

The door let go so suddenly the Colin lost his grip and fell back. The blast of air that came through, almost as though it had been trapped out there, almost as though it had been *waiting*, rushed at Gwynn and was so foul that for a moment her sight darkened, her breath caught in her throat, and she staggered backward before it. The rain spattered around them, the sound sharp on the damp and dying leaves. The smell of decaying wood and grass and leaves filled her nose, and she wiped a hand across her face, trying to rid herself of it. The smell clung to her, to her hair, her clothes.

"Come on, then," Colin said.

He had pulled the door open perhaps a foot, and now he squeezed through the opening. Clasping the metal bar tightly, Gwynn took a desperate look around the overgrown garden and followed.

"Do you smell it?" The fetid stench would not leave her nostrils.

He looked down on her speculatively. "What?"

His expression gave nothing away. Gwynn felt defensive. "The air— the smell—something rotten, dead. Dead for a long time."

Instead of answering, he pushed his way forward.

Out here it was darker and wilder. The trees grew together overhead into a canopy that kept the light dim and weak and sickly. The rain beat on the remaining leaves as though on a metal roof. Gwynn was surprised to find no brambles—they had apparently confined themselves only to her side of the wall. Most of the trees that lined a vaguely defined path were young, their trunks not that thick around. She had the sudden feeling that if she were to shout, the sound of her voice would be deadened, swallowed.

She could no longer hear the doves.

Colin was waiting, looking about them measuredly.

"Never been out here," he said. "Which way?"

It was, after all, her determination that had brought them through the wall, though it had been his brute strength. Still holding the pry bar as a weapon, she stepped past him and made for a path, dimly visible through the ferns. Further along she could see a shadow, a structure whose definitions she could not quite make out.

It was like walking through cotton batting. The air was thick and damp and silent. Even their footsteps were muffled. Gwynn's skin felt clammy, and she shivered despite her coat. She hefted the iron bar in her hands, testing out its weight for a weapon, and unable to explain to herself logically why she should feel the need to carry one. She only knew she had to have a look at this dovecote—she knew instinctively that the shadowy building would prove to be just that—and at the same time she felt anxious at the thought of it, and fought the urge to turn back. She knew Colin was just behind her, but she dared not turn and look at him, in case—in case—it wasn't in fact him. Or that he'd disappeared entirely. She wanted to speak to him, if only for the reassuring sound of her own words, and his reply—but her voice was trapped in her throat.

The building was in a slowly-shrinking clearing; the trees had not yet overtaken the sky above it. She and Colin burst into it, but with surprisingly little change of atmosphere: the sky was still ominous, the rain falling steadily. The dovecote was long and low, wooden, unlike the stone ones she had seen online, with the roof sagging in the middle, tiles broken and fallen away. A door at the near end hung half-off its hinges; next to it, a window had lost most of its small panes of glass, the remaining ones jagged like broken teeth. A ragged piece of canvas, black with age, flapped listlessly against the frame at the side.

The only sound was the rain against the broken roof, and the sharp sound of Gwynn's own breathing in her ears. The dark maw of the door beckoned her. Unable to look away, she took an unsteady step forward.

"Don't."

Colin's voice, and yet no. He gripped her arm.

She stared down at his hand, then up into his face. His jaw was set, and he was not looking at her but at the dovecote.

"Don't go in there."

The sound in his voice made the hairs on the back of her neck prickle, and it shocked her to realize how close she had been to breaking away and entering the black unknown of the door.

"WHERE ARE THE doves?" she gasped at last, shaking.
He looked around the small clearing, and up at the sky.
"There haven't been any here for years," he said.

BACK AT THE cottage, Colin put the tea kettle on while Gwynn
went upstairs to change. Her clothes and hair were soaked, and she used
one of the rough towels to try to rub some warmth back into her skin.
It didn't seem to help: the cold was embedded in her very bones. She
donned a fresh pair of jeans and a thick sweater, and left the bedroom
light on when she went back down.

Colin had stoked the fire. He handed her a cup of tea. There was a
surprising sharpness in it, to her tongue.

"Whisky," he said at her expression. "Bottle in the cellarway."

She didn't ask how he knew that; probably he had been Gwynn
Chelton's alcohol supplier as well.

"Drink it." He had his own mug, which he lifted slightly to her in a
wry toast before taking a drink.

She let the fire spread, down her throat and into her belly, then
outward.

"I shouldn't have had you open the gate," she said at last, staring
at the fire behind the stove's isinglass window. "We shouldn't have
gone there." She felt confused, angry, surprised at her own reaction.
Fearful. How could there have been such menace in an abandoned,
falling-down building? Yet she had been drawn there. Mesmerized. She
thought of how her feet had wanted to keep going, through the door
into the depths of the dovecote's darkness. How it had taken Colin's
restraining hand to keep her from entering. She had been seduced.

Melodramatic ass.

Gwynn tried to shake the feeling that would not quite let go.

"Finish the whisky," Colin said, his grey eyes on her. The clock on
the bookshelf rang the hour. "I've got to get to the gig. And I think
you'd better come with me."

10

GWYNN RODE IN the cab of the truck with a guitar case between her knees.

"Gig?" she managed at last.

The Compass was down by the water; when they eased the truck off the road, the lot was nearly full.

"Pig Iron," was all Colin said.

She was still shaky as she slid out of the cab, but he took the guitar case from her, and held her by the arm. Inside, the pub was warm and noisy; at the far end, three men were setting up on a small stage.

"Pat, Mike, Davy." Colin nodded at each by way of introduction. "Gwynn."

"You're late," the man named Davy said. He wore a watch cap over his grey hair, and had an unlit cigarette clenched between his teeth. He held out a hand to Gwynn. "Pleased."

"Held up," Colin said, setting down the guitar case and grabbing a loop of cord.

"Can see that." Davy laughed, and Mike grunted. Pat barely looked up.

"Get yourself a pint," Colin suggested. "I've got to help here."

AT FIRST GWYNN didn't recognize any of the songs Pig Iron played; seated at a small table in the corner, nursing her pint of Swift One, she found she was barely paying attention anyway, and she felt vaguely guilty about that. She looked up as they launched into a cover of "Lullaby of London." They were, she thought, pretty good.

What had happened out there at the dovecote? Gwynn wished she knew. She might have been able to convince herself she had imagined the entire thing, but for the fact that Colin had been there with her. He had felt it. Or at least, he had felt something. And he had seen her reaction. She felt again his hand on her arm, and looked down. She looked up at the stage once more, and he was watching her, his hands moving between chords as though with a mind of their own.

He had warned her. He'd warned her on the phone, and again before he'd pried the latch of the gate and dragged it open. His words hung with her: *we might not get it closed again.* Nothing had been out there, save the building, slowly falling to ruins in its tiny clearing. She didn't know what she had expected, but it hadn't been—this. Maybe to have her curiosity satisfied, that was all. To be able to turn to Colin and say, "Oh, a dovecote. I'd heard there was one out here," and then to return to the cottage. All done. Yet despite there being nothing out there—*there had been something.*

Now the gate was open.

When they'd returned to the garden, Colin had put all his weight against the gate and shoved it back into its place in the wall, where, the hinges buckled, it no longer fit. The latch destroyed, there was no way to lock it back up again.

Gwynn wished there was.

She wished she hadn't urged him forward.

And where were the doves?

SHE FOUND AN answer in the final song of the second set. Pat stepped forward to the mic, Pat, who, she had noticed, had remained as far in the background as one could get on such a small stage, with his bass guitar. His voice, when he sang, was a high tenor, lighter and higher than Davy's had been—Davy, who, looking sulky now, had picked up a melodeon.

> *O, don't you see that lonesome dove*
> *That flies from vine to vine*
> *He's mournin' for his own true love*
> *Like I will mourn for mine*
> *Like I will mourn for mine, my love*
> *Believe me what I say*
> *You are th' darling of my heart*
> *Until my dying day.*

The song, despite the beauty of Pat's rendition, called up goose bumps on her arms. Gwynn looked up, and found, once again, Colin watching her.

WHEN THEY RETURNED to the cottage, well after midnight, Colin seemed uncomfortable. Wary. Gwynn let him go inside first, let him look into every room.

"I'll be fine," she said when he returned to the entryway.

He looked unconvinced. "I don't like this house." He had his hands shoved into his coat pockets.

"Really." Gwynn wished she could convince herself. She opened the door for him and stood aside. Suddenly she felt the truth of the matter. "The house is just sad. It's the dovecote that's—angry. I'll be fine."

UPSTAIRS, IN THE bed which had been her great-aunt's, she found herself wondering what it would be like to sleep with Colin Moore.

The thought was strangely upsetting.

She hadn't slept with anyone since Richard, and he'd been dead these past six years. Celibate six years. That in itself was unnerving.

Not, perhaps, as unnerving as the idea of that other Gwynn, widowed young—how young?—and who had lived on for fifty or sixty more years, sleeping alone in this bed. Perhaps her great-aunt had taken a lover at some point—she didn't have to be alone just because she was widowed. Somehow, though—just somehow—Gwynn knew she hadn't done that.

Suddenly Gwynn was terrified. What if that happened to her? What if she spent the rest of her life repeating the history of her great-aunt? Widowed young, no children, always alone. Until she died, unhappy, friendless.

In the darkness she clenched her eyes shut, trying to envision Colin Moore. Just his face, the steady gray eyes, the dark hair going to gray at the temples. But the image swam away from her mind's eye, and she was left with nothing but emptiness.

Damn you, Richard, she thought. *Damn you for doing this to me.*

11

"I'M GLAD YOU could see me on such short notice," Gwynn said to the solicitor as he ushered her into the office after instructing his secretary to bring tea.

James Simms waved her into a chair before his massive desk. "Oh, no, no, that's not a problem at all." He looked mildly uncomfortable. "As a matter of fact, I'm glad you telephoned. I've had a bit of a disturbing contact I'd like to make you aware of. Thank you, Miss Devlin." This directed to his secretary, who looked about sixteen; she set the tea tray on the side table and swished out of the office, closing the door behind her softly. The tea ceremony occupied the solicitor for a few moments, during which, Gwynn noticed, feeling mildly paranoid, he glanced at her frequently, as if measuring her reaction to the *disturbing contact.*

"I think I may be able to guess at who that might have been," she said, accepting the cup and saucer from him. "Paul Stokes, from The Stolen Child?"

Mr. Simms looked relieved as he slid behind his desk. He had poured himself a cup of tea, which he now set carefully to the side. He slid a large folder onto to his blotter, but did not open it; rather, he folded his long-fingered hands over it.

"He has approached me, in my capacity as your great-aunt's solicitor"—he cleared his throat and picked up a pair of reading glasses, which he perched low on the bridge of his nose—"as your mutual great-aunt's solicitor, I should say, to make enquiries about the validity of her will." For a moment he looked affronted. "As though there would be any question at all, as I drew up the document for Mrs. Chelton." He glanced up across the polished expanse of the desk. "Have you met Mr. Stokes?"

Gwynn nodded slowly. "I have. It was not a pleasant encounter. He was angry that I—a stranger, as he put it—would inherit over him, who had lived here all his life and had known our great-aunt. His last words were that I would be hearing from his solicitor." She grimaced.

"Could you tell me about it? From the beginning?"

So Gwynn went through the story, thinking of the waves of fury rolling off Paul Stokes. "He said he wasn't through. He said he would contest." She set her cup of tea on the saucer, and it clinked. Punctuation.

"He has expressed a wish to challenge the will in court," Mr. Simms agreed. "I have yet to hear from his chosen solicitor, if in fact he has been able to find one to take his case, but I suggest, should you be contacted by one, you refer the matter to me."

"What are the chances of his success?"

Mr. Simms shook his head gravely. "Very small, I would say. Mrs. Chelton owed no debt to Mr. Stokes. She owned her property clearly and without encumbrance, and was free to leave it to anyone she chose. The RSPCA, for example, had that been her desire. However, she chose to leave the property to you." He pursed his lips, looking suddenly like the old man he would eventually become. "The will has been probated. I don't see how any self-respecting solicitor would take on his case." Again he looked insulted, as though it were unthinkable that anyone would question his work. "We made perfectly certain that everything was ship-shape and Bristol fashion before you were even contacted, Mrs. Forest."

"So he's just blowing smoke, as they say."

Mr. Simms raised his fine eyebrows at the turn of phrase, but nodded. "As they say." He opened the file before him and sorted through the papers inside, glancing at a sheet before setting it aside and picking up another. "Mrs. Chelton, as I've said, was of sound mind when she made her will. It was signed and witnessed right here in this office, with all due care." He paused, looking again at her, waiting for the next gambit. He closed the folder and placed his hands on it. "You told my secretary over the telephone that you wanted some further information about Mrs. Chelton," he prodded after a moment, glancing at the wall clock. Time was money, after all, Gwynn supposed, and she wondered what time his next appointment was scheduled for.

"Yes. Some questions have arisen during the past few days in the cottage. I thought to ask you, so that I could avoid the gossip asking in the village would cause." She looked up at him over the rim of her tea cup; he seemed to have caught and lightly savored the veiled compliment.

"Go on," he only said.

"My great-aunt. First, how did she die?"

Mr. Simms cleared his throat. "You know she was nearly ninety. She'd lived a good long life by anyone's standards."

Gwynn nodded, waiting.

"She died at home. The housekeeper, Mary Tennant, found her seated in a wing chair, a cup of tea gone cold on the table beside her."

"At home." But not in her bed. For that one thing, Gwynn found herself suddenly grateful. Still—poor Mary! The sympathy welled up. She wondered why Mary had not mentioned it. It had to have been difficult for her. It would be, Gwynn knew all too well, difficult for anyone.

"Yes." Mr. Simms looked properly mournful. "Despite the shock, Mrs. Tennant did the right thing: she telephoned for the paramedics, but it was already too late." He glanced down again to the papers before him. "The coroner's verdict—it was an unattended death, you see—was a heart attack. Her heart just—stopped. Because, I suppose, she'd just worn out, poor woman. As we all do eventually. And thus you are the beneficiary."

For a moment the misery of her great-aunt's situation struck her. To live nearly sixty years alone, unhappy—only to die alone, kept company by a single cup of cooling tea. What would have happened had she not had a housekeeper? She might not have been found for days, weeks. No one would have known.

Of course, there was always Paul Stokes, across the way at The Stolen Child. How long would it have taken him to notice the light left on, the newspapers piling up? According to Colin Moore, Stokes had made little effort with the elderly woman, but surely he would have noticed? Abruptly she set her teacup on the desk before her, pushed it aside.

"But I don't know why." Gwynn looked up at him, puzzled. "Why me, I mean."

Mr. Simms took off his glasses for a moment and rubbed his eyes, a gesture Gwynn found strangely endearing. "I don't think any of us knew why she chose to do what she did. She was not a woman who took people into her confidence. However, she obviously had her own reasons for what she was doing. The result was, of course, in your favor." He replaced the glasses slowly, but looked over them at her. "Believe me, Mrs. Forest, when I say that you are safe in possession of Gull Cottage. Your cousin may believe he deserves more, but under the law, he has no claim." He cleared his throat. "Will there be anything else?" he asked after a pause, again with the surreptitious glance at the clock.

Gwynn nodded, deciding to take the plunge. "Yes. *Mr.* Chelton. He that would have been my great-uncle."

This was not the question the solicitor had expected, and his eyebrows rose over his reading glasses. "Yes? He's been dead a very long time."

"How long?"

Mr. Simms frowned, again sifting through the pages in the file before him. "I'm afraid I can't say for certain," he hedged, the crease between his eyebrows deepening. "He died before I was born. My father would have been the one to answer that question to the year, if that's what you're looking for. Sometime in the 1950s, I believe."

"And you wouldn't know how he died?" Gwynn didn't know why this suddenly seemed important.

Mr. Simms only shook his head. "Again, before my time. Without research, I'm afraid I don't."

"Your father?" she asked. "Would he know?"

A soft clearing of the throat, but no other falter. "He most likely would have known. Sadly, however, he's been dead these two years past. I will, however, find the answers to your questions, should you wish me to." Those questions, though, seemed to make him uncomfortable, and now he stood. "I'm sorry, Mrs. Forest, to rush you, but I'm expecting another client shortly."

Gwynn retrieved her cup and saucer, then stood to replace them on the tray. "Of course. I'm sorry for keeping you."

Full recovery. "No, no, that's fine." Mr. Simms moved to open the door for her. "Please," he said as she slipped into the outer office, "remember to get in touch should Mr. Stokes, or a representative from him, make contact."

"I will do that," Gwynn said, and left, feeling distinctly dissatisfied.

WHEN ALL ELSE fails, make a list. Gwynn had always done that in the days she spent in the office of the construction company she had started with Richard, all those years ago. Now the dictum surfaced again as she tossed the boxes she'd collected in town into the guest bedroom; clearing there could wait at least until she tried to settle her mind. She made herself a pot of tea and brought the tray to the dining room table. The clutter here was dissatisfying, too, and not conducive to clear thinking, so she gathered up everything that wasn't a drawing in progress, stuffed it into the wood stove, and threw a fistful of kindling on top. In a moment the morning's embers flared up, and after adding a stick of fire wood, she closed the door on the flames.

Now she drew her sketch block toward her, tore off the rough drawing on the top sheet, and began to write.

Thomas Chelton died in the fifties.

She stared at the words, remembering the *T* incised into the note in the bedside table drawer.

How? She wrote. *When?*

Then, *why is that important?*

Everyone who had spoken to her about her great-aunt had been sure to mention the same thing: Gwynn Chelton had never married again, had never had any children.

How long were they married?

Why did she never marry again?

Not for the first time, Gwynn wished she had a picture of her great-aunt as a young woman. She glanced up, her gaze darting about the room. Surely there must be photographs, somewhere. She hadn't seen any, though they still might be tucked away someplace she hadn't cleaned. Now that she thought about it, she wished she had a picture of her great-aunt as an old woman. Or at any time in her life. Gwynn squeezed her eyes shut and tried to remember whether her grandmother Lucy had any old photographs of the three siblings, but she couldn't bring anything to mind.

The reflection in the window.

She looked down at the pad and was surprised to see she had written that. She thought of the moment, just the other evening, when she had seen that face surrounded by white hair, the raised hand—a greeting? A warning? The reflection and the memory solidified. She had not imagined it. That had been Gwynn Chelton. She was certain of it. The other Gwynn, standing behind her. The reflection of two Gwynns in the front window.

She shivered, looking up at the window now. The lights were beginning to come on, early evening that it was. Down in the road before The Stolen Child, a couple passed, slowed, and continued, arm-in-arm. Gwynn tried to will herself into the state she had been in when her great-aunt had stood behind her, tried to unfocus her eyes slightly. It was no use; she couldn't even see her own reflection.

"Gwynn," she said out loud, holding her face in her palms. "Gwynneth."

No one appeared.

One half of her wasn't at all surprised. She didn't believe in ghosts, after all. Never mind that, if there were ghosts in the world, this would be the house in which to find one. Never mind that her great-aunt, so far in all descriptions, had been a lonely old woman—and weren't unsettled spirits the kinds which were supposed to return to the places where they had lived?

The steps on the stairs.

She had heard them her first night. She had convinced herself that she had simply imagined them, being overtired and overexcited as she had been. But—had she? If Gwynn were still here, then of course she'd go up and down the stairs. However, her great-aunt was dead, and this line of thought was purely imaginative. She shook her head.

What else?

The brambles.

This was a stretch, of course. She really knew nothing of brambles, or any kind of plant, come to think of it, except perhaps household geraniums—and even those she killed every time she brought a plant home, thinking this time would be different. Yet she couldn't shake the feeling that the brambles in the rear garden grew up more quickly than they should have, almost malevolently. They hadn't wanted her to get to the gate; they hadn't wanted her to open it. This time she really shivered where she sat, and quickly took a sip from her tea cup. That was it, wasn't it? The brambles had not wanted her near that gate.

"Stop it," she told herself sternly.

THIS LIST WAS getting creepy. Gwynn got up to feed another piece of wood to the fire and to refill her tea pot. As she passed through from the dining room to the sitting room to the kitchen, she turned on lights: let Harvard down at the shops think she was throwing yet another party. Somewhere deep in her gut she wished Mary were here. Or Colin. Returning through the sitting room, she ran her hand along the back of the sofa where he'd spent the other night. The pillow she'd clasped to her that morning was gone, back up to the guest room as Mary's parting shot. However, Gwynn had, before abandoning it, pressed her face to it, breathing the male scent of the sleeping Colin.

The realization that she wished she had awakened to the male scent of the sleeping Colin on her own pillow nearly made her spill her tea.

She closed her eyes and tried to steady herself. Yes, that had been a rogue wave of lust washing over her, she told herself briskly. *Get over it.* He was an attractive man, tall, long-limbed, with those unreadable gray eyes, and that dark hair going gray over the temples. In her mind's eye she pictured him going upstairs that night with her, undressing, undressing *her.* Kissing her. She caught her breath. She'd fallen asleep thinking this way last night, and she hadn't thought like this about a man in a long time. She hadn't let herself think like this, not since Richard's death.

"Stop it," she said again, aloud.

Gwynn tried to imagine instead the face of her dead husband, his golden hair, his blue eyes. She tried to remember the feel of his skin, the way he smelled. But after six years, she could not call him up in her memory, could not bring him back to her. The face was still Colin's, the dark hair, the gray eyes. The build. And—though she had never seen much of it and it was only wishful thinking, she could imagine his bare skin, could almost feel her fingers tracing their eager way over it.

No. Colin had better stay away this evening. He would be a complication she didn't have the inner resources to deal with, and a complication she was certain she wouldn't be able to resist.

No matter how easy it had been for him, the other night, apparently, to resist even the thought of her. *I'll stay down here,* he'd said, after checking all the rooms, the doors, the windows. *To keep an eye on things.*

She'd brought him the blankets, the pillow, and retreated upstairs, tired, frightened, unquestioning.

He hadn't kissed her good night. He hadn't even touched her.

GWYNN SAT BACK down to her list. It was full dark outside, and she thought perhaps she should fix something for dinner: an omelette, maybe. That would be easy and filling. The lights outside drew her gaze again down to The Stolen Child. She thought perhaps she could hear music, a bass line—but it seemed far away and inconsequential. Did the pub do live bands on Friday nights? It seemed more than likely. She wondered momentarily what music Paul Stokes would book, but she couldn't even guess. Maybe he didn't book the bands. Maybe he left it up to someone else. The woman Sarah, perhaps. Gwynn supposed that would have to remain an idle wondering for now, because it seemed highly unlikely she'd make her way across to the Child to check, at least for a while. Until her cousin got over his great fury. *If.*

She put her chin in her hands again and gazed out. She was saddened by Paul Stokes and his anger. To think that she'd come all this way to find a relation she had no idea existed—and he already despised her. It seemed a waste. *Great fury.* He felt short-changed, cheated of something he thought he was owed. Yet Colin had insisted Stokes had not earned the inheritance of the house through any great effort toward caring for the cantankerous old lady, their great-aunt, any more than she had earned it. Still, some people, she knew very well, felt entitled, and thus always felt cheated. Those people very rarely overcame their feelings of being treated unfairly, and never got over their great fury at the unfairness of the world. Gwynn frowned at the pub's facade, knowing that this was one such instance. Perhaps her one sojourn to The Stolen Child would be her last, because it was unlikely her cousin would ever accept her inheritance of Gull Cottage with good grace.

Sighing, Gwynn again let her eyes drop to her list.

Doves, she'd written.

She stared at the word, stared at the pen in her hand, then wrote beneath that:

crying
dead
And shivered again.

12

"MARY," GWYNN SAID, "we have to talk."

Mary looked pointedly at the clock on the mantle. It was ten o'clock, spot on. Her two hours were up, to the minute. Even now she was pulling on her dark coat, having removed her apron and folded it away into her bag. Her jaw hardened.

"If I don't suit—" she began stiffly.

Gwynn held up a hand. "It's not that. Nothing like that."

Mary waited, tying the kerchief under her chin; it was not raining yet, but looked as though it might shortly.

Now Gwynn felt wrong-footed, as she did so much of the time with Mary. She clenched her fists, then opened her hands and rubbed her palms down her jeans. "I just wanted to ask a question. Whether you knew something."

Now Mary's expression was guarded, measured, back to the vaguely suspicious gaze Gwynn had come to know so well. Mixed with something that bordered on relief? Still Mary waited.

"I went to see the solicitor," Gwynn said. "Mr. Simms. Friday afternoon. He told me"—and she looked into Mary's broad unreadable face—"that you were the one to find my great-aunt. When she died."

Mary nodded. She pointed to the wing-backed chair facing the sofa. "There."

Gwynn's eyes were drawn to the chair, the one she always chose, the one she felt most comfortable sitting in. The chair in which her great-aunt had taken her last breath. Why had she not known that? Felt it?

"It must have been hard for you."

Mary only shrugged. "She was in her eighties. She could have gone at any time. It's not like it wasn't expected."

"But still—"

Mary had gone still, then, in remembrance. Her eyes were still on the chintz-covered chair. "She was just sitting. Her eyes still open. A book on her lap. There was a cup of tea. It was stone cold."

She tilted her kerchief-ed head, still looking at the chair, as though she could see her former employer still seated there. "She must have sat down for her nightly read and cuppa before bed, and it came upon her. Just like that." Now she shook her head sadly. "Just like that, poor soul. And no one there for her."

Gwynn felt a lump in her throat. Unpleasant and angry though her great-aunt might have been, here was a woman, unimaginative as she seemed, who loved her in a strange, quiet way. Despite being pushed away repeatedly.

With a quick intake of breath, Mary became herself again. Her industrious fingers began to do up the buttons on the black coat. "There wasn't anything I could do. She was cold. Long gone. I called the paramedics and waited."

For a moment they both gazed on the empty chintz chair.

"What book?" Gwynn asked suddenly.

Mary's head swiveled, her eyes widening in surprise.

"What book was she reading?"

Mary set her purse down on the coffee table and crossed to the shelf, where the books ranged neatly: none of that haphazard piling on her watch. She ran her hands along the spines until she found the one she wanted and pulled it from its place between its brothers. She handed it to Gwynn. "This one. I put it back when I cleaned. Afterwards. But I marked the place." That, apparently, was the only logical step—as though the next reader might want to pick up where the last had left off. Later. Or as if the last reader might be back—but Gwynn thrust that thought away.

Grimm's Fairy Tales. Gwynn was struck by the oddness of her great-aunt's choice. Fairy tales? In her hands the book felt warm. The cover was worn, a uniform, faded green.

She carried the book to the wing-backed chair and sat, holding it on her lap. Afraid to open it to the marked place.

"If that's all—" Mary retrieved her purse and threw another look at the clock atop the bookcase. Wherever she was meant to be, her expression plainly said, she was already late. The entire conversation had been a sacrifice, throwing her off her schedule.

"Wait." The book made her speak. "Tommy Chelton." Gwynn cleared her throat. Why were the words so slow in coming suddenly? Her throat felt thick. "Do you know when he died?"

Mary now settled her black purse over her arm.

"I don't recall," she said. "I was only a child. I wasn't paying attention at that point."

As though she had been paying careful attention to the goings-on of the village since then, was the implication.

Mary stopped at the front door and turned partway.

"My old father, though," she said slowly, "might have your answers." She was frowning, as though trying to work through a difficult decision. "I'll ask him."

She let herself out, shutting the door with a decisive click.

SLOWLY GWYNN LOWERED her eyes to the book in her hands, then let it fall open to the place Mary had marked.

The Sleeping Beauty.

13

THERE WERE NO windows, Gwynn suddenly realized, at the back of the house, no windows overlooking the rear garden. Nonsensical. What was the point of a garden behind the house if there was no way to see it? Even the kitchen door had only a tiny clouded pane of glass, impossible to see out of; otherwise the door was solid, stout oak.

From her seat in the wing-backed chair, Gwynn examined the rear of the sitting room. The wood-burning stove in its alcove took up most of the wall. She stood and crossed to the dining room. On that back wall, a framed print of a man reading, a bowl of grapes at his elbow, but no window. There were none in the bedrooms upstairs either, where there might have been dormers, but weren't. The cottage made no sense, architecturally speaking. None.

The curious thing, Gwynn realized as she sank back into the chair, was that, with all her years working with and then without Richard at the company—a construction company, for heaven's sake—she had not thought of this before. Gull Cottage was totally blind on one side. Gull Cottage faced Eyewell Lane and steadfastly turned its back on the garden, the wood, and—the dovecote. Just as, it would seem, her great-aunt had, for half a century.

Gwynn bit her lip and turned back to the front window, where she could see The Stolen Child, and its bow windows encroaching on the pavement. Not an overly cheerful view in that direction, either.

COLIN MOORE APPEARED an hour later, knocking briskly. "I've brought clippers," he said without preamble, as she opened the door to him. "To do something about the brambles in the back garden."

Gwynn nodded. "I think just clippers might be optimistic. We probably need an exorcism."

"I guess we'll find out." He cocked his head. "Can I come through? It's the only way into the garden. We're going to have to throw the brambles over the wall."

"Or carry them back through the kitchen." Gwynn stopped, reminded forcefully of her morning's musings, then turned to stare up into his face. "Hold on." She shook her head. "Hold on. Colin. That's another thing that doesn't make sense."

"It doesn't," he agreed. "There should be another way into the garden. From the path up from the road. On the side."

"But there isn't."

"There isn't."

Gwynn pushed past him, out onto the tiny terrace, around the side of the house and past the woodshed. Here the high garden wall met the hillside, and turned to surround the back, where the gate was now broken, open to the woods beyond. Colin had followed her.

"Why have I never thought of this either? Why?" Gwynn shook her head, held her hands out helplessly. "There should be a gate on this side."

Colin scuffed his boot into the ground. "Look at the path."

She did as she was told. It ran up from the road, where Colin's work truck was parked, the back empty of wood this time, the barrow strapped down inside. Well-worn, a path that had been used for years, for decades. It met the terrace and moved to the woodshed. Turned right into the woodshed.

"Did there used to be a gate here?" Gwynn asked, reaching an unsteady hand to the woodshed door. "Through here?"

"Looks like."

"Someone built the shed here and blocked it off. The only way into the garden, unless you went into the house."

"Looks like."

Brambles, thorns, gateways blocked off.

Sleeping Beauty.

"Something is very wrong here," she muttered.

"It is." Colin's gaze was steady.

HE WIPED HIS boots carefully on the mat before making his way through the sitting room and kitchen to the rear door. His was the ease of familiarity, but then, he had slept, the other night, on that sofa. She felt herself flush at the thought. Colin had also worked for years for her great-aunt. Had filled that woodshed, the one built to block the side entrance to the rear garden.

"How long did you work for my great-aunt?" she asked, trying to make sense of this new nonsensical thing.

Colin tossed her a look over his shoulder. "That's a bit strong a term, 'worked for.' I did odd jobs for Mrs. Chelton when she asked." He looked over the brambles thoughtfully, his eyes resting for a long time at the space in the wall where now they knew to look, they could make out the newer stonework, fitted carefully into the space where a gate had once been. "Sometimes when she didn't. And I brought her wood."

"Of course." Gwynn swallowed, shutting the kitchen door behind her. "You didn't build the woodshed?"

He shook his head. "That's been there as long as I remember. From before my time."

"So someone blocked off the exit a while back." *Why would anyone do that? Who had done it? Had Gwynn Chelton hired someone? Had Tommy Chelton done it?* The questions piled one on top of another in her mind. Then she realized what he had said. "Sometimes when she didn't ask?"

Colin shrugged, again with that offhand look tossed over his shoulder. "She was an elderly lady. She needed help, and for the most part, she wouldn't ask for it."

There was something in his tone which implied things not given words. He stepped further into the watery November light, she following. The stoop was damp, and the brambles reared their ugly heads, glistening darkly from the rain overnight. Gwynn thought of the thicket of thorns which surrounded Sleeping Beauty's castle, keeping suitors at bay: the story her great-aunt had been reading when she died. The story Mary had marked in the book. The thorns had overtaken the garden at the end of the long-widowed, long-lonely Gwynn's life; but she, Gwynn Forest, was no princess, and she felt no need of suitors, nor protection from them. She did, however, feel the need to see the end of the brambles, especially as they caught at her clothing, and at her skin. She swore lightly, and, seeing the loose threads where the thorns had pulled at her sweater, swore more loudly. As she moved along the overgrown path, this kept happening, so she kept swearing.

Colin looked at her with something akin to interest. She looked away quickly, stuck her hands into her pockets.

"This is going to be some job." Colin lifted his chin toward the side wall, the path on the other side. "We should start over here, clear the way to throw the canes over the wall. Do you have gloves? A heavy coat? If you're going to help with this work, you'll need them both."

Chastened by his tone, and by the thorns, she fought her way back to the house.

THE WIND WAS picking up; it was cold. Despite the gloves and heavy coat, the brambles continued to scratch at her like wild things: between the glove and the sleeve, through the legs of her blue jeans, across her cheek when she turned too quickly. They pulled up the canes, piled them, threw them over the high stone wall. Colin got the barrow from his truck, and she could hear him filling it, rolling it down to the road, wheeling it back up again. For her part, she continued to build the pile, pulling until she had an armful of thorny canes, and throwing them next to the wall. Each time she returned to the spot where she'd been dragged out the last handfuls, she looked around her, feeling more and more hopeless.

"The back of the truck is filled," Colin said at last, returning through the kitchen. He pulled off his gloves and wiped his forehead with his rough sleeve. His look at the garden was calculating. "I don't know how many more loads it will take to finish."

"Where will you take them?" Gwynn too wiped at her forehead, knowing herself to be flushed, hair a mess, bleeding where the thorns had dragged across her skin.

"Farm tip," he said, tossing his head in the general direction of the village outskirts. "A friend's. He doesn't mind." He slapped the gloves against his leg. "Won't take long. Want to come?"

Gwynn threw a glance around, knowing she could keep working, feeling it was of no use.

"All right," she said.

The corners of his eyes crinkled. "Might want to wash your face first." He reached out a finger and touched her cheek. Then he showed her the blood.

They both washed up at the kitchen sink, and he examined her face under the light. "Little scratch. Don't think you'll die of it."

"Am I scarred for life?" she asked.

Colin cocked his head. "You tell me."

14

THEY HEADED INLAND, away from the estuary and the village, the sun now pushing the shadow of the truck along in front of them.

"Just watch out for Giles, is all," Colin warned as he turned left down a long farm track. A five-barred gate blocked the way; Colin climbed down from the truck, opened it, drove through, closed it behind them. "He fancies himself a bit of a ladies' man." The look he cast sideways at her was unreadable.

They bumped along the track toward a low stone farmhouse in the midst of a cluster of outbuildings; as they neared, two geese lifted their wings and made an angry show of getting out of the way. Colin tapped the horn twice, but did not stop at the house. He skirted the barn, where an elderly man in an overall raised a hand—the ladies' man's father?—and followed the track up the hill toward a pile of wooden scrap and litter. He swung the truck around and backed up to the mound.

"For Bonfire Night," he explained as she came around to join him at the bed of the truck. "Giles always throws a good one." Colin reached under the pile of canes and pulled out a rake. "Stand clear." With a couple of sweeps, he pulled the canes from the bed of the truck and into the pile.

Gwynn reached in a gloved hand, pulled out a few stragglers, and tossed them with their brethren. "Party?"

Colin nodded, closing the truck gate. "Ceilidh. After a fashion. Bonfire. A bit of cider."

The elderly man was stumping up the track toward them, a border collie to heel. Colin raised his hand, and remained standing next to the truck.

The old man wore a cap and had a snowy beard, and, Gwynn noted, fingerless gloves, as though his hands were cold, but he needed his fingers for fine work. He leaned against the side of the truck and appraised her with black eyes like currants. The dog lay down at his feet.

"You're Gwynneth, then," he said, nodding. "Pretty little thing, aren't you?"

Colin shook his head sadly. "I warned her, Giles."

Not Giles' father.

The farmer threw up his hands.

"You're Giles," Gwynn said. "You're the ladies' man."

He held out his hand, and when she put hers into it, he covered it with his other one. The grin split his wide red face. "He spoils everything, does our Colin. Can I help it if I'm full of charm?"

"Full of something," Colin retorted, tossing his gloves into the cab of the truck.

Still Giles held onto Gwynn's hand as though on to some sort of lifeline. "Giles Trevelyan. Of Trevelyan Court Farm since the dawn of time." He nodded to the dog, who lay still save her brown eyes, which studied each of them in turn. "This is Star. And you're Gwynn Chelton's niece, come to live in her house now, I hope."

Gwynn shrugged, smiled noncommittally. "We'll see how things sort themselves out. I've just been here a few days."

The snapping dark eyes widened, and then the farmer winked at Colin. "A few days, and already fallen into the clutches of our Colin." He laughed. "And he calls me a ladies' man, does he?"

"Just cleaning up the back garden at Gull Cottage," Colin said. His voice was still pleasant, but he shifted slightly. "Mrs. Chelton—it got away from her. Brambles."

Finally Giles let go of Gwynn's hand, but only to reach into his side pocket and withdraw a short-stemmed pipe. He searched his other pocket, then patted his trousers. "Blast. You haven't got a match anywhere about, have you?"

Gwynn shook her head, and Colin laughed.

"Best you find a match by Bonfire Night, then, Giles."

"You be coming, then?" A second time Giles searched all his pockets, as though certain he had had matches only moments before. Perhaps he had. "And you'll be bringing your lady here?"

Again the shift. "Gwynn's not my lady, Giles."

Again the wink. "Then the field's wide open for such as me." Giles leaned closer to Gwynn. "You'll be coming? Fine *craic*."

He was charming, that was for certain. She smiled at him warmly.

Giles jerked his beard at Colin. "Get the lug to give you a lift. Least he can do, the unchivalrous bastard."

Now Colin looked up at the sky, where the weak sun was drawing the afternoon along. "Have to get going. Give you a ride back down?"

Giles shook his head, the pipe stem clamped between his teeth. "Best not. I'd just cramp your style. I'll walk." But instead of heading downhill, he turned up to circle the burn pile, raising a genial hand over his head in farewell.

They climbed back into the work truck, and Colin turned the key.

"What's your style, then?" Gwynn asked as they bumped back down toward the farmyard.

He kept his eyes steady on the track. "Haven't got one."

WHEN THEY PULLED back up in front of the Gull Cottage, the first thing Gwynn saw was Paul Stokes, leaning against the stone front of The Stolen Child, smoking his ever-present cigarette. He kept his eyes on them as they climbed out of the truck; Gwynn could feel his angry gaze on the back of her neck all the way up to the terrace. Her hands fumbled as she attempted to unlock the front door. Then she turned, and found him staring at her. As she met his eyes, he took the cigarette from between his lips and flicked it away contemptuously. His expression, even from this far away, was clear, making plain he'd like to do the same with her: flick her away contemptuously, like so much trash.

"Ignore him," Colin murmured, leaning close to her ear.

Inside, she offered Colin coffee, knowing he'd refuse, knowing what he'd say.

"Best get back to work. Not much time before sundown."

They had, she realized as she opened the kitchen door to the back garden, forgotten to shut the gate in the stone wall; but then, since they'd pried it open, it had refused to close all the way anyway. Still— and somehow she had expected it—somehow she had feared it—the brambles seemed to have returned, growing closer now to the kitchen door, growing more thickly across what formerly had been the path to the gate.

"How can this happen?" she whispered, dumbfounded.

"More things in heaven and earth, Horatio," Colin said thinly, pulling on his gloves once more and stepping outside.

15

"DINNER?" HE ASKED as the sun began to fail them, and their courage began to flag.

Gwynn looked around the rear garden hopelessly. In her mind's eye she could see it laid out properly, with borders, roses in the spring and summer, perhaps a garden chair or two around a table. Now she felt defeated: her romantic imaginings of a walled garden—her own secret garden, perhaps—looked as though they'd never come to fruition in the face of this stubborn jungle of brambles.

She sighed heavily. "I'm hardly in any shape to go anywhere." She spread her hands and looked down the length of herself, scratched skin, torn jeans. She blew her hair out of her face, and it fluttered back down and stuck to her sweaty forehead.

"Me, neither." Colin, she though appraisingly, did not look any worse for wear; if anything, he looked more rugged, his dark hair glinting with that silver at the temples in the fading light. "But neither do I feel like fixing tea, and I expect you don't, either."

Gwynn's shoulders slumped. Her back ached, and she was bone-weary, but hungry, too—the kind of hungry that woke a person in the night and held her hostage if she didn't eat before bedtime.

"Leave this," he said. "We'll walk to the harbor."

Again they washed up at the kitchen sink before setting out. After she locked the front door carefully behind them, Colin led her down Eyewell Lane to the corner, where they turned left, he taking the outside of the pavement, near traffic. What traffic there was, of course, which was next to none. The shadows were long and deep, the whitewashed buildings hulking toward each other. As they walked, a streetlight flickered on ahead of them, and then another, and soon they were following lights like a string of pearls down the winding street.

"Here." Colin touched her elbow at the end of a block, where two wide plate-glass windows fronted on the pavement. He opened the wooden door for her. Inside, two granite steps led to a second door. Beyond this was a narrow space with a handful of well-worn tables and mismatched chairs along one wall, and a counter at the back. Two men at one of the tables nodded in greeting; one had, in front of him, a paper plate mounded with fish and chips.

The man behind the counter was round and red-faced, wearing a grease-spattered butcher's apron. He grinned as they approached.

"Colin," he said, nodding.

"John," Colin returned. He glanced at Gwynn. "Cod and chips do you?"

She nodded.

"Two, then, John, please." Gwynn reached into her pocket, and Colin put a hand on her arm. "On me."

"I can't—"

"On me," Colin said again. He handed some notes across the counter, and John rung up the order and passed back a handful of coins. Then Colin pulled out a chair from the nearest table and held it for her.

"You've put in a hard day's work," he said as they settled to wait. "I should pay you."

"It's my garden."

"I guess there's some that'd dispute that."

His tone was light, but she saw again her cousin leaning against the wall of the pub, and she winced. "Let's not go there."

"Sorry. Bad joke."

The two men finished their meal, and there was much scraping of chairs as they rose to leave. "Have a good evening, John," one called. Again he exchanged nods with them. "Colin. And you, miss." Then they had the shop nearly to themselves. From the back they could hear John whistling as he banged the fry baskets around.

The cod and chips came in paper—not newspaper, but printed to look like it. Colin poured vinegar liberally over his; Gwynn was a bit more conservative, shifting the paper cone from hand to hand, as it was hot.

"Night, John," Colin called as they left. "Cheers."

Full night had fallen in the short time they'd been inside the chippy. The streetlights glowed, each with its own nimbus, leading the way down to the harbor; they followed the lighted path, again Colin taking the outside of the pavement.

"Everyone knows you," Gwynn mused.

"Small village."

The sound of the tide grew louder as they crossed the small stretch of grass to a deserted bench. A handful of seagulls scattered before them, skittish, but then turned and watched suspiciously, small pale ghosts under the street lamp. Gwynn sat, trying to see beyond their circle of light onto the shingle, and out to the water beyond, where she knew small fishing boats bobbed on the swells. The smell on the cold air was salty, vaguely fishy. A seagull approached warily, but took a few fluttering steps back when she turned to him.

"You grew up here?" she asked, dipping into her paper cone for a chip. The fish was still too hot to eat.

From his jacket pocket, Colin drew a handful of napkins and held them out. Gwynn took one gratefully, and tucked it under her leg on the bench to keep it from blowing away.

"I did."

"Why aren't you a fisherman?"

"Can't swim."

She couldn't tell from his voice whether he was joking.

"Have you always lived here?"

Colin held up a finger, mouth full. "Went to university away. Bangor. Read linguistics."

Gwynn glanced at his profile curiously.

He lifted a brow. Waited.

"It didn't take?" she asked at last.

"Oh, I liked it. Didn't fancy myself a teacher, didn't know what else to do with it. Then there was a girl. Back here."

The sirens went off in her head. Of course. There was always a girl, wasn't there? How old was he? The silvering at the temples suggested early forties. Most men of that age were unavailable.

"*That* didn't take," he said, eying her face in the angled light cast by the street lamp. He shook his paper packet, peered down into it, pulled out a last bit of cod. "*Since* you ask."

"I didn't ask."

"Your expression asked." He laughed, licked the salt and vinegar from his fingers in a way she found vaguely disturbing, so she looked away, toward the black water.

Gwynn was surprised to notice that her cone of fish and chips was nearly empty. One last chip. When had she eaten them all? She pulled the napkin from beneath her leg and wiped her hands. Colin took the wrapper and tossed it a few feet into a waste basket.

"You? Husband at home? Children?"

"No husband. No kids."

"Thought so. No ring. Means nothing, of course, nowadays."

"He died. He left a small construction business. I ran the office side until I got an offer of a buy-out from a bigger company. Then I sold it." Why was she saying this? And to him? "Now I'm trying to figure out what else I can do instead." She wasn't ready to talk about Belinda's drawings.

Colin nodded. "The house came at the right time."

"Yes."

An odd shadow had grown up to their left, lumpen and misshapen, with two heads. Gwynn looked up and saw the moon rising in the east. Not quite full. Bright. She looked down again, held her left hand out before her and watched the shadow do the same.

"And that may be how I spend the rest of my natural life," she said. "Pulling up brambles in that back garden."

Colin took the crumpled napkin from her and tossed it toward the basket; this time, it fell wide. He stood to retrieve it from the grass and dropped it in before speaking.

"Maybe," he said quietly, "we're not supposed to pull them up."

The air was growing colder as the night and tide moved in on them, but it was the words, and his tone, which made the chills run along her spine.

ALL UPHILL, THROUGH the village, up along Eyewell Lane past The Stolen Child, and up the path onto the tiny terrace. The stones underfoot rang as though hollow, the cold autumn air throwing back the echo of their steps.

"I wish you'd stop that," she said at last.

"Pardon?"

"Speaking so prophetically." Her hands, even stuffed into her coat pockets, were cold. "First it's the gate: *maybe we're not supposed to open it.* Now it's the brambles: *maybe we're not supposed to pull them up.* What's that all supposed to mean?"

Colin shrugged in the darkness, and she sensed the movement more than saw it. She wished she'd thought to leave a light on in the front window, to welcome them back to the house. There was a swell of noise from the pub as the door opened and closed; she looked down to see a couple linking arms and heading off into the night. Not Paul Stokes this time. Not those unfriendly black eyes watching her every move.

"I'm not sure."

"That's a help." She fumbled in her pocket for her keys, and in the darkness, dropped them on the flagstones, where she heard them skitter away into some dead leaves. She cursed softly.

Again the shrug. "Really. I just don't know. There's something—strange—about the whole situation." He bent down. "Here, let me." More rustling in the dead leaves. She really had to sweep the front terrace. Before Mary came and decided that as a house owner, Gwynn was definitely a lost cause. In a moment Colin straightened, key ring looped over his index finger. "When I pried open that gate, the sound it made—remember? Like a moan, or a cry. A warning."

"Now you're being fanciful," she said impatiently. Then stopped, remembering the stench in her nose, in her mouth.

"Probably," he agreed without rancor. "It's just that I don't like the feeling of this house. That's all."

"It's not the house," Gwynn protested.

"I know, I know. You said the house was sad. I don't agree."

The conversation was making her nervous. Anxious. Gwynn could hear the peevishness in her voice, but couldn't stop it. "So now I guess you're going to tell me you don't want to keep working at those brambles."

Colin took her hand and set the key ring in her palm. "I think you know that's not it."

She curled her hand into a fist around the keys. "Then what?"

He sighed, looking up at the three-quarter moon. "I'll come back tomorrow, if you like. Work all day at the brambles, if you like. But I think you're going to find that it won't make any difference."

Gwynn stomped a foot in frustration, then turned away to jam the key into the lock. "That doesn't even begin to make sense."

"I know."

"That's all you can offer? 'I know'?"

"I don't understand it, either."

Another wash of noise reached them, as more customers left The Stolen Child. They must have downed a few, from the sound. Suddenly extremely tired, Gwynn pushed the door open and reached inside for the light switch.

"Listen," she said wearily. "Do you want to come in for a nightcap?"

Colin laughed. A small laugh. "Probably that's not the best idea. You're exhausted and edgy—"

"I'm not edgy—"

"—and you should probably just go on up to sleep."

Gwynn thought, in the light from the front hallway, that he was smiling slightly, at least with that tiny quirk of the lips that passed for a smile with him.

He bent down and kissed her cheek. "And do not—I repeat, do not—check on those brambles tonight. Tomorrow morning will be soon enough."

She let herself in, then locked the door behind her. She got to the front sitting room window just in time to see the work truck pull away from the curb and head down Eyewell Lane.

16

AFTER SHE'D BRUSHED her teeth and donned her pajamas, Gwynn returned to the sitting room for her great-aunt's book of *Grimm's Fairy Tales*. True to form, Mary had tidied it away, back to its erstwhile home on the bookshelf. Gwynn knew she should be searching for something lightweight, something she didn't have to think about, something that might give her pleasant dreams. Fairy tales in the original didn't always do that—but she knew she was looking at that book for another reason.

She hadn't forgotten just how grisly the stories could be. Her great-aunt's book was well-worn, the green binding faded to a soft spring pastel. The title was stamped in gold: *Fairy Tales Old and New*. Not too new, obviously; and as she thumbed through the yellowed pages, she remembered just how little these had to do with their Disney counterparts. The line-drawn illustrations, which she studied curiously, were not comfort-inducing. She paused at one page, where a burly hunter in a feathered cap was busily carving up a wolf with an axe, blood spurting. How could parents read these to children? Unless it was to steel them for the hard cold cruelties of life ahead.

She snorted at her fancy and flipped through another couple of pages, to Mary's bookmark.

Another illustration, this of a crumbling tower, surrounded by and perhaps choked by a thicket of wild, thorny brambles.

Just like mine, she thought wryly.

Gwynn shifted the page back and began to read. Sleeping Beauty, the cursed princess who pricked her finger on a spindle and fell into a hundred-years' sleep. Over time the thicket of brambles grew up and hid her castle from view, and no one could penetrate the thorny overgrowth.

Just like mine.

There was a happy ending to this fairy tale, of course. After the hundred years, a prince came to fight his way through the thorns and awaken Sleeping Beauty.

This was the point where Gwynn thrust the book aside and turned off the light. That part wasn't like hers, that was for sure. Her former prince was dead, by his own hand. As attractive as Colin the wood man was, she didn't need another prince—and Colin couldn't fight his way through the brambles anyway. He had even admitted it.

With her hand to her scratched cheek, Gwynn fell asleep.

Part II
Fairy Tales

17

SHE WASN'T AFRAID, Gwynn told herself.

For some time after Richard's death, she'd dreamed of the apple orchard, the looming trees with their low-hanging skeletal branches, reaching for her, always reaching for her. In those dreams she'd feared them, and everywhere she'd turned, there had been another. The cold, gray, scaly bark. The occasional fruit, well past its season, which clung to a branch like a tiny yellow shrunken head. The dream knowledge that something terribly wrong, terribly evil, was just out of sight along the path. In these dreams she knew she could not turn back—could never turn back. In these dreams she knew that all paths led to a horror.

But the dreams had faded. She had not had the nightmare of the orchard in years. And she was not afraid now, she told herself. Still, the day was cold, and she pulled her coat more tightly about her, pulled her sleeves down over her hands. The dead leaves crunched and skittered underfoot, the bones of the dead summer. She shivered and forged her way on.

There was blood on her hand, she realized suddenly, feeling the trickle between her fingers. The thorns had scratched at her, again trying to hold her back. She didn't even pause now, but walked on, holding the scratch to her mouth. She wouldn't think about the blood. She wouldn't think about the brambles. She wasn't afraid, and she would look inside the dovecote.

Don't.

The voice was Colin's, soft in her head, but with some urgency. Gwynn had let him convince her to come away that other afternoon, but she would not be swayed today.

The clearing came as a surprise, as it had the first time. In the center of it hulked the low barn, its beams worn, the ragged canvas hanging like a black distress signal in the window. There was no sound. The dovecote was black with age, the roof sagging slightly in the middle, and menacing, like a monster prepared to leap. Gwynn shook herself, a hand to her breast. It was not a monster. It was not a hulk. It was a building, old, abandoned, and unused for ages. She was simply going to look inside; she would not go into its bowels too deeply, not with the way the ridgepole sagged. She was curious, she told herself, but not stupid. She patted the flashlight in her pocket. Reassurance.

There was no sound. The clearing, as she crossed it slowly, was silent. No birds. Perhaps they were disturbed by her presence. Well, she would not be here long. Just long enough to look, long enough to prove to herself that, despite the chills the place gave her—it was simply abandoned, and she was simply suggestible, and there was nothing more to it than that. Despite the urgency in his voice when Colin had told her to leave the door alone—she was master of this, her own property, left to her by her own great-aunt, for reasons she would probably never understand. She pulled the flashlight out and flicked the switch, turning it up to look at the bulb, which glowed slightly orange. No doubt the batteries *were* weak after all this time; she'd simply have her look around, and put batteries on the shopping list when she'd returned to the cottage.

Gwynn hadn't brought the remains of the penetrating oil, because, as she remembered, the door here was not latched, and in fact hung slightly askew on its hinges; there was probably no need of it. Now she put a hand to the wood and pushed gingerly. The bottom plank was driven into the ground by its own weight, and at first it resisted her. She pushed harder. The crack widened. Slowly. With an ugly dragging sound. She glanced down and saw the arc it traced in the dirt. She shoved even harder, and suddenly the door swung open to slam against the inside wall. She nearly fell into the dimness.

The flashlight beam was indeed weak, yellow instead of the strong clear white of full power. Gwynn cursed herself for not checking the batteries back in the kitchen. A thin pale rectangle of light fell at her feet from the grey day outside, and though she shone the hopeless flashlight beam further into the dovecote, it took a few moments for her eyes to accustom themselves to the darkness.

Cages lined the walls at the edges of the light, their occupants long gone, their doors, for the most part, hanging open like hungry mouths. Patches of rotten hay were scattered over the dirt floor. She shone the light overhead and it picked out the great black beams that crisscrossed beneath the sagging roof trusses. Dust motes filtered their way past, into the beam and out again like flurries. The mustiness made her sneeze, once, and again.

Deserted. Gwynn had no idea what had so spooked Colin. Or why she had allowed herself to absorb his uneasiness. There was nothing here.

She turned slowly, looking at the dove boxes, at the beams overhead. Everything was deathly still.

A slight movement of air touched her cheek. There was a creak behind her. She spun, and the flashlight died.

"Who's there?

Gwynn shook the flashlight, retreating quickly toward the pale rectangle of daylight on the floor. Impossibly, the door to the dovecote swung shut.

No, it didn't. She blinked, confused. Took a quick panicked step.

Gwynn stumbled, fell to her knees. The flashlight beam, reviving, gave out a feeble light. She looked up, and for a moment thought she saw feet. Swinging gently in the movement of air, the toes barely dragging across the dirt floor.

With a strangled cry, Gwynn scrambled toward the door. She clawed at it with her fingers, and then threw herself out into the clearing, into the air, away from the creaking darkness.

18

"HE DIDN'T WANT a care home," Mary said, unlocking the front door of the semi-detached cottage with one of her many keys. "Can't blame him, though it surely would make life easier for the rest of us. Didn't want to come live with us, either." She pushed open the door and stepped into the entryway, calling. "Dad? Hello?"

There was a weak shout from the end of the hallway. Mary shut the door behind them and led the way forward until they reached the solarium at the back of the house. It was crowded with furniture: a sofa, a reclining chair, a large-screened TV. The view was into a garden where the shrubs were wrapped up in burlap for the winter, as though in heavy coats. On the sofa, a whip-thin old man, shrunken into a dark green bathrobe, leaned against a mound of cushions. Gwynn had the impression he'd just taken his feet off the coffee table before they came in, but couldn't quite pinpoint why she thought that.

"Dad," Mary said briskly, setting aside her purse and unbuttoning her coat, "I've brought you a visitor."

He had brilliant blue eyes, brighter even than the pillows against which he leaned. The eyes were huge in his bony face, like a bird's eyes set above the sharp beak of his nose. He looked over Gwynn curiously. "Gwynneth Chelton's niece, living up in Dove Cottage—excuse me, *Gull* Cottage. Never got used to the new name." He eyed her curiously, measuring her up and down. "You've got her nose. And her chin. And those green eyes. But the hair's not right."

"Dad," Mary remonstrated.

"Just an observation, girl," Mr. Scott replied. He turned again to Gwynn. "She thinks I'm being rude. I think if I want to be rude at my age, I've earned that right." He waved a hand toward the recliner. "Have a seat, young Gwynn. Mary tells me that's your name as well. Hope you don't mind me calling you by it."

Gwynn slipped in behind the coffee table piled high with books and settled. "Not at all, Mr. Scott." The old man did not seem to share his daughter's cagey ways. She must have come by her nature from her mother.

"Martin. Call me Martin. Nobody calls me by my name anymore. That's one of the horrors of old age. They turn you into your father."

"You *are* my father," Mary shot back.

"Go fix tea, you obstreperous girl," he ordered.

Mary glanced at Gwynn with the slightest raise of the eyebrows before disappearing back down the hallway.

"And don't you be raising your eyebrows at me, girl," Martin called after her. He winked at Gwynn. "Blasted girl. Always has to have the last word." He shifted against the mounds of pillows, and a spasm crossed his face, quickly bitten back. "I'm an old man. She oughtn't argue with me so much. But she's the most argumentative child there ever was." He laughed. "Got it from her old mum. That woman would argue with me until she was blue in the face, even when we both knew she was as wrong as could be. Contrary, that's what it was."

"You miss her," Mary shouted from somewhere down the hall.

"And she eavesdrops. All the time. Where'd she learn that?" Martin shook his head. His hair was fine and wispy, snow-white, standing about in clouds.

"Mr. Scott—Martin—you called it Dove Cottage."

Doves. Again.

"Oh, aye, that it used to be. Until Tommy Chelton died, and Gwynn changed the name. Took some getting used to." He frowned, then shook his head, as though he had no idea he'd provided a vital piece of information. Though perhaps he didn't know. Gwynn wasn't sure, either, why it was vital, just that it was. "So what is it you want to know, then?" He leaned forward, lowered his voice. "You haven't got a bit of whisky on you, have you?"

Gwynn shook her head, surprised.

"Damn." He winked at her again and sat back. "So. Is it Tommy Chelton I hear you're interested in?"

"Tommy Chelton," she repeated, nodding. But she was still distracted. Dove Cottage. Doves.

Mary returned with the tea tray. She shoved the pile of books aside and slid the tray onto the table. Her face was still stern, though there was an unfamiliar quirk to the corner of her mouth.

"It's Earl Gray," Martin said, holding out his frail hands for his cup. "I hope you don't mind. It's the only kind I like anymore." There were tiny cookies on a plate next to the tea pot, and he nodded to them.

"Try those. Lemon drops. Nobody makes them like Mary—she has her mother's secret recipe."

"He can't eat them," Mary said. "Gets his blood sugar up. But if I don't put them on a plate for a visitor, it gets his blood pressure up."

Martin shrugged. "One way or another, it's all going to kill me anyway."

"He's always saying that," Mary said, handing Gwynn a cup, then pouring one for herself before perching on the edge of the sofa. "But he's far too ornery to die, this one."

"Listen to her," Martin said, feigning shock. "Just listen to this child of my blood." He took a sip of his tea, slurping mightily. "Now, back to business, young Gwynn. You want to know about old Tommy Chelton. Or I should say, young Tommy Chelton that was."

"He died young, didn't he?" Gwynn asked. "The solicitor said he thought sometime in the 1950s. That would have made my aunt a widow in her twenties, wouldn't it have?"

"1951, it would have been." Martin nodded, took another slurping drink of tea.

"You're awfully sure, Dad," Mary said suspiciously.

"Looked it up, didn't I? After you asked me?" He snorted. "Had that battle-axe of a nurse you keep having drop around here get out my scrapbooks for me. A lot of noise she made about it, too, as though I were asking her to do something obscene, or against union regulations." Again that sly look in Gwynn's direction. "I finally had to pretend to a heart attack to get her to do what I asked."

"Dad!" But Mary wasn't as shocked as she sounded.

"1951. July of that year. Tommy was never quite right after the war, everyone said. I don't think they quite remembered what he was like before the war, actually." Martin gazed up at the ceiling, as though trying to read history there. "He wasn't really a nice man. I never knew what Gwynn saw in him. Older than she was, too, by some ten years or so."

"How long had they been married? In 1951?"

He pursed his lips and thought a moment. "Seven years? Something like that. He was home on leave, recuperating from some wound I don't remember. They married up, and he went back to the front. Not sure where he was stationed. I think he might have been a gunner of some sort." His blue eyes flickered to Gwynn and back. "I was only here off and on myself, anyway. I was stationed outside of London."

Mary shook her head. "All that secrecy. The war's been over for a few years, Dad. You can say it." She put her tea cup in her saucer and sat back. "Bletchley Park. Dad was C and C." There was pride in her voice, and a bit of marvel.

"All I know is that I had a bit of an eye for Gwynn myself back then," he said, as though Mary had not spoken. "Came back on leave and found her married off, just like that." The expression in his brilliant eyes grew mournful. "She looked terrible when she told me. As though she'd had the life squeezed out of her. Never heard her laugh again."

Now Mary drew back, and the tea cup clattered gently against its saucer. Her face was drawing in, closing down in that look Gwynn found so familiar. The measuring face. "You never told me this, Dad."

Martin lifted his pointed chin. "Not something you tell your daughter, is it? About your first love?" He coughed gently. "But then I turned my eyes elsewhere, and they lighted on your mother. A good woman. And there you have it." Yet he seemed to have withdrawn momentarily, into a past where they could not follow, and at least on the part of Mary Tennant, certainly couldn't understand. "And then there you were, my Mary, a prize worth keeping."

For a long time no one said anything. From the corner of her eye, Gwynn watched the color wash in and out of Mary's face. Mary sat stonily, her hands gripping her tea things. She saw Gwynn watching her, and she put her cup and saucer back on the tray on the table. Her lips were pressed together, her jaw fixed.

"Then he died," Gwynn prodded finally. "Tommy Chelton. In the summer of 1951. You said he had a difficult war?"

Martin shrugged, and in that moment, he looked like his daughter. "As difficult as anyone else's, I suppose—except mine, of course, because Bletchley was a relatively comfortable berth." His mouth, too, thinned out. "A bully, Tommy was, before he joined up. All through school. Sometimes the army's a good place for someone like that—a kind of legalized working off of aggression. But he came home, after he was mustered out, and he was worse than before. People don't remember that part." He sighed, his lips still tight. "You come home a war hero, and everyone forgets what you were before. Everyone forgives your behavior afterwards. And he played it, too. Oh, yes. Tommy knew how to profit from people's sympathy."

The bitterness in his voice was a surprise.

"He was an angry, cruel man, was Tommy Chelton. Don't you believe anything other, young Gwynn," Martin said. "That's why his killing himself like that came as such a surprise to everyone."

Gwynn caught her breath.

"He *killed* himself?"

The blue eyes blazed into her face.

"Hanged himself. Up in that old dovecote behind the cottage."

19

"I NEED TO sit down," Mary said as they crossed the park and came upon a bench.

Despite her own disquiet, Gwynn looked at her with concern. She had never seen Mary Tennant shaken out of her steadfastness, not even at finding a stray man sleeping on the sofa when she let herself in to Gull Cottage first thing in the morning. Unflappable. Until now. Mary planted her feet squarely on the grass—no crossing of legs for her—and gripped her purse with both hands. Gwynn herself felt unwell: dizzy, a bit frightened by what she'd learned.

"Did he—did what your father said about my great-aunt—upset you?"

Even more surprisingly, Mary laughed. "That old goat? Oh, never. Flummox me? Always. He can't help himself. He loves to wind me up."

Gwynn sat back. "But you said—he'd never told you that—"

Mary shrugged, her eyes on the gulls which strolled about them brazenly. "And wasn't he adorable, the way he tried to reassure me?" She laughed again. "He comes out with these things, you know. Maybe they're true. Maybe he was friendly with Mrs. Chelton before they both married others. Who really knows? He cut a figure back then, that old man. Doesn't look it now, but he was quite the blade." She shook her head, tossed a glance back at the row of cottages they'd just left.

"I believe you," Gwynn said.

"It's just exhausting sometimes, keeping up with him. He's always trying to get a rise out of me."

"And succeeding?"

Mary tilted her head in assent. "But I can't let him see that, or he crows over it abominably." Now she turned her brown eyes—obviously inherited from her mother—on Gwynn. "But he managed to give you a shock, didn't he?"

He hanged himself. In the dovecote. Behind Dove Cottage.

Gwynn had forced herself to go back, to look inside the dovecote. There had been nothing there. No feet scraping the dirt floor. Nothing. She had imagined it all. She had imagined it.

She nodded, swallowing.

"Do you suppose it's true?" she asked, her throat thick. "That part, about Tommy Chelton hanging himself?"

She had imagined it.

Mary looked thoughtful, her dark brows drawing together. "Probably that part is true. I wonder why I didn't remember that? We'd have to check."

"The newspaper?"

"I don't think so. 1951? Even if it were in an obituary, the language would be coded. Subtle. 'Died suddenly at home' or some such thing. Cagey back then, newspapers were." Mary was still frowning, sorting this out. "No. I'll have to ask around, see if anyone can back up Dad's story. How about Jamie Simms?"

Gwynn shrugged. "He said he'd research that if I wanted—but I thought I'd dig around a bit myself before I paid him to do it. And you really don't remember? You said you were just a child then."

Mary shook her head. "I have a sense about it, his dying and people talking, hushing when we children came into a room. But I might be imagining things, too."

Gwynn didn't think so. A less imaginative, more practical person she had never met. She wished desperately to be more like Mary. She also wished that the visit with Martin Scott had not been cut so short— that the visiting nurse had not made her daily appearance and hustled them out of the room. "I'd really like to see a picture of him. Of them. All of them. I need to know more."

Mary levered herself up from the bench. "I know. I'll try to wrestle those scrapbooks of his away sometime." She looked at the sky. "Let's go, before the rain starts again."

THE WEEKEND WAS the most difficult, when Mary didn't come in for her two hours in the morning. Gwynn busied herself Saturday with rearranging more furniture, with boxing up things and setting them by the door for the next run to Oxfam. The wood in the shed was getting low, though she put off calling Colin Moore for another load; she wasn't sure why she felt uncomfortable, but she wasn't quite ready to speak to him again. She had not seen him since the night of the Pig Iron gig; she wanted to talk to him about what she had found, but she wanted, too, to pretend none of it had ever happened. She wanted to tell him about the dovecote, but she did not want to admit she'd gone back. Twice.

What would he think about the former name of the cottage? About Tom Chelton? She remembered the almost irresistible pull toward the half-closed door of the dovecote, toward the darkened maw, and shuddered. She remembered Colin's hand on her arm, the urgency in his voice when he held her back. She remembered the cold. Most of all, she remembered the feet, swinging gently, toes in the dirt—feet which were not there, feet which she hadn't known had ever *been* there. She didn't think she needed any verification of Martin Scott's story beyond that: evil had occurred in that dovecote. Thomas Chelton's suicide. If there were actually such a thing as an unhappy spirit leaving an imprint—and she didn't believe it, she *didn't*—surely there would be one there.

Unhappy spirit. Yet—yet. The dovecote didn't give off the sense of unhappiness. There wasn't the miasma of despair one might expect. It was something else. Something angry, vengeful. Something malicious. She thought of the putrid stink that forced its way in through the gate they'd broken open. The smell of evil.

The more she learned, the more she wondered: had Tom Chelton really been an unhappy man? A bully, Martin Scott had called him. Who had had a bad war. Martin had thought her great-aunt Gwynn the unhappy one. *I never heard her laugh again.* He had spoken with such sadness, too, as though all his memories of the other Gwynn, up to that point, had been filled with laughter. Then, a sudden marriage to a cruel, angry man without explanation—and then, seven years later, an unhappy death, and the beginning of a miserable widowhood. Surely, though, if the marriage had made her great-aunt Gwynn miserable, then her husband's early death would have freed her? Yet both Mary and Colin had told her that Gwynn had remained miserable, had tried desperately to hold people at arm's length, and had, for the most part, succeeded. What had truly happened there?

Death and the dovecote.

And what did the dead dove on the step have to do with anything?

GWYNN DID NOT sleep well.

Her great-aunt came to her in a dream, her hair white, her eyes hidden behind steel-rimmed glasses. Her face and hands were lined.

How can you keep him out now?
Who?
Tom.
Where is he?
He walks. You opened the gate. You've let him in.
He's dead.
That doesn't matter to him.

Gwynn wrenched herself awake, trying to escape the old woman. The bedroom was dark save for a rectangle of reflected light on the ceiling from the street below. Beneath the duvet her skin was damp with sweat, and she found herself breathing heavily, as though from a run. The travel alarm on the bedside table showed 1:47. Her ears were straining for any sound, but she heard nothing save the roaring of her blood in her skull. She was alone, she told herself. She was alone. Slowly she tried to regulate her breathing, her racing heart.

"Calm down," she said aloud.

Then the bedroom window burst, glass splinters flying everywhere.

20

GWYNN CLUTCHED THE duvet around her shoulders, huddled in the chair. The lights of the police car still strobed through the windows, splashing color across the ceiling, flashed back again by the mirror in the dining room. An officer in a yellow safety jacket pressed a cup of milky tea into her hands. She took a sip automatically and found it liberally sugared. Overhead, she could hear the other officer moving around in the bedroom.

"Are you sure there isn't someone I could call?" The officer had taken out a small notebook and pencil.

She shook her head, reaching up to touch the side of her face where she felt an itch, and found blood. She stared at her fingers dumbly.

"You must have taken a bit of glass there," the officer said. "Are you hurt anywhere else?"

He suggested the paramedics, and she waved the idea aside.

"So tell me again what happened."

"I don't really know. I was sleeping. Something woke me, and then the brick came through the window."

"Something woke you. A sound? Could it have been someone moving about out in the road? On your terrace?"

The second officer came stomping down the stairs and entered the room. "Whoever threw that didn't throw it from the road, unless he was some sort of Olympian. No, he came up, probably onto the terrace." He cleared his throat. "You were here alone, Mrs. Forest?"

"I live alone, yes."

He looked at her. "That wasn't what I was asking."

Gwynn met his gaze, a dull anger in her chest. "Yes. I was alone. I woke. Someone threw a brick through my bedroom window." She held out her bloody fingers for him to see.

"Some hoodlum from the pub?" the first officer suggested.

"Probably," the second answered.

"The pub was closed," Gwynn objected.

There was a sharp knock at the front door. Slowly the second officer turned back into the entryway and slid the bolt.

"Gwynn?"

She hadn't seen Colin Moore for almost a week. He pushed past the officer, into the sitting room and circled the sofa to her side. His grey eyes went immediately to her face, and she put the hand up again.

He dropped to his knee before the winged-back chair and pushed her hand away from her cheek. With gentle fingers, he probed the cut, and she gasped at the sharp pain.

"Glass?" he asked, throwing the question out to the room at large.

"And you would know that how?" the burly officer demanded.

If Colin Moore ever tossed contemptuous glances, it would be now. "The curtains waving *outside* the bedroom window." He turned back to his examination of the cut at her temple. "There doesn't seem to be any in there now. It's not a big cut—I don't think you'd need stitches, but I'll take you to the surgery in the morning just to be sure."

It was the most words, Gwynn thought, she'd heard out of him since she'd met him.

"And you are?" the younger officer asked, pencil at the ready.

"Moore," he said, not looking up. "First aid kit? Kitchen?"

Gwynn nodded. He drew a folded handkerchief from his pocket and handed it to her.

"Hold this there. I'll be right back." He straightened and pushed past the policemen, one of whom put out a hand to detain him.

"Just a moment, Mr. Moore, if you would, please," he said mildly.

Colin only looked down at the hand as though it were something noxious. "I'll be right back." Then he pushed through the kitchen door.

"You know this man?" the officer asked.

A rather obvious question. "He's my wood man," Gwynn said.

THE OFFICERS TOOK the brick along with their statements and departed, the strobing light disappearing.

"Why'd you tell them about the dead dove?" Gwynn demanded. She still huddled in the wing-backed chair, still wrapped tightly in the duvet from the big bed upstairs.

This time it wasn't tea or coffee, but milk he'd warmed in the kitchen. He handed her a mug. The steam coming off the drink smelled vaguely of vanilla. "Drink this. No caffeine. Maybe you can get back to sleep."

Gwynn shook her head. "I don't think I'll sleep again tonight." She didn't really *want* to sleep again, perchance to dream. She took a sip from the mug anyway, felt the warmth of the milk glide down her throat and spread. She glanced over at him where he sat on the sofa, leaning forward, his own mug untouched on the coffee table. Waited.

"Because you didn't," he said, when she remained silent.

There was a question there, one he didn't need to ask, but she refused to answer. She didn't know why she hadn't told the officers about the dead dove on the front step.

"It happened," Colin assured her. "I was there. I saw it. You didn't imagine it."

His words were pointed, and prescient.

"I know I didn't imagine it," she retorted defensively. "Of course I didn't."

"They were going to dismiss the brick as hooliganism. Some drunken yob late out of the pub, tossing bricks. You know how it goes. They wouldn't have stirred themselves further." He turned his mug in a circle, and, seeing the damp ring it left, wiped the surface with the heel of his hand. Absently he took a coaster from the holder and slipped it under his drink.

"And the dead dove matters?"

Colin eyed her. "It's a pattern. Someone is targeting you."

Gwynn took another drink from her milk, savoring the vanilla. She didn't think she'd ever feel warm again. Or safe.

"I opened the gate," she murmured.

He turned to face her with those steady grey eyes.

She felt her face flush.

"My great aunt said that," she whispered.

"You'd better tell me," he said.

GWYNN TOLD HIM about the dream, about the conversation with the woman she'd known was the other Gwynn, though she'd never seen her in life. Only in reflection.

"How do you know it was her, then?" he asked.

Carefully she described the woman to him, down to the steel-rimmed spectacles.

"Yes. That's Mrs. Chelton." He glanced quickly toward the door to the dining room and back again.

She caught the look. Remembered what he had said when he'd arrived that late afternoon with the tool box. *You've got company.*

Remembered how she thought she'd seen the reflection beside her own in the dining room window.

"You've seen her," she said.

Instead of answering, he picked up his mug as though to take a drink, but then set it down on its coaster again. He looked into the cup of his own hands.

"Once," he said finally.

He knew what she meant. He knew *when* she meant.

"So it wasn't *nothing* that afternoon."

"No. It wasn't nothing."

The realization hung between them, filmy, nebulous.

"Then what was it?" Gwynn asked. She was clutching her own mug so hard her knuckles ached. "I don't believe in ghosts. I don't believe the dead are still with us. I won't believe that."

Slowly Colin stood, walked to the doorway, and looked into the dining room. He had his hands in his pockets, and he leaned now against the door frame as though waiting for a visitor to come through. Or for the vision of Gwynn Chelton to reappear, to make herself known to them. In the light from the table lamp, his face was shadowed, his cheekbones chiseled.

"You know," he said, each word weighted, "you might not have a choice."

21

"I THINK," COLIN said slowly, "that we can separate things into two categories."

Gwynn looked at him over the rapidly cooling milk. Waiting for more.

"The things we can't explain," he said, a challenge in his expression, "and the things we can attribute to human agency."

Still she waited.

"Footsteps on the stairs when you're alone in the house, doors opening and shutting, crashes from upstairs. Mrs. Chelton in the window, once for you, once for me. The brambles, the gate, the *feeling* at the dovecote."

"We don't need to explain *feelings*," Gwynn protested.

Colin held up a hand. "Just listen to me. Then there's the dead bird and the brick. I know you don't believe in ghosts. But the first list is in the realm of the unexplainable. The second is in the realm of angry human action."

"Who is angry enough to do that?"

Colin cocked his head, raised an eyebrow. "I think we both know, don't we?"

Gwynn grimaced. "I guess we do. But why would Paul Stokes do those things? It's not—*normal.* He could just wait and see what the challenge to the will does for him."

"You said the James Simms told you there was very little case for Stokes and his challenge," Colin reminded her. "Perhaps he's just taking a two-pronged approach. If he can't get the property legally, he'll try his damnedest to drive you out. To make your life here miserable."

She drove a distracted hand through her hair. "That's ludicrous."

He only shrugged. "The other alternative is that it's a random stranger or strangers, just tossing things at your cottage on a whim. Do you buy that?"

Colin had a point. She set the empty mug down.

"I've never met such—malevolence."

He came back slowly to his seat on the sofa across from her chair.

"There is malevolence in the world," he said. "There is evil. And it's not some disembodied idea. Evil is done by people. Regular people."

GWYNN WOKE UP stiff and groggy, with the duvet wrapped around her and pillows tucked under her head. For a moment she kept her eyes closed, feeling surprisingly warm, until she heard the muffled thunk of the wood stove door and realized the fire was burning full-force. She smelled bacon. Something with eggs. She opened one eye.

For a large man, Colin went about the room with little noise; he barely disturbed the air through which he moved.

"For a moment I thought you were Mary," she said, yawning.

"Not half so good-looking," he replied, skirting the coffee table to look at her with narrowed eyes. "How's the cut feel?"

She rose slowly to a seated position, put a hand to her temple, and winced. "About that good." She pulled the comforter more closely about her shoulders. "Do I smell breakfast? That's why I thought you were Mary. Had nothing to do with your looks."

Colin shot her a glance. "It's Sunday. She's at church."

"You don't do church?"

"Should. After a gig." He left the room. She heard him moving softly around the kitchen.

"You were playing last night?" she called after him.

"Over to the White Hart," he answered. After a moment he returned with a plate, which he set on the table before her. Bacon and an omelette. "Eat this. Good for shock."

"That's how you happened to be by at two in the morning?"

He shrugged. "Village is dark. You see police lights, you go look." He sat down, looked toward the window. "Especially if you have a bad feeling."

Her head shot up.

"What do you mean?"

Colin only shook his head. "I don't know." He did not look at her. "You keep asking me that question, and I don't know the answer." His gaze remained focused on something beyond the glass. She turned her head. All she could see was filmy gray October sky.

"LAST NIGHT," HE said thoughtfully, "you said several times that you don't believe in ghosts."

"I don't. I can't." Gwynn sounded desperate, even to her own ears.

"Can't?"

Gwynn shook her head violently. "If there were ghosts, I'd be haunted."

"By?"

Colin still wasn't looking at her. She refused to answer until he did. She waited. After a long moment, he turned away from the window and she glared into his grey eyes.

"My husband. He died six years ago."

Colin was very still. He seemed to recognize her sudden anger as having no fixed direction, and he simply stood and let it swirl around him.

"I didn't love him. I failed him. He was bipolar, and I wanted to leave him." The words were garbled, confused, and they tumbled out any which way.

"Did you?"

"No." She swallowed. "I stayed with him. Until he died. Chose to die. But he knew."

Suddenly Gwynn saw again the orchard, saw Richard, the inexpertly fashioned, but effective, noose. Her angry husband, who had hanged himself. She dropped her head in her hands.

Gwynn Chelton knew. She had to have known.

"What is it?"

She drove her nails into her skin. "I was widowed young. No children. I never remarried."

SHE HAD NEVER admitted all of that to anyone, and now she felt shocked at the words. Richard. She hadn't loved him at the end. She had failed him. Her love had simply worn out. She had wanted to leave him. Then she had found him in the orchard behind the house. Hanging, neck distended. Dead. Beyond what help she could give when she screamed and tried to hold him up, tried to scrabble for the knot.

Colin had not moved. He still gazed on her face, expressionless.

"So he would haunt me. My husband. If I allowed it. If there were ghosts."

I might as well have killed him, she thought.

"Eat your breakfast," Colin said.

Gwynn stared at him. "God damn it! I've just told you this and all you can say is to eat my breakfast?" She wanted to hurl the plate across the room at him.

"You need your strength," he said calmly. "Gwynn. Listen to me. You might not believe in ghosts—you might not allow yourself to believe in them. But" and he took a deep breath—"that doesn't mean they don't believe in you."

SO GWYNN ATE the omelette, finding it filled with tomato, cheese, and onion, and surprisingly fortifying. While she ate, Colin went upstairs with a broom, a dustpan, and a box he brought in from the back of his truck. She heard him moving about in the bedroom overhead, cleaning up the glass. He'd done a quick fix in the middle of the night with a plastic bin liner, but now, in the light of Sunday morning, she could hear him taking care of the rest.

"Only one pane," he said when he reappeared, the box of glass clinking with each step. "Shattered the living hell out of it. But it's easily replaced. If I can get hold of Harvard—he can cut a piece down to the shop if he's about."

He made the call on his cell, the conversation brief, terse, and barely intelligible. While she listened, Gwynn ran her hand idly through her hair, finding more bits of glass.

"I'm going to get it, and I won't be long." Colin retrieved the box, his hand on the door. "Lock this behind me."

Leaving the plate on the coffee table, Gwynn did as she was told, then took herself up to the bath for a quick wash. She pulled on some jeans and a sweatshirt; toweling her hair, she examined the broken window. It was, as Colin had said, only a single pane; he'd pulled the jagged edges from the frame and scraped out the putty. She put out a shaking finger to touch the scarred wood, and as she did, her eyes caught the movement in Eyewell Lane below.

Paul Stokes leaned against the door frame of The Stolen Child, the smoke rising lazily from his cigarette. As though he sensed her gaze, he slowly raised his head to look up to the bedroom window. And then, equally slowly—and Gwynn could not be mistaken about this—he smiled and raised a hand in salute.

22

"COME ON, THEN," Colin said, the window freshly glazed, the dishes washed and put away. "We'll get away for the day. Different place, different ghosts." He looked down at her bare feet. "Wear sturdy shoes."

Gwynn glanced at him sharply, but his face was impassive. Still. Again. Always.

"What if he throws another brick?"

"Nothing we can do. But he won't. No fun if you're not here for it."

He had a point. Gwynn donned her hikers, shrugged into her wool pea coat, and followed him out the door, checking twice to make sure it was securely locked after her. He had the work truck, but the front seat was clear, and she snapped her seat belt into place as he climbed in behind the wheel.

"A bit of a ramble, and maybe a pub lunch," he suggested, pulling out onto Eyewell Lane and heading down to the intersection. He took a sharp turn onto Alexander Road.

"I don't know as I feel all that up to walking," Gwynn protested, looking out the window as the houses thinned and the trees thickened.

"You will," Colin said. "Trust me."

Did she? Trust. What an awkward idea. She turned it over in her mind, as though examining a rock or a brick thrown through the window. She supposed she trusted Colin Moore as much as she trusted anyone, but then, she hadn't been all that close to anyone since Richard's death. It was easier just to keep her head down, keep pushing forward.

My husband died young. I never married again.

That was the first Gwynn. That was her, too. She pondered now: how much *had* her great-aunt known about her? Had the other Gwynn recognized the parallels in their lives? She would never know for certain, but she had an inkling.

THEY DREW INTO a carpark and followed the signs to the path, Colin stopping to pay the entry fee. Gwynn was glad she'd worn her hiking boots; the day was damp, and the path was, too. She followed close behind Colin, who kept his hands stuffed into his coat pockets until they came to a particularly steep stretch; then he put out a steadying hand to Gwynn, which she took. His grip was firm, no-nonsense. He released her when the path eased up, and she discovered she missed his hand as soon as it was gone.

She heard the rush of water long before she saw it. The falls opened out before them suddenly, and she gasped.

The air was full of water, mists rising up and falling down. She held her hands out, lifted her face up. It was cool, soothing. The rush might have been the blood in her veins, the thoughts in her head.

Colin was watching her. "Trust me?"

Gwynn looked up at the falls, the water tumbling from somewhere up in the greenery. There was no one else around. Then she looked up into his face, the water beading up on his forehead, his cheeks. She could feel the condensation on her own skin.

"Yes," she said.

For the first time since she had met him, she saw Colin smile fully, a slow deliberate lifting of the corner of his mouth; his grey eyes acquired more depth.

He took a step forward, took his hands from his pockets, and cupping her chin, bent to kiss her.

"I love this place." His hand found hers, and he turned to gaze up at the falls.

Gwynn said nothing. She had no words.

"TELL ME HIS name," Colin said, still staring upward to the point where the water leapt from its rocky stream bed and tumbled down whitely to them.

Again Gwynn reveled in the feeling of the moisture on her face, clinging to her skin. It was a baptism. The mist felt green, alive, like the mossy stones they'd clambered over to get to this pool, like the undergrowth, like the trees. She wondered how long it would take her, standing here, to grow moss between her fingers, to become the female version of the Green Man.

"Take me up there," she said instead of answering, following his gaze with her own. "Can you?"

He nodded once, his grey eyes flickering to her and away again; then he turned toward a path that snaked away into the trees. His hands were tucked into the pockets of his coat in the way he had, and she found herself shoving her own fists into her pockets like him as she fell in behind.

They were silent as the sound of the waterfall quieted behind them, muffled by the greenery. The path passed further into the trees before turning slowly back to the left and following the contour of the hillside. It was faint, but Colin walked it confidently, as though it were more than familiar to him. His steps rustled in the damp leaves underfoot; liking the sound, Gwynn shuffled a bit to emphasize it. Colin threw a glance over his shoulder at her, his expression knowing. One corner of his mouth lifted again. Soon the muscles of her thighs began to burn with the effort of climbing, and she placed her feet more carefully.

Atop the hill, the rush of the water grew louder again, and they followed the sound and the path until they reached a level clearing. The ground was soft and slippery now beneath their boots. The air tasted of fecundity; her lungs felt opened. She ran her hands through her hair and felt it curl slickly around her fingers.

The top of the waterfall was deserted, and Gwynn followed Colin wordlessly until he stopped at the edge of the stream and stooped to thrust his hands into the rushing water. She too squatted and put her fingers in, feeling the bone-chilling cold, feeling the power of the movement as the water sped up in its quest to hurl itself over the rocky ledge.

"Can you feel it?" Colin asked, raising his voice to be heard over the rush of water.

Gwynn nodded, not knowing what he meant, not caring.

Colin lifted a hand from the stream, and, turning slightly, touched his wet fingers to her forehead, then pressed his wet palm to her cheek. The slightest of touches, only lasting a moment, a kind of benediction. A blessing.

"The spirit of the wood and water be in you," he said, leaning close.

She was unsure what he meant by that, either, but it was comforting. She closed her eyes and listened for the spirit of wood and water. The sound was mesmerizing. She felt her breathing deepen; she felt larger, expanding into a surprising and beautiful universe.

Slowly he stood and held out a hand. She took it, and he helped her up. He slipped his arm around her, almost without seeming to think, and they leaned together, watching the water rush past them to the falls.

"His name was Richard," she said at last.

Colin nodded.

"He died."

"Six years ago."

Gwynn nodded gently. She kept her eyes on the water, trying to let it wash the unhappiness away—but then she realized that what she was feeling wasn't as sharp as unhappiness, but rather, sorrow. A softer feeling. With its sharp edges worn away, as if by the water. Or time.

He didn't ask anything further, though Gwynn waited. Most people were curious. Most people wanted more. Most of the time she didn't give it to them, because she couldn't. But, as she stood at the edge of the falls with Colin's arm around her, she felt the hum of him on the air: he didn't need to ask. He would accept what she needed to offer, and not demand more. She let out a sigh and found herself leaning against him; it was comfortable. It was comforting.

"He took his own life," she said.

Colin nodded. "He must have been a very unhappy man."

Gwynn weighed his words carefully. Sometimes there was judgment: what role had she played in Richard's unhappiness? She didn't feel that here. Colin's words were all about Richard. There wasn't even a question.

"He couldn't see his way at the end. And I couldn't help him. Sometimes I think I failed him, because"—and she stumbled, still unused to saying the words aloud—"I wanted to leave him. So many times I wanted to leave him."

She felt Colin's slight shift beside her, but she did not take her gaze from the roiling water.

"But you didn't."

"I didn't. But in the end it didn't matter. Richard took his own life when I stayed. He might have taken his own life had I gone."

"How long did it take you to figure that out?"

"A long time." Gwynn pushed her damp hair back from her face and felt the slight touch of a breeze on her cheek. "Sometimes I think I'm still figuring it out. Intellectually, I understand it. But there are other levels, other than intellectual. And that's where my relationship with Richard lives, on those other levels. That's where I have to deal with it."

Gwynn was surprised at her own words and stopped. She was so unused to admission, so unused to speaking the ideas she'd lived with for six years.

"Six years is a long time to feel guilt," was all Colin said.

THEY LEFT THE truck in the carpark and entered the pub in the falling darkness. The tide down on the strand roared gently; the windows glowed with a soft welcoming light. The dining room looked out over the cliffs at the incoming tide. Candles burned in hurricane lanterns on the tabletops. They ordered the Sunday carvery, and, after the waitress had brought their pints, Gwynn took a long drink and sank back into her chair.

She couldn't bring herself to look at Colin. Instead she looked down on the night on the Celtic Sea. In the early evening darkness, the reflection from the dining room on the glass grew more defined, and after a few moments, she saw that he was watching her. That odd half-smile curving his mouth.

Gwynn felt the heat rush into her cheeks, and she ducked her head quickly to her drink once more.

"Steady on," Colin advised.

She set the pint glass down on the table with a click. "I'm not like this. I don't—"

He looked quietly amused. "I know."

She threw up both hands. "You don't know. You can't. You've known me for a couple of weeks."

"I know what you told me."

"I could have lied."

"But you didn't, did you?"

The waitress came with their steaming plates and set them on the table before whisking herself silently away.

"Six years," she said in a small voice.

"I know." He touched a finger to the back of her hand. "Eat your dinner." He took up his own knife and fork.

COLIN CLOSED THE door behind them and slid the bolt, and Gwynn found she was shaking.

He had only turned on a single light. The room was in shadow as he came to her and took her in his arms.

"Don't be frightened," he whispered into her hair.

With warm fingers he pushed aside the hair at her temple and pressed his lips to the sticking plaster beneath it.

"I won't hurt you, Gwynn," he said.

She nodded dumbly, sudden tears pricking behind her eyelids. Then his mouth found hers again, and her hands moved under his shirt, and she forgot to try to remember how this all worked.

23

COLIN WALKED HER to the front door, took the key from her, and let them both in. He shoved the door closed behind them with his hip.

"Wish I didn't have some jobs," he said, running a hand along her chin.

"Wish you didn't. I'd like to be your job." Gwynn's skin felt electric, as though she had been turned inside out, and the very air shocked her. She put her own shaky hand to his unshaven jaw. Skin, she thought, surprised. Remembering.

That small half-smile. "I'll be your handyman," he sang, quietly.

He leaned forward to kiss her.

From the kitchen doorway, Mary cleared her throat, the feather duster held before her like a weapon.

Gwynn would have leapt away from Colin, but he held her tight.

"Out all night, have we been?" Mary's voice was arch.

"Don't know about you, ol' Molly," Colin said, "but I have been."

"Damned kids."

Gwynn buried her hot face in Colin's shoulder. She felt like laughing. Maybe singing.

"Hope to God you at least took your clothes off this time," Mary said.

At this Colin laughed, full-throated, and attractive—and happy—sound. He released Gwynn and bounded to Mary. He took her stiff body in his arms and kissed her soundly on the cheek. "Oh, and you're just jealous. I'll talk to your old man for you, if you like."

"Damned kids," she repeated, pushing him away with both hands. "I've got my work to do." And she disappeared back into the kitchen with a sniff, waving the feather duster before her.

The kiss before he slipped back out into the street was thorough.

"I'll call you," he whispered against her mouth.

She raised her eyebrows. "Don't say that. People always say that."

He smiled. "All right. I won't call you." He stepped outside. "I'll just show up."

"I'll be waiting."

Gwynn leaned against the door frame, watching his retreating back as he made his way down to the road where the truck was idling. Before sliding in, he took a hand from his pocket and raised it, slightly, palm out, his level eyes on her.

24

GWYNN ENTERED THE stores from the garden entrance, her cloth bag over her arm. She passed through the low-ceilinged rooms holding shelves of aprons, of wash buckets, of boxed matches—which made her think of Giles Trevelyan. On impulse, she picked up two small boxes; she never knew when she might need some, but she always knew when Giles would. A new package of tapers for the candle holders on the shelf, in case she wanted to throw an intimate dinner party: the idea was rather pleasant. A bit further toward the front of the shop was a shelf full of emergency oil lanterns. There hadn't been a power cut since she'd been in the cottage, but it was now November, and that was the Atlantic Ocean at the end of the village, and the forecast for this evening had been especially grim.

"How are you settling in, then?" Leah at the counter asked as Gwynn set her lantern, tapers, and matches down. Leah's look was kind, concerned. Again Gwynn thought how motherly she seemed. "A bit lonely in that old cottage, I should think."

Gwynn looked up, surprised at the tone. "It's all right," she said quickly. "Mary Tennant comes in every other morning, you know. Like she did for my great-aunt."

Leah nodded. "Ah, that's so. A good woman, Mary. Keeps you company, like? Someone to talk to."

"Yes." Despite the oddness of the conversation, Gwynn didn't want to appear unfriendly. "Everyone's been kind. Mary's taken me to meet her father, up to his cottage. I'd need some batteries for the flashlights, too, I think. And have you any wax buttons, for the candleholders?"

"I think we might still have a package or two," Leah said thoughtfully. She frowned for a moment. "Had a bit of a run on them lately."

It was difficult to imagine there being a run on anything in this shop—in this village. Except, in the summer months, on postcards and ice cream cones and sunscreen. But the season was long over, summer visitors having left the village to the residents and to its own devices. Gwynn followed Leah through a wide doorway, ducking her head under the low lintel as the hand-lettered sign above warned her to.

Leah turned to the right, still frowning, pausing to hand off a couple of packages of batteries, and led the way to a heavy oak dresser, the shelves of which held tea towels and sponges. She opened one of the deep drawers in the lower half and smiled.

"Here they are," she said triumphantly. She pulled out a pair of cellophane wrapped packages and held them up. "How many do you need? Fifteen buttons each package."

"I'd better take them both. It's always nice to have candles on the dinner table, isn't it?" Gwynn smiled brightly at Leah. Probably she wouldn't use that many buttons in a year, but then again, who could tell? Candle-lit dinners for one, Leah probably thought, unless Mary wanted to bring her father over to keep her company, like. In her lonely old cottage. Gwynn breathed a sigh of relief that no one knew about Colin—though they probably would before long in a village this size.

At the counter once more, Leah totted up the purchases on the block. Gwynn handed her a note and took her change. She tucked the purchases into her cloth bag and said her thanks. She turned to go. "You're welcome to come on down here any time, if you'd like someone to talk to," Leah called after her. "We could have tea, like. You know. Another woman to talk to when you're feeling a bit down?"

"Thanks," Gwynn said, puzzled. "That would be nice."

25

THE WIND PICKED up while she was shopping, and as soon as she let herself into the cottage, the rain spattered against the front windows. Her timing was perfect.

Gwynn put the kettle on for tea; the tray, as always, was already set—Mary had left it out as her last act before leaving that morning. There were ginger biscuits, too, but Gwynn decided to leave them for afters. She moved one of the small boxes of matches from her cloth bag to her purse, in case she ran into Giles Trevelyan with his unlit pipe. She slid the emergency candles and the extra flashlight batteries into the drawer beside the sink, then unwrapped a pair of tall green candles and the wax buttons, and pulled the brass sconces from the shelf beside the garden door. She warmed a couple of buttons between her fingers, rolling them about until they were soft and pliable, then dropped them into the holders—polished and gleaming, no doubt under Mary's ministrations—and jammed the tapers in after them. Then she stood back and examined her handiwork: neither of the candles listed drunkenly. Pleased, she brought them out to the low table in the sitting room.

The rain had picked up and now thrashed violently against the windows. Gwynn turned on the lights and drew the front draperies against the encroaching storm. A gust of wind rattled the glass in the casements as she did this, a protest at being shut out of the light and warmth. That reminded her, and she opened the door on the stove and examined the embers, which still glowed red. She laid a few scraps of kindling over the coals and blew on them gently, urging them to flare up and catch. Satisfied, she fed the fire a small split and closed the door.

Gwynn had bought a steak and some mushrooms at the market, and dug a potato out of the darkness under the sink. There was a half-bottle of red wine left over from the previous evening, and as she cooked her dinner, she drank some from a balloon glass she'd found in the back of the cupboard. She flicked through the music on her iPad and called up *Never Stop Moving* by John Jones; her little Bluetooth speaker on the bookshelf put out just enough sound, and she found herself swaying lightly, singing along to "Ferryman." Laughing, she twirled. For the first time in a long time she felt like dancing.

It was like dancing, wasn't it? Sex, done right. She laughed again.

She mashed the potato with butter and garlic, then dumped a bit of the red wine into the steak pan, to deglaze it. Then she poured the result over the meat and potato both. After taking her dinner through to the sitting room, she lit the tapers. She adjusted the volume of John Jones' voice, and then, because it seemed the thing to do, she flicked off the lights, leaving only the candles' wavering flames to illuminate her romantic dinner for one. *There, Leah. A dinner date with myself. And John Jones.* Who needed anything else?

Well, maybe one thing.

Gwynn paused, fork in midair, imagining Colin's tanned face, his watchful gray eyes, his narrow hips. Then she scolded herself. He had a life. She had a life. He was off with Pig Iron. Where would he sit, anyway? She'd have to rearrange everything again, clear off her work on the dining room table, perhaps even pull that table away from the window to allow two to sit there comfortably. It seemed, here, with the draperies closed against the storm and the fire burning cheerfully in the stove behind her, to be far too much trouble. She lifted her wine glass, took another sip, and raised it in toast to herself.

She wasn't lonely. She didn't really know why Leah at the shop would have thought so. Perhaps Leah was thinking about Gwynn Chelton, living up here in Gull Cottage on Eyewell Lane for nearly all her adult life, nearly all of it alone. Still, from the sounds of things, the old woman had been quite capable of living with herself. Gwynn toasted to that and took another drink as the last of John Jones' songs faded out.

AS GWYNN SET down her glass, she heard a sudden wild pass of wind along the narrow street outside the front window, and with a half-hearted flicker, the electricity cut out. At almost the same moment there was a crash from the kitchen, and a sudden blast of air through the cottage snuffed the candles. She was surrounded by total blackness.

After her first small shriek—surprise, she told herself, not fear—Gwynn pulled herself to her feet and looked around the small room. The fire in the stove still blazed through the glass window, throwing a small red shape on the floor before it. As she stared, trying to gain reassurance from it, it darkened and disappeared, then reappeared again, in a wave, much as though someone had passed between it and her.

She felt the hair on her arms stand up.

"Who's there?" she demanded sharply.

There was no answer. She fumbled on the table for the matches and knocked the box to the floor. She knelt to find it, struck her kneecap on the table, and the silverware clanked against the plate. She swore, straightening up with the box in her shaking hand; several matches fell out before she was able to grip one and strike it against the side. The flame flared up and she touched it quickly to one wick and then the other. She grabbed one of the candle holders and turned, holding it aloft like a weapon.

She was alone in the room.

For a moment she merely stood there, candle in hand, her other palm pressed to her chest where her heart pounded against her ribs. *Calm yourself.* She took a deep breath and let it out slowly through her mouth, then took another.

At the window she pulled the curtain aside. All of Eyewell Lane was dark and indistinct beyond the rain-streaked glass. Another wave of air bent the candle flame sideways, and she quickly turned to the kitchen.

The door to the garden had blown open, and rain hurled itself in on the wind, puddling across the kitchen floor. Gwynn cupped her hand around the candle flame and hurried to slam the door against the storm. She had to lean into it, and then, at last, she threw the bolt.

Hadn't she thrown the bolt already?

Gwynn set the candle on the countertop, then pulled tea towels from the top drawer to throw onto the floor. Then, for good measure, she took the flashlight from the cupboard and flicked it on. The beam was sickly yellow—she'd forgotten. She dug out the new batteries— thank God for foresight—and hurriedly changed the old for new.

Then she looked over her shoulder at the door. She hadn't opened it today, hadn't had the heart to look out on the thorns. Had she locked it yesterday? Had she checked the bolt before going to bed? Perhaps Mary had unlocked the door when she had been in this morning. Perhaps. That had to be the answer. Had to be. Repeating this mantra to herself, she retrieved the dirty dishes from the sitting room and piled them in the sink. No electric, no water. Mary would sniff in the morning, but a power cut was hardly Gwynn's fault.

She took the flashlight and one of the candles upstairs with her.

HER CELL PHONE rang as she was finishing an awkward brush of her teeth with a dry brush. She still couldn't recognize the jumble of numbers that showed themselves on the lighted screen, but, needing to hear another human voice, she answered anyway.

"Gwynn."

The human voice she wanted to hear.

"Power cut up there?"

"It is," she said.

"You're all right?"

"I am." Despite her earlier fright, she had to laugh at the monosyllabic conversation. What was it about that man that turned her so laconic in speech? It wasn't just Colin, though; Mary spoke in the same short declaratives as well. Nearly everyone she'd spoken to in the village did. Perhaps it was just in conversing with her, the woman from *off.* Perhaps they were more forthcoming with one another? She had no way of knowing.

"Need anything?"

You. "No," she said. "Thanks. I'm fine."

"All right, then. Lock your doors."

Gwynn bristled slightly at the order. She was an independent, intelligent person. Surely she could be trusted to lock her own doors. Surely she could be trusted to take care of herself. *Unless.*

"Already did," she replied tartly.

There was a sound that might have been impatience, or might have been a laugh. "Phone if you need me."

Then the call was cut, and she was left holding the phone, staring at the glowing icons on the screen. She hadn't told him about the kitchen door, and probably wouldn't, either. Why admit to the stupid shock? To be frightened in a strange cottage by a little wind: she felt foolish enough thinking about her spleeny reaction, without sharing it with anyone. He'd only think she was angling for him to come spend the night with her. Which, upon reflection, would not have been a bad thing.

So there it was, she told herself, waving a hand dismissively in the dark. She made a circuit then of the house, checking the kitchen door again by the light of the flashlight and the sound of the storm, checking the front door as well. She imagined everyone else doing the same to the sound of the wind and the rain, women like Mary Tennant passing silently through their houses like ghosts, making sure their families were secure against the wild world and its storms.

It was—almost—a comforting image. Gwynn took the flashlight upstairs with her again, balancing it on end on the nightstand as she drew on her pajamas and crawled under the duvet. Despite all her protestations on the phone, she wished there was someone here for her to keep secure. More than that, she wished there was someone who, after checking the locks, would curl up in the wide bed with her, and protect her as she slept.

Except she didn't need protection. She didn't.

26

IN THE GREY light of morning, the path was nearly overgrown. Slowly Gwynn closed the door on the rear garden, defeated.

Wordlessly, Mary handed her a cup of strong black coffee, and then returned to cleaning the oven.

"DRESS WARMLY," COLIN had said over the phone.

Now Gwynn wished she had thought to pack thermal underwear for the trip over, but she had never thought to be standing in a high field in the West Country in the dark, waiting for an old farmer to touch a match to a burn pile. The pile itself had grown, she thought, five-fold since she and Colin had last added to it; and the November wind which cut past them on its way to bedeviling the valley below was giving Giles Trevelyan a hard time, snuffing out his brand before he had a chance to touch it to the pile.

Colin pressed a heavy bottle into her gloved hands, his eyes glittering in the dark. "This'll warm you up—and the fire, too, once old Giles gets it going."

Gwynn took a cautious sip.

"Cider. A bit more potent than you'd think. Best be careful." Colin turned to look back down into the farmyard, now filled with cars and trucks parked haphazardly, abandoned when their occupants had wandered up into the pasture. "Giles makes his own. He's got a press down there in one of the outbuildings."

She nodded. The taste was sourer than she had expected, but then, she hadn't ever drunk a cider which had fermented. She took another sip from the bottle, holding the slow warmth on her tongue for a moment before swallowing.

There was a shout, and she turned back to where Giles was straightening up, backing away from the licking flame. "I think we got her that time," he announced cheerily, waving his brand in the air before tossing it in a flaming arc into the pile.

"Throw some petrol on her, that'll do," someone shouted.

Giles only laughed and waved off the suggestion. He was plucking his pipe from his pocket, clenching it between his teeth, patting down his pockets. "Any of you yobs have another match?" he called.

Gwynn had left her purse at the cottage.

The field was crowded. Gwynn had not seen this many people in the village itself, even on market day. In the light of the ever-growing fire, she saw them now, moving in and out of groups, forming and breaking apart and reforming in twos and threes and fives. She felt awkward, an outsider. She took another swig from her bottle.

"Colin. And how's your lady friend?" Giles asked genially around the pipe between his lips. Then he laughed. "Sorry, sorry, *not* your lady friend. How are you, then, Gwynneth?" He didn't wait for her reply. "I see our Colin's got you a drink." He peered at the bottle. "I think that might be from season before last. Strong stuff. Mellowed, but with a bit of a kick, he has. Best take care with him."

"I've already warned her," Colin said.

Giles was patting his pockets again. "Got a match, would you have?"

"You just lit the bonfire, for God's sake."

Giles shrugged. "Used 'em all up."

GWYNN DID NOT know how much later the music started. Colin had found her a stray kitchen chair with the caning blown out, and he himself was seated on an upturned pail, guitar in hand. Her head was buzzing as he started to play; too much cider too fast, she realized. *Deceptive.* There was another bottle in her gloved hand, though she had no idea how it had got there, or from whom it had come. The music was soft, welcome, a gentle underlayment to the roaring of the bonfire a few yards away.

"Here comes the Guy," someone called.

Gwynn glanced up in time to see a handful of people—slightly drunken young men—rush up the hill from the farmyard, carrying what looked like a scarecrow seated on a chair. There was much shouting from the waiting crowd, and the circle around the fire opened enough to let the little procession rush through.

"Careful, then," a voice called, and the men came to a ragged halt and hurled the seated Guy up onto the blazing mound.

The circle closed again, the crowds cheering all the more loudly and atavistically, several people breaking away to congratulate the effigy burners as though they personally had saved Parliament from destruction. Someone broke into a raucous song Gwynn didn't recognize, and several voices shouted along. Beside her, Colin's guitar belted out the chords. Another guitar joined in, and a fiddle, and the song rose louder and louder, taking on a life of its own.

"Sing it, then," someone shouted at her, clapping her on the shoulder.

"I don't know the words," she protested, lifting the cider bottle.

"Then come and dance."

Someone grabbed her free hand—one of the men who had run the Guy up the hill on his throne, she thought, though she could not be sure—and swung her to her feet. Suddenly there were more guitars, another fiddle, someone playing a melodeon, and more people joined in the dancing, wildly, many of them drunkenly. Her head still buzzing, Gwynn tipped her bottle up and let her partner swing her about in steps she knew as little as she knew the words people were shouting up tunelessly. As she whirled past the knot of musicians—a piper had joined them now—she saw Colin shaking his head at her. She turned her back and danced away with her partner

THE WIND WAS still blowing, Gwynn realized suddenly, though the fire still burned strong, and the singing and dancing continued nonstop, lustily. Someone set off some fireworks, and the snap and ensuing explosion startled her so she stopped dead in her tracks. A couple of dancers plowed into her, apologized, and whirled on.

She didn't know where the bottle had gone; and now she didn't know where her partner had gone. She didn't think she would recognize him, actually; so many men had cut in that she no longer could keep track. Another round of fireworks went off, closer, and she cringed away from the sound. The noise, the movement, the fire, the explosions—she was suddenly quite dizzy with it all, dizzy and nauseated: the hillside was suddenly spinning, beyond her control.

Someone was moving toward her, a dark shape looming, backlit in red by the fire. Someone who would no doubt wish to whirl her back into the dance. Gwynn staggered away quickly, away from the devilish light and into the safety of the darkness.

The ground sloped downhill dramatically, the grass uneven in the dark, tangling at her boots. She stumbled, fell to her knees, and skidded across something damp which she did not dare think about. The noise had faded somewhat, and she turned to look over her shoulder to see whether anyone had witnessed her fall, the hellish view swam before her eyes. She closed them tightly and took a deep breath, her mouth and nose full of the stink of grass and manure and smoke. She was going to be sick. Sick.

"Hup," someone said close to her ear. Gwynn felt the hand on her elbow, lifting her, steadying her. She thought she recognized the voice, but wasn't sure. More fireworks went off in the distance, and she clapped her hands to her ears. Her eyes refused to focus; everything spun. Then she was on her feet, and the hand was leading her further away from the crowd, the fire, the explosions, and noise. "Come along, then."

The grip was forceful and tight, and the voice seemed somehow less than pleasant. Gwynn's hackles rose, and she tried to right herself, tried to pull away. "I'm all right now," she said thickly. "You can let me go."

The hand only squeezed tighter on her elbow.

"You're hurting me," she protested.

"You need to come sit."

In the light from the waxing moon, the stone wall at the end of the field glowed slightly, a pale gray worm against the darker ground. She staggered again, scraping her palms against the rocks, and fell roughly to a seat. Her rescuer did not sit, but stood between her and the fire and the people in the distance.

"Don't want you to sick up, now," he said.

She looked up, but the looming shape was indistinct. There was a rustle as he drew something from his pocket, then a flare as he lit the cigarette he held to his lips.

"Seen enough drunks sicking up in my time." He shook the match out and flung it away. "You wouldn't be the first."

Her cousin. She shifted on the stone wall, preparatory to getting back to her feet, and was struck by a wave of dizziness.

"I'm not drunk," she said.

"Could have fooled me." Stokes looked back over his shoulder at the party on the peak of the hill. There was distaste in his voice.

Gwynn made another move to stand, but Stokes put out a not-so-gentle hand and shoved her back down.

"Not so fast," he said. His touch on her shoulder was heavy and hot. "We've got business to discuss, you and I."

"No, we haven't."

He shook her a little bit, not hard, but enough to let her know he could be rough if he felt like it. "Don't be difficult. Our great-aunt was difficult. Don't be like her."

"I don't know what you're talking about," Gwynn said, her voice rising. "Take your hand off me."

Stokes did, holding both hands up innocently. "Just a little family love between cousins. Nothing more than that. I'm helping a girl out when she can't stand on her own feet from the drink." Now he bent over her, uncomfortably close. "And now you can help me out."

Gwynn leaned away. There was something to the smell of him— not drink, not even the smoke from his cigarette—something sour and unpleasant. The smell of constant anger and resentment. She put a hand to her mouth.

"I saw you talking to the solicitor. I saw you with him."

"Dancing." She vaguely remembered Mr. Simms as one of her partners. What had he been doing there?

Stokes sucked at his cigarette, and the end glowed like a red star in the darkness. He was too close. She tried to edge around him; perhaps someone else was near, someone she could appeal to for help. There was no one. No one knew she had disappeared from the bonfire. No one knew she was missing.

"Whatever." Stokes blew smoke out, not exactly into her face, but close enough that she found herself coughing. "You know I'm challenging the will."

She didn't answer. He moved closer, looming over her threateningly. "You can save us all the trouble of dragging this through the courts." He reached into the pocket of his windcheater—how had she not noticed the red jacket back there at the fire?—and drew out a sheet of paper. "Sign the cottage over to me. I'll make it worth your while. I'm a fair man."

"Gwynn Chelton didn't want you to have it." She looked around again, desperately. Her hands scrabbled on the stone wall, her fingers searching for a purchase. "She wanted me to have it."

"Undue influence. Or balance of mind." He thrust the paper at her, nearly in her face. "You know that's what the courts will find. And you'll lose it, all of it, and it'll come to me the way it should have in the first place." He flicked the cigarette over the wall behind her and leaned in until his face was nearly touching hers. His hand was on her again, gripping her upper arm in a vice that hurt. "Just sign the paper, *cousin.* Just make it easy on us." He squeezed harder, twisted.

Gwynn tried to wrench away. "You're hurting me."

"Sign the paper."

She felt his hot breath on her cheek and tried to turn away.

He pulled her back. "Just sign it and go on back where you came from. Because I'm telling you: if you try to stay here, your life will be miserable. *Miserable.* I'll make sure of that."

Gwynn's fingers dug into the wall around a small stone, and she suddenly strained and swung it upward. She felt the shock in her arm as the rock connected with Stoke's shoulder. He swore, staggered backward, and fell to one knee in the grass.

"BITCH!"

"Gwynn!"

The voices were a confused jumble in her head. Gwynn leapt to her feet and ran, dodging the swinging arms of her cousin, taking a circuitous route back toward the bonfire. As before, the grass tugged at her feet, and she stumbled but kept on. She heard someone calling her name—Colin?—and she fled blindly toward the sound. She heard grunting and thrashing behind her, and prayed she could get to the circle of light before that hand gripped her arm again.

"Gwynn?"

She ran into his chest. His arms came around her. She struggled wildly to escape, but he held on.

"Gwynn, what is it? *What is it?"*

Sanity returned slowly. She ceased her struggles and pointed over her shoulder. "I hit him," she panted. "With a rock."

"Who?"

She looked around, panicked. She could see no one else. "He was here," she whispered. "He was *right here."*

"Who?" Colin demanded again. "Gwynn, what happened?"

27

"WHAT ON EARTH was he thinking?" Mr. Simms demanded. "The paper would have been worthless. No witnesses to your signature? What was he thinking?"

The rocking chair in the corner, in which Giles sat, creaked gently on the tile floor. Beside him, Star lay still, but alert. "Oh, the paper's secondary, you know. Men like Paul Stokes—it's all about the threat, all about the intimidation." He eyed Gwynn over his unlit pipe. "Hit him with a rock, then, did you, our Gwynneth? I'd say the intimidation didn't quite work as planned."

Bel Trevelyan probed the bruising gently with a capable hand, shaking her head, and Gwynn winced. "Not a man, that one. Roughing up a woman." She pressed her lips together.

Gwynn took the proffered ice pack and held it gingerly against her arm and the ugly bruising, already going to blue-black. "I just don't understand. Why does he want the cottage that badly? Why does he hate me over a house?"

"He hates over everything," Giles said. "He hates everyone. Surprised to see him here tonight at all."

"You didn't see him, old man," Bel reminded him tartly.

"All the same," he retorted mildly. He was frowning. "That he was here at all—he's never come up to the farm for Bonfire Night as long as I can remember. Too many people, and all of them he doesn't like."

"He's in the wrong profession, then, as a publican," Gwynn observed bitterly.

"Only thing he knows. Left the business by his old dad, he was." Giles patted his pockets down in the familiar gesture. Finding no matches, he plucked the pipe from his mouth and glared at it as though the lack were the pipe's fault.

"But me," Gwynn protested again. "Why me?"

"It would have been whomever your great-aunt left the property to," Mr. Simms said. "It's nothing personal."

Giles' laughter was a sharp bark. "I'm sure, James, that that's a real comfort."

"Not really," Gwynn said darkly.

"Meanwhile," Colin cut in, shifting slightly on his chair at the table, "there's Gwynn's real question: what's going on with Paul Stokes that he wants the house so badly?"

"Everyone tells me he had little to do with our great-aunt, so it can't be some kind of emotional attachment—as in he wants it because it reminds him of her." For her part, Gwynn had little attachment to the cottage emotionally either—she hadn't even known the house existed before receiving the legal notice of *something to her great benefit;* she grimaced at the irony of the situation. Now, it was the mare's nest of *whys* that plagued her. *Why* had Gwynn Chelton chosen her to inherit the house? She thought she was beginning to understand that, at least. But *why* did Paul Stokes want it so badly?

That led down a rabbit hole of new thought. Had Stokes come at things from a different angle—had he suggested, for example, a buy-out of half the property value—would she have been so resistant to his claim? Had it been his immediate attack on her right to inherit that had made her dig her heels in so stubbornly? Probably. But now her desire to stay had evolved into something deeper. She had to stay until she found out why Gwynn Chelton had chosen her. She had to find out what Gwynn wanted of her.

"Follow the money is what I always say," Giles said, his tone deliberate as he scowled into the bowl of his unlit pipe. "Follow the money. That's a trail that always stinks."

Mr. Simms made a noise.

"Am I wrong?"

Despite the hay tangled in his thin hair, Mr. Simms managed to look a bit prissy and secretive as he pursed his lips. "I'm not at liberty to say what I know."

"Oh, Jamie," Bel said, as though to a foolish and recalcitrant child.

"So I'm not wrong," Giles crowed. He turned to Gwynn and Colin, his black-currant eyes sharp and squinting. "That's where you look to find out what's up with Stokes. Find out what you can about his finances. I bet you find he owes a bit here and there. Probably more than a bit."

Gwynn nodded—the old farmer seemed to expect it—and felt her head throbbing; she knew that when the sun rose she'd have one hell of a hangover. Try as she might to accept his reasoning, she resisted Giles' thoughts.

Giles was watching her with interest, and a bit of disappointment. "This is a waterfront village, my girl. In case you hadn't noticed. That cottage of yours, for better or worse, is a veritable gold mine. The owner—you, in this case—could sell out, or even just let out to folks from off, and come away from it with a hefty profit."

"And if Paul Stokes needs money—" Gwynn looked at Mr. Simms, his lips still pursed. He was, so obviously, *not at liberty to say.* "You're not representing him, Mr. Simms. You're representing the interests of my great-aunt, and by corollary, my interests."

"However, I might have dealings with other parties involved," Mr. Simms said primly.

"Oh, Jamie," Bel said again. She handed him a cup of tea, plucked a bit of twig from the hair above his ear.

"I'll have a cup of that, my dear," Giles said to Bel, waving a hand in the direction of the teapot on the table. He looked out the window into the farmyard, where the gray light of the pre-dawn shadowed everything. "Since there's no point in toddling off to bed now." He took the cup from Bel with a broad wink. After the first sip, he wiped his beard, and cocked his head. "It might be worth it to find out just how deep the money troubles go, if there are in fact money troubles behind this story. How far into the past they reach. Just in case our Paul Stokes had been biding his time waiting for the old woman to die."

Bel turned to him, her hands on her wide aproned hips. "That's a terrible thing to say, Giles Trevelyan. Just terrible."

He looked up at her with his beady black eyes. "People are terrible, Isobel. You know that for a truth."

Bel turned away, disgusted; she bent over the refrigerator and shuffled foodstuffs before bringing forth a pair of white-paper-wrapped packages. "We'll have breakfast, then." She drew a bowl of eggs toward her on the countertop.

Gwynn's stomach roiled. "None for me, thanks, Mrs. Trevelyan."

"None for me, either," Colin said. "I've got to be getting back down into the village. I've got a few jobs to tend to this morning, and unlike Giles, I'll need my beauty sleep." He stood slowly, holding out a hand to Gwynn.

They said their good-byes, but Giles stood to see them out to the truck in the farmyard.

"Just watch out for your cousin, our Gwynneth," Giles warned, jamming his cold pipe once again between his teeth and leaning heavily on his stick. He looked up into her face, his dark eyes hard. "Just you watch out for him. Because if he's in the trouble we think he might be, he might not have been simply *waiting* for your great-aunt to die."

"Giles, what are you saying?" Colin demanded sharply.

But Giles had turned away, waving a hand over his head in farewell.

"YOU WERE VERY quiet in Bel's kitchen," Gwynn said as they drove back onto Eyewell Lane and toward the village.

"Listening," Colin said.

She glanced at him. There was a crease between his brows, and he seemed to be gripping the steering wheel as though he wanted to strangle it.

"What conclusions has your listening brought you to?"

His lips twisted. "Not good ones." He slowed the truck as they neared the cottage. In the gray of early morning, the blue door seemed to float above the terrace. Colin, however, was looking at the shuttered front of The Stolen Child, and his frown seemed to harden. He shifted the truck into park and pulled on the handbrake before turning to her, and his gray eyes were dark, troubled. "Between all the things we know and all we don't, I can't see how you can stay in this cottage."

Gwynn snorted. "You're not going to tell me you think I should leave."

Colin didn't answer.

"Besides, what does that even mean? 'Between all the things we know and all the things we don't'? What does that even *mean?*

He skewed her a look. "I just don't think it's safe."

"I know how to lock a door, thank you very much."

"Some of the things here can't be locked out, can they? They're already inside."

"Stop it," she said, shoving open the door of the truck roughly. "Just stop it."

Colin too got out, and crossed to her side. "Listen, I don't necessarily want you to leave the cottage," he said quietly, looking up at the house with a certain intensity. "I just want you to be careful."

"I can handle myself," she retorted. "I've been doing it for years."

Colin reached out a hand to touch her lightly on the upper arm, then dropped it just as quickly. Still, she felt it, and winced.

"I know. I know you can." He sighed, and met her eyes. "I just don't want you to have to swing any more rocks, all right?"

She forced a smile. "All right."

Still, that feeling of foreboding stayed with her as she let herself into the house. She greeted Mary—who looked as though she had forsworn Bonfire Night parties for years, if not forever, and refused the cup of coffee Mary offered.

"I need sleep, more than anything," Gwynn said.

Mary only tipped her head laconically.

On the way up the stairs to the bedroom, though, Gwynn caught herself looking into the sitting room at the wing-backed chair, the one in which her great-aunt had died. She heard again Giles Trevelyan's warning: *he might not have been simply waiting for your great-aunt to die.*

28

THE KNOCK STARTLED her. Despite having been working at the table before the window, she had seen no movement from the street, so engrossed had she been in the miniature on the block before her; she had made several unsatisfactory starts this afternoon. She leaned forward wearily and drew the curtain aside.

A dark suit. A fedora?

Gwynn made her way into the hall and snicked back the lock. She opened the door.

Her visitor turned and winked. "Let me in off the street, young Gwynn, before someone sees me."

Dumbly she stood aside, waiting for Martin Scott to enter before closing the door again. In one hand he held a carry-all; with the other, he doffed his hat.

"I'd tell you to lock it," he said over his shoulder as he entered the sitting room, "but I know our Mary has a key."

"What—?" She followed him into the sitting room, where he'd set the carryall on the coffee table. "Mr. Scott—Martin—what are you talking about? Why are you here?"

"Busted out," he said, and laughed. "Have to be back before Mary knows I'm gone." He settled onto the sofa, tucking his trousers up at the knee. He took a deep breath, and then blew it out. "Haven't been out and about without a minder in I don't remember how long. It feels good." He unbuttoned his suit coat and eyed her speculatively. "You haven't got a spot of whisky about, then, have you?"

Gwynn shook her head, sinking slowly into the wing-backed chair. "They don't know you're gone. Mary. The visiting nurse?"

"Damn right, they don't." His blue eyes sparked. "And don't you be telling them, either." He looked up again. "Whisky?"

"Tea?" she countered.

Martin sighed mightily. "You're as bad as our Mary."

Gwynn eyed him warily. "Are you supposed to be out?" She caught herself. "Of course you're not."

If he could have spat, Martin would have. "I'm old, not senile, not sick. Definitely not bedridden. And now, thanks to you," and he pointed at her with a bony finger, "I'm curious." He lowered the finger to nudge the carry-all. "So I had that old battle-axe of a home health carer get the scrapbooks down from the closet shelf again, and didn't she make a fuss." Again his eyes darted around the room. "That tea, then, young Gwynn?"

"Oh. Oh, sorry."

She slipped into the kitchen, where Mary had already laid the afternoon tea tray, as she always did before she left; all that was needed was a second cup and saucer. After the electric kettle came to a boil, Gwynn rinsed the pot, spooned in the tea, and poured the hot water over the leaves. Then she returned, tray in hand, to the sitting room. Martin shifted his carryall to the seat beside him, and she set the tray on the low table. He had, she saw, an album open on his knee. She turned back to the wing-backed chair, but a sudden guttural noise from him stopped her.

"Don't sit there," he said quickly. His blue eyes were not on her but on the chair.

She took a step back, and now she sank into the overstuffed chair at the other end of the sofa.

"What is it?"

He shook his head and didn't answer. His jaw worked.

"I was sitting in the chair earlier," she protested.

"And you looked good in it," he answered, but automatically, as though from a distance. She saw his gaze still locked upon the wing-backed chair. For a moment he seemed to be wrestling, then he looked at her. His smile was forced. "I meant to say that earlier." He cleared his throat. "Will you be mother, then?"

Gwynn poured the tea carefully and handed him the cup and saucer.

"Not English enough to put milk and sugar in first," Martin observed, reaching for the tongs.

"I've been away all my life," she countered. "But you're not getting off that lightly. Tell me why you didn't want me to sit in the chair just now."

He pressed his lips together, dropping one sugar cube into the cup, then a second, as though sugaring his tea against shock. His eyes flickered to the chair, then back to the matter at hand.

Then she knew, with a sudden realization.

"You saw her," she said.

He lifted his tea cup to his lips and took a sip. He put it back down in the saucer, the china clinked a bit. Shaking? He placed them both on the low table.

"I don't know what you're talking about," he said.

"Martin." Gwynn took a sip of her own tea, black. "Don't lie to me. You saw her. While I was in the kitchen." She took another sip. "Maybe you still see her. Is she in the chair now?"

Instead of answering, he folded his hands together and leaned back against the sofa cushions. "Is who in the chair?" he asked at last. Cagily.

Gwynn had to place her cup and saucer on the low table to keep from throwing it at the old man's head. "My great-aunt. The other Gwynn. The woman you used to be in love with. She was sitting in her chair while I was in the kitchen. Wasn't she? And that's why you didn't want me to sit there." She shook her head. "That's it, isn't it?"

"You've seen her?" Martin countered. "Have you?"

"Yes. Once. And heard her. Several times." It felt good to admit it. "I'm not the only one. Colin has seen her."

"Has Mary?"

"I don't know. She hasn't said."

Martin closed his eyes. "Probably she hasn't. Too practical to be haunted, that daughter of mine. She misses a lot that way."

For a moment they fell silent, both watching the wing-backed chair. To Gwynn it looked perfectly empty. No one sitting there at all. But she was coming to learn that that meant nothing.

"Yes," Martin said at last. "She was there."

"She's not now?"

"No." He sighed. "It was just for a moment."

"Did she say anything?"

He turned his head quickly. "No. Does she speak to you?"

"In dreams."

"You're lucky, then." Martin looked as though he meant it, looked as though the thought brought him sorrow. "I miss her. I miss her voice. I miss the way she moved. Even when she was alive. I missed her as soon as she married Tommy and he turned her into someone else."

With her eyes closed, Gwynn could almost imagine what her great-aunt would have looked like, sounded like, walked like as she moved across the dance floor toward a much younger Martin. She felt him place the scrapbook in her lap she looked down at the page to which he pointed.

"That's her," he said, his voice low. "Down at the Palais."

It was the dance floor she had imagined, and the younger Gwynn was wearing the flowered dress with the puffed sleeves from the vision in her mind's eye—but by now she scarcely even thought about the strangeness of that. She stared down at the girl waltzing in the arms of a barely recognizable Martin Scott in his uniform, her chin tilted up in the laugh she threw over her shoulder toward the photographer, her shoulder-length hair swinging about her face. In the way one recognized colors in black-and-white photographs, Gwynn knew the girl had red hair, knew the dress had blue flowers, knew the curtains on the long windows in the background were deep crimson.

"She looks happy," she whispered.

"I thought she was," he said sadly. "Then I was gone, and when I came back she was with Tom, and I don't think she was ever happy again. I don't know how that happened. I don't know how everything changed so quickly."

Again they fell silent. Gwynn looked down at the picture of her laughing great-aunt, feeling an unaccountable sorrow for a young woman who died long before her own death. She reached out a tentative finger to touch the black-and-white face, the laughing cheek, the bright eyes. What had happened? *What happened, Gwynn?*

"Tommy," Martin said, flipping the page quickly.

Again the dancing couple, and off to the side and slightly back, another uniformed man had his eyes firmly on them. For a moment Gwynn stared in shock, seeing not eyes, but burning dark holes in the stranger's face. She put out a hand, this time as if to ward off a blow, and the sorrow was replaced by fear, waves and waves of fear. Animal loathing, and a need to escape something that she knew she never would. There was screaming in her head; she pressed her hands to her mouth to keep the sound in, though she knew it was not her own voice she was hearing. *What happened, Gwynn?*

The scrapbook slipped from her lap to the floor, and landed facedown on the worn carpet. Only then did she look up, to find Martin Scott watching her with his blazing blue gaze.

"Steady on, young Gwynn," he murmured. He put a hand on her shoulder.

She jerked away convulsively.

"DRINK IT," MARTIN ordered sharply, pressing the glass into her hand.

She raised it to her lips, and the smoky acridness filled her nose before spreading across her tongue.

"Where—"

"Cellarway, shelf overhead. I knew she had to have some here, and that seemed a logical place." He glanced at her, up and down, appraisingly, then resumed his seat on the sofa.

"You knew it was here all the time," she whispered.

Martin shrugged. "I'll tell you about it sometime. But not now. Now you have to tell me about what you saw. After you drink the rest of that, I mean."

Gwynn's eyes slewed to the scrapbook where it lay on the carpet. *The pits of hell.* She raised the glass to her lips and took a longer drink, letting the fire of the whisky burn its way down the back of her throat. It was a picture, she told herself. A photograph, sixty-some years old. With a dead man. It couldn't hurt her. It couldn't threaten her.

Unless she let it.

She wouldn't let it.

She drank down the last of the whisky and set the glass on the table. Then she took a deep breath, and leaned forward to pick up the scrapbook, closed it carefully, and set it next to the empty shot glass.

"I didn't see anything," she said slowly, "except Tommy's eyes. And they scared me."

Martin nodded.

"But I heard something."

Martin's gaze hardened, his eyes narrowing. "What did you hear?"

Gwynn took a deep breath. "Screaming. The word *no* over and over. A woman's voice."

Martin looked stricken. "Was it Gwynn's voice?"

"I don't know." She pressed her hands to her face.

"You *do* know," he insisted. "Was it your great-aunt's voice?"

She nodded, biting her lip. "I think so. I *think* so. She was frightened. Maybe hurt." She couldn't bring herself to say the rest: she was sobbing.

"*Bastard.*" Martin looked away, toward the chair, his hands clenched into fists on his knees. Gwynn could see him blink, once, twice, several times; his Adam's apple worked up and down. She thought he might be crying.

29

"WHATEVER YOU DO," Martin said, leaning quickly toward her as she held the door, "don't tell Mary I've been here. She'll tighten security if she finds I've been out." He shook his head in disgust. "Thinks I'll hurt myself, she does." He was down the steps to Eyewell Lane with a surprisingly quick step; as he made his way along the pavement, he raised a hand in farewell, and Gwynn thought, under the fedora, his eyes were scanning the windows of the house.

SHE TURNED AWAY from the front door and went back to the sitting room. The tea things on their tray still sat on the table; Martin had offered to help her clean up, but she had waved that suggestion away. The afternoon was drawing down, oppressively, and she needed something to keep her occupied; she didn't think she could concentrate on the drawing any more. Now she stood, her gaze lifting beyond the table to the wing-backed chair.

The chair was empty.

Of course it was. Gwynn shook herself, trying to get rid of the prickly feeling on her skin. Her great-aunt was nowhere to be found in this house, because she was dead. Gwynn told herself she was simply becoming infected by the irrationality of others. No ghosts. No.

Martin's voice: *You've seen her.*

And Colin's: *You might not have a choice.*

Gwynn stared at the chair. Floral Chintz. A perfectly normal chair, with antimacassars on the arms. There was no indent in the cushion indicating an occupant, no pressure of an unseen head on the chair back. She could go over and sit there now, now that Martin was gone and would not stop her with his strange urgency.

Yet she wouldn't. Instead she picked up the tea tray and took it through to the kitchen. She filled the sink and washed the cups and saucers mechanically, listening hard for the sound of anyone else in the house. The footsteps, perhaps, of her first night, after the sound of the door closing.

No.

There was no sound. Of course there was no sound.

Dishes dried and put away, Gwynn hung the dish towel on the rack. The mantle clock rang the hour, and a sudden gust of wind rattled the glass in the window frames. She jumped. She couldn't help it. Was that the sound of someone at the kitchen door? It was growing dark outside, twilight, the time in between. Resolutely she straightened and wrenched the door open to look into the garden.

There was no one there. Of course there was no one there.

Brambles. Still. *Always,* she thought in disgust. She'd have to see if Colin would be ready for digging up the entire back garden, to get rid of the roots which she imagined snaked beneath the surface, sending up ten tendrils for every one cut back, a horticultural many-headed hydra. She pushed that idea aside as well: one hired a handyman, but did one hire the handyman who had become a lover?

The gate in the wall was creaking. From here she could see that it was partially open, though she knew she had shoved it as much closed the last time she'd come through there, and she knew she checked it compulsively every time she was in the garden.

"Damn it," she hissed, ignoring the frisson along her spine, pushing her way out into the brambles.

You opened the gate. You let him in.

"Shut up," she said aloud.

The thorns caught at her jeans, and tiny knives scraped their way across the back of her hand. She shoved her way through to the gate, pushed at it with all her strength.

It didn't move.

Gwynn leaned her entire weight into it. The bottom scraped along the ground, but still it refused to close all the way. Of course it did. Eight inches of space, maybe twelve, through which she could make out the shimmering boles of the trees on the hill between her and the ruined dovecote. She pushed again.

Then she heard the doves.

Gwynn stared out into the falling darkness, out there, beyond the wall, for only a moment before turning on her heel and fleeing back into the cottage. In the kitchen she slammed the door and locked it, leaning her back against it, trying to catch her breath.

SHE DIDN'T KNOW how much later the telephone rang.

"The gig's on," Colin said, as soon as she picked up. "At the Holly Bush."

There seemed to be an opening in his pause.

Gwynn looked around the sitting room, feeling panic rise. She hadn't realized how much she had been looking forward to Colin's appearance this evening, and now she was faced with several hours filled with only—something she couldn't quite identify. Something she didn't want to identify.

The vision of Martin's photograph rose up in her mind. Of Tommy Chelton, standing in the background, watching with those black pits of eyes. Waiting.

"Come get me," she whispered quickly.

"Gwynn?" A question. Urgent.

"Just come," she pleaded.

30

SHE OPENED THE door to him, and he immediately enfolded her in his arms.

"Get your things," he said into her hair. "Let's go. Tell me on the way."

And yet, on the way out of the village on Clear Street, Gwynn could hardly formulate the words. Colin listened without interruption until her voice petered out.

"He left the scrapbook with you?" he asked. "Martin?"

Gwynn nodded, clasping her shaking hands together between her knees. "I hid it. Upstairs. In the bottom drawer of the dresser."

"I don't know." Colin downshifted, turned into a side street, then sped up again. "I don't want it in your house."

She glanced over, and in the green light from the dashboard, there was a hard set to the line of his jaw.

"I think—" Gywnn bit her lower lip. "I think you need to look at the pictures. I need to see if you have any reaction to them." She turned away, caught a glimpse of her white face in reflection in the side window, and clenched her eyes shut against it. "I need to know if I'm crazy."

Colin took one hand off the wheel to cover both of hers. "You're not crazy."

"I heard screaming," she protested.

"And doves."

"And doves."

"You're not crazy." His hand remained atop hers and the warmth of his skin slowly seeped into her cold fingers. She couldn't remember ever being this cold. "Something crazy is happening, but that's not the same."

THE HOLLY BUSH filled slowly as the band set up on the miniscule stage at the far end of the low-beamed room.

"We'll try not to blast you out," Pete said to her, plucking the strings of his guitar, his head bent to listen. He frowned and adjusted a tuning peg. Gwynn took her pint to the stage corner and slid into a chair at a small table. She watched Colin over the rim of her glass as he bent to some plugs. In the dim light she couldn't make out his features, but she could imagine them, and the thought was comforting. His gray eyes, plain, honest, watchful. Kind. The way he looked at her, as though offering safety.

Not Tommy Chelton's eyes. Gwynn wondered what her great-aunt had thought, looking into the eyes of her husband for those seven years. *She never laughed again.* She thought of the blazing blue of Martin Scott's eyes, and the tears she saw when he spoke of Gwynn Chelton's unhappiness. The unhappiness which clung to her throughout her widowhood. Fifty-odd years of widowhood.

Now Colin knelt beside her chair. "You're not crazy," he repeated, looking up into her face.

Gwynn reached out a hand and touched his brows, featherlight, and swept from one eye to the other. "I want to believe you," she said, leaning close so he could hear her above the growing din. She almost did believe him. It was easy to believe his words now she was away from Gull Cottage.

He ran a hand up into her hair and cupped the back of her neck. His kiss was long. He pulled away. "You won't go back there tonight." Then he leapt away and took his place behind the other band members at the back of the stage.

Colin read her mind. There was something comforting in that, too.

FOR THE FINAL number of the last set, Pete picked up his melodeon and said, "We're going to try a new song out on you, never been heard before in public." He stepped away from his mic, and Colin, much to her surprise, stepped forward. Gwynn did not know he ever sang at these gigs. He looked mildly uncomfortable.

"I wrote this one," he said. "For somebody. Wish me luck. It's called 'No Ghosts.'"

She held her breath and clasped her hands together in her lap.

GWYNN HAD NEVER seen his house, had only the vaguest idea of where it might be in the village, and when he pulled the work truck to a stop in front of his door, she still was unsure, in the dead of night, where she was. She fumbled with her seat belt, then pushed her way out of the truck before Colin could make his way around to help her.

"What do you want me to carry?" she asked.

She saw his quick smile before he turned away to the back of the truck. "Can you take the guitar?" He handed her the case, his fingers lingering on the back of her hand. He gathered up an amplifier and a couple of heavy bags, then led the way to a set of stairs climbing the side of what looked like stables or a garage. "Careful," he said over his shoulder. At the tiny landing, he paused to unlock the door and pressed back to the rail to let her pass.

He flipped the light switch, and she found herself in a single loft room, economically furnished, with a kitchen at one end and a sitting room at the other. "Toilet through that door, if you need it," he offered, jerking his chin to the left.

Gwynn did need it. She washed up quickly, toweling her wet face, tucking her damp hair behind her ears before emerging to find that Colin had stowed his gig bags and amp on shelves in the corner, leaning the guitar case against the wall.

"A drink?" he offered. "Beer? Wine? Not much else. Ice water?"

Gwynn laughed nervously, moving to sit on the futon beneath the dormer window. "I'm fine."

He was bent to the refrigerator beneath the counter. "Are you hungry? I can do a cheese sandwich, I think. Or a sausage or two."

Gwynn suddenly felt an emptiness in her stomach; she couldn't remember when she had last eaten. "Cheese and crackers, maybe?"

Colin nodded, and economical of movement in the tiny space, pulled a packet from the refrigerator and a box from an overhead cabinet. In a moment he took a seat beside her on the futon, balancing the plate on his knee. His thigh touched hers, and again she felt grateful for his warmth, for the clean scent of his soap.

"Why are you nervous?" He loaded a cracker with cheese and a daub of red relish and handed it to her. She took a bite: cranberry, sweet. The cheese was sharp.

"I'm not nervous," she said.

He only waited. He fixed himself a cracker, heavily laden with cheese.

"What kind of cheese is this?"

Colin grinned, slowly.

She threw up her hands. "I'm not nervous. This is just—strange for me, that's all. To be here. With someone who just sang a song to me in public."

"Did you like it?"

What Gwynn really liked was the way his face was suddenly boyish. Hopeful. Back at the Holly Bush, he had not said a word once the song was over, but had bent to his amplifiers and cords, as though embarrassed. Shy. "I liked it. Very much."

Colin looked pleased. He smiled, ate another cracker, looking down at the plate.

"And now you're going to bed with me," he said.

She opened her mouth, closed it again, and looked away.

"As soon as you finish your midnight snack, because you need your strength."

Her eyes slewed around quickly.

"Because I can't open this futon by myself."

Gwynn burst into laughter. The plate slid to the rug as he caught her face in his hands and kissed her.

LONG AFTER COLIN'S breathing had evened out and deepened, Gwynn lay awake beneath the weight of his arm curing about her waist. With the curtains drawn across the windows, the room was dark, but her eyes slowly grew accustomed to the varying grays. She found her gaze skirting his contours where he lay next to her: his tousled hair, the curve of his cheekbone, his jaw, his shoulder, his flank. It was so strange, and yet how quickly it had become familiar.

Somewhere outside along the road she heard the hush of the incoming tide; a bell rang in the distance. Otherwise, it was quiet, calm. Colin's house seemed to sleep, without the anxious waiting feeling her own cottage gave out, as though it were breathing, or holding its breath.

"Sleep," he murmured against her forehead. "Worry about it tomorrow."

"Yes," she said, and did.

Part III
Exes

31

IN THE MORNING they made love again, then rose and dressed and slipped out into the cool air that smelled of salt tide. There were a pair of seagulls in the drive next to the truck. They complained loudly before lifting into the sky on their strong white wings.

"ANYWHERE IN PARTICULAR, Penny?" Colin called as they entered the little restaurant at the end of the alleyway.

"Anywhere you can find," the woman with the long blonde braid behind the counter answered, then returned her attention to the customers seated before her. Fishermen, they looked like.

Two tables at the back were empty, one piled still with dirty dishes. Gwynn slid into a chair at the clean table, but Colin leaned over the end of the counter, pulled out a gray plastic bus tub, and cleared off the dishes from the table across the way. One of the fishermen at the counter nodded to him.

"Can't take the restaurant out of the boy, then, can you?" he asked genially.

Colin nodded in return. "Not if you yobs insist upon leaving the poor woman a mess like this."

The fisherman laughed and turned back to his plate. The man beside him elbowed him in the ribs, leaned close to say something. They both glanced quickly back at Gwynn, and then away again. The noise of the breakfast wave rose and fell about her.

Colin wiped the table down, returned the bus pan to its place, and then slipped behind the counter to pour two mugs of coffee. Gwynn saw the waitress throw him a wry but grateful look on her way to the kitchen pass-through.

He slipped into the white chair across from Gwynn and pushed the cup of coffee across the table to her. "I should have got you a menu, but I can never remember where Penny keeps them. Nobody here reads them anyway." He shot a look back at the fishermen at the counter. Two of them stood, tossing some money down, and made their way to the door. The noise level fell momentarily as people turned from their conversations to wish the two a good day on the water. "Think of something you want for breakfast, and you can probably have it."

"Eggs Benedict," Gwynn suggested.

Colin made a face. "You'd do that to a self-respecting egg?"

"No, but I was testing your theory."

"Thank God. I thought we were going to have to have a break-up when we've barely just begun this thing." His lips quirked.

"This thing?" She laughed. "What the hell is this thing?"

Still the odd smile. "I haven't got a clue, but so far it's been rather interesting, wouldn't you agree?"

Gwynn lifted her coffee cup to her lips. It was scalding hot, but black and fierce, the way she liked it. "I would agree." She sipped some more. "You're quite comfortable here." Of course, he was comfortable everywhere. "Have you worked here before?" Cooking and waiting were probably among his talents, she mused, rather like delivering wood, wielding a crowbar, playing a guitar.

Colin glanced over at the waitress, who now was bent over the table of a wizened old couple, laughing as she wrote their order on a yellow pad. "Penny and I opened the place together. A lot of years ago. She always wanted a little restaurant, hidden someplace where only locals could find it."

Gwynn leaned back in her chair. "You opened this restaurant."

Then Penny appeared at their table. "Thanks for that," she said, indicating the other table with the hand that held the pencil. Her voice was rich with good humor. She bent down to kiss Colin's cheek. Her smile at Gwynn was wide and welcoming. "I'm glad he finally got around to bringing you along. He's taken long enough, he has." She scratched at the order book quickly. "I don't even know why I'm writing this down—ol' Bob knows what you're eating as well as I. And you, Gwynn? What'll you have this morning?"

"Have the sausage," Colin suggested. "It's from Trevelyan's."

"Oh, and have you met Giles, then? Did you make it up for the *craic*?" Penny glanced at Gwynn as she wrote some more.

"I have."

"He's already propositioned her." Colin chuckled. "Maybe twice."

Penny laughed.

He leaned across the table conspiratorially. "Penny's probably the only woman in the village he hasn't propositioned."

"Neither has he me old Ma," Penny retorted. She leaned in as well. "Ma is his niece, that's why. It'd be a bit weird, that." Her smile was wide. "What'll it be for you, then?"

Gwynn smiled, disarmed. "The sausage, then. And eggs, scrambled? Some toast?"

Penny swung away as the door opened and slapped closed again in its frame.

Gwynn sipped some more coffee. "You know each other well."

Colin shrugged. "She's my ex-wife." He too lifted his cup to his lips.

GWYNN WAS FUMING, angry, and feeling guilt as she ate the breakfast Bob had piled high for them. They ate in silence, and she could feel Colin's gaze on her, but she kept her attention stubbornly on her plate. He at last gathered their coffee cups and went for more—the tiny restaurant had filled again, conversations roaring about them, punctuated by Penny's calls to Bob at the pass-through, Bob's shouts in return—Gwynn sat stiffly at the back table, twisting her napkin between her fingers. Colin had told her, hadn't he? Some of it, anyway. That there had been a girl, that it hadn't worked out. She *could* have pressed him, asked for more. She could have learned his entire history before tumbling into bed with him like a wanton. Gwynn kicked herself for her reticence—for shying away from the conversation when she could imply have asked. You know, she cursed herself idiotically, asked something like *hey, did you marry her?* Or *did you play the guitar for her like you did for me?* Or how about *that song you played last night at the gig—did you really write it for me, or was it hers first?* Then there was always *was that just one big pick-up line, one I fell for, hard?*

Gwynn bit her lip, feeling unutterably stupid. She watched Colin pause with cups in hand to exchange a quick word with Penny—*with his ex-wife*—saw Penny toss her blonde braid over her shoulder as she touched his sleeve familiarly, smiling up at him. Suddenly he set the cups on the counter, pulled his mobile phone from his pocket, looked at the screen, and stepped toward the door. Penny shrugged and gathered up the cups. She breezed toward Gwynn's table.

"He thinks you're upset with him," she said, setting the mugs down, black in front of Gwynn, milky at Colin's empty place. She reached over and piled the empty plates. Gwynn said nothing, watched Penny crumple their napkins into her apron pocket. "I can guess why. He probably didn't tell you he had an ex-wife."

"He said there was a girl. After university."

"Ah, me." Penny shook her head. She had sympathetic brown eyes. "Damn fool. Yes, that girl was me. We lived together for a while, opened the restaurant, got married, woke up one day and realized it wasn't right. So that was that."

"He never mentioned marriage."

"Oh, he wouldn't, you know, unless you'd asked him outright. He's not proud of divorcing. He's old-fashioned enough to think a marriage should be for life. His parents' was. *My* parents' is, though they still have time to screw it up." She laughed.

"People get divorced all the time." Gwynn felt raw, like she'd been scraped.

Penny stopped in the midst of gathering the dirty dishes, staring. Her expression was of intense disappointment. "Colin's not people."

The rebuke was firm, and obvious.

Gwynn felt suddenly ridiculous, and petty. She looked down at her hands, still twisting her napkin into oblivion. Embarrassed, she dropped the pieces on top of the pile of dishes. "I just wish he'd told me," she mumbled at last. "I told him—about my husband." She raised her eyes to Penny's face, where the expression had softened once again to a good-humored kindness. "Did he send you to talk to me?"

Penny shook her head. "Learning about him, maybe, but you haven't learned it all yet, if you'd think he'd do that." Then she relented. "But it's because he would never ask me to intercede on his behalf—in anything—that I always think I need to. Or that I want to." She lifted the dishes, looking around the dining room. "We've been friends, Col and I, for more than half my life now. I guess I know him as well as any self-respecting sister would. We might not have made it as a married couple, but it's better this way, you know? And one thing I can tell you about that man, Gwynn. He's incredibly loyal. *Incredibly.* If he's made up his mind you're worth his effort, he'll stick by you until the end of time." She laughed softly and took a step back, glancing over as the man in question came back into the restaurant, pocketing his phone. "And if I'm not mistaken, he thinks you're worth the effort." She smiled that open grin again. "I'm glad." Before she moved away, she leaned closer and lowered her voice. "I'm glad, Gwynn. Take care of him."

"I'M SORRY I didn't tell you," he said as they slipped out into the lane and turned toward the strand. A wind blew sand at them in the tunnel between the tall houses.

Just words, Gwynn.

"I wish you had." She sighed. "I mean, is there anything else I should know? If this is just a little thing you forgot to mention, what are the big things?" She shook her head, the hair cascading around her face. With a hand she shoved it back and took a deep breath. "What was your phone call?"

Colin shrugged. "Some work. Later this week. Nothing to worry about this morning." He reached for her hand, then stopped. "Do you mind? Are you still angry with me?"

"Yes. No." It was difficult to explain. "I told you everything. Things I've never said to anyone. Then I find this out—a rather important thing you neglected to tell me, the woman you're sleeping with. I just don't know."

"It's in the past."

"It's in your past."

"Yes." He stopped, scuffed a foot at the ground. "But a long time in my past. You're in my future."

Gwynn shrugged. She felt disappointed, discouraged. As though the ground, never firm to begin with, was shifting beneath her feet. Again. She watched a pair of gulls wheel overhead; the same pair from Colin's yard? "I'd just like to be sure there aren't any more surprises. I don't want any more surprises in my life."

"I've got no more surprises, I promise." He held out a hand. "That's everything, you know. I have no other wives, no other stories." He sighed. "Can we go back to the flat? You can ask me anything."

But Gwynn shook her head. "I've got to get home," she said without looking at him. "I've got work to do for Belinda. I think I should probably just go on home."

The words were lifeless things, an excuse dropped between them.

"All right," Colin said slowly. He sounded tired. "I wish you wouldn't. I wish you wouldn't leave it like this. I'd like to fight this out and be done with it." She wasn't up to responding. Again the sigh. "I'll give you a lift back up."

"No need. I'll walk up." She wanted to be away. She wanted to think.

"It's no trouble—and I'd feel better if you'd let me see you home."

Gwynn shook her head. "No. There's really no need." She took a quick step away, but threw one look back. "I'll call you."

She walked briskly along the narrow street, forcing her shoulders back.

"Don't say that. Everyone says that," he called after her.

She didn't answer.

32

GWYNN UNLOCKED THE front door and nearly stumbled into the entryway.

The flow of cool air caught her by surprise. She checked the watch on the inside of her right wrist, puzzled. The fire had long ago gone out, but the draft? Quickly she shut the door, and after half a second's thought, locked it behind her. The movement of air slowed and stopped, like she'd shut off a faucet, but still it felt cool. Something was still not right. Her neck prickled.

She was not alone.

Gwynn stood back to the door, waiting for the feeling to solidify. Was it her great-aunt, making herself known again? She didn't think so; she had become used to the feeling of what she imagined to be Gwynn Chelton: sad, at times unbearably sad, but not threatening. Right now she found it hard to breathe. There was something menacing in the cottage this afternoon.

No. She shook herself, steeling her spine. She was being fanciful. She was making things up. It was only the rain, which had begun to fall fitfully, the unrelenting steeliness of the sky and the water, just visible to her left on most of the walk home. *Stop it,* she ordered herself.

You shouldn't have let him in. Gwynn Chelton's voice. Again she shook herself and hung her coat on the hall tree before heading for the kitchen and tea. Again she looked at her watch: it was tea time, wasn't it?

Paul Stokes was sitting in Gwynn Chelton's wing-backed chair.

She pulled up short, shocked. Horrified.

There were muddy footprints leading from the kitchen, across the carpet, to the chair. But the chair wasn't where it was supposed to be. Stokes had pulled it closer to the window, and now sat, for all the world as if he owned the place, thumbing through Martin Scott's scrapbook.

He looked up, his black eyes unfathomable. "You left the gate open." He placed both of his broad hands on the pages before him.

"Which gives you the right to come into my house?" she demanded, more shrill than she intended. "I don't think so."

"I believe the ownership is still in question, actually," he said, closing the scrapbook and rising slowly from the chair. His stocky frame seemed to shrink the sitting room until there was no room for her, no room to breathe.

"Only you question it," she corrected. "And until something changes in the probate courts—if anything does, which I sincerely doubt—this is *my* house. Mine. You need to get out before I call the police."

Stokes tossed the book contemptuously onto the table, where it slid halfway before coming to a rest. He smiled in a way that she recognized all too well—but how could she recognized it? She bent quickly and grabbed the scrapbook to her. Martin Scott's scrapbook, with his photographs of the young Gwynn Chelton. The scrapbook she had hidden upstairs in the dresser. So, she had told herself, that Mary would not find it, the evidence of her father's illicit visit.

She clutched it now to her chest, her eyes lifting furiously to Stokes' face. "You broke in here, You searched my things." The thought of his beefy hands sifting through her belongings made her skin crawl.

He shrugged, still smiling. "The ownership is still in question." He turned, pushed the wing-backed chair—*Gwynn's* wing-backed chair—a few inches closer to the window. "I like this better over here."

"Leave it alone," she cried. "Get out. *Get out.*"

He took a step closer, ran his hand along her arm, where the bruises still lingered. This time it was like a caress. Gwynn shrank back from him. He tucked his hands into the pockets of his red windcheater and pushed past her roughly.

"See you," he tossed over his shoulder as he passed into the front hall, "*later.*"

She heard the latch at the front door, heard the door open. She did not hear it close. She steeled herself to look into the entryway and saw that he'd left the door wide open behind him Rain was splashing over the sill.

SHAKING, GWYNN FOLLOWED the muddy footprints into the kitchen.

The curtain over the tiny window in the garden door fluttered, the pane broken out, shards of glass littering the tiles. The door itself was ajar, much as if, having broken his way into the house, Stokes had been too contemptuous to shut the door after himself. The gate in the stone wall was open as well.

How had he got around there?

He had to know a way around.

Gwynn slammed the door shut. Her shoes crunched on the broken glass. She hurriedly opened a bottle of red wine and poured herself some The bottle clinked against the wineglass and set her teeth on edge.

She wanted to call someone. The police? Paul Stokes was gone. What would be the point? Perhaps James Simms—perhaps the solicitor could give her some advice? She felt dirty, violated. Stokes had walked into her home, had treated it and her with—there was no other word for it—contempt. The contempt of ownership. That he felt he could do that nauseated her. A violation, she thought again. A willful violation, meant to establish dominance, power. *Look what I can do to you.* She quickly swept up the glass, pulled out the mop, and wiped up his footprints, erasing his progress across the kitchen floor. In the sitting room, it was more difficult, and she panicked. The hoover took up most of the now-dried mud from the carpet, but she went over it again and again until she could no longer see any trace of his footsteps.

Gwynn felt the hot angry tears behind her eyelids, and she forced them back. Just another thing to add to the downhill slide the day had suddenly taken. Just another thing.

She wanted Colin, and despised herself for it. Even if they were to regain their footing, how could she possibly tell him about Paul Stokes' invasion of her home, of her security? He'd be furious. He'd demand she leave the cottage. Perhaps he'd go after Stokes. Dumbly she poured a bit more wine into the glass. The curtain over the broken window lifted again, fell. How could she not tell him? She'd need him to fix the window. She didn't know how to glaze. He'd ask about the damage.

Her hands were still shaking, and she spilled wine on the counter. As she grabbed the sponge to wipe it away, the movement of damp air from the broken window touched her hot cheek. In the days of the construction company, she hadn't had to know how to fix broken windows; she'd only had to make sure there *were* windows, and that the people responsible for them were paid. Colin could fix it, if he had glass and tools. But again, that meant she would have to call him, to tell him what had happened. She shrank from having to do that. She shrank from having to speak Paul Stokes' name. Just that thought brought forth a wave of revulsion. Gwynn leaned over the sink, praying not to be sick.

33

THE BOTTLE, BOTH Colin and Martin had told her, was in the cellarway. Tonight, Gwynn decided she needed it. Wrapped in a blanket against the chill, the fire having long since gone out, she felt her way down the stairs, through the sitting room, and into the kitchen. The door was in the wall beyond the counter; she flicked on the overhead light and was momentarily blinded. The fluorescent ring buzzed. She opened the cellar door and could find no light switch there, so she turned back to the cupboard and grabbed the flashlight. The beam showed her the glitter of glass bottles of the shelf at the foot of the steps. A veritable arsenal of drink. *Good on you, Gwynn.*

She pulled the blanket tighter about her, navigating the stairs slowly, leaning into the rough stone wall for balance. She reached for the bottle of whisky—the only bottle not covered in a coat of dust—and with a sharp creak, the cellar door closed behind her. She swung around quickly.

An old house. A drafty house with a broken kitchen window. A house uneven on its foundations after all these years. Gwynn took a steadying breath, collected the whisky bottle, and carefully ascended the stairs.

The door wouldn't open.

Gwynn lifted the latch and shook it. The door would not budge.

Not another one. The doors to the house, the garden, the dovecote conspired against her.

A gate that would not close. A door that would not open.

Gwynn leaned her forehead against the door, trying to think. The blanket slipped from her shoulders. There was no point in pounding, no point in pushing or pulling or shouting. Gull Cottage would not acquiesce. She knew this. Yet a part of her brain fought against it. She tried to picture the latch on the other side, tried to imagine how the door might close itself, latch itself shut. The latch wouldn't open. It had to be stuck, that was all. She lifted the handle and shook it some more. She leaned her weight into the wood. Nothing. Despite knowing it would do no good, she set the bottle on the step beside her, then kicked at the base of the door. Still nothing. Of course.

That was that. Gwynn slumped. She was locked in the cellar. No one would hear her if she shouted, pounded. No one until Mary came at eight. Quickly she checked herself, making sure what tomorrow was: Monday. 'Ihank God. Mary came on Monday mornings. At eight. What time was it now? In answer, the mantle clock, far away in the sitting room, rang once. One? Or twelve-thirty. Or one-thirty? She closed her eyes, gripping the flashlight in her sweaty palm. She wished she had thought to look at the travel alarm clock on the bedside table. She wished she had turned on a light, passing through the sitting room. She wished—*damn it, Gwynn*—that her great-aunt had updated her appliances to include a stove, a microwave, a coffee-maker with an LED clock. Anything.

The blanket had come to rest at the bottom of the stairs. Gwynn retrieved the whisky bottle, and trod back downstairs, again leaning into the white-washed stone wall, gray now with age and neglect. She wrapped the blanket around her once more and huddled on the second step, her feet firmly on the packed dirt floor. She would not panic. She would wait it out. Mary would come at eight and everything would be all right.

Gwynn set the flashlight on the step beside her, the beam shining straight up to the low ceiling, where spider webs glistened. She let out a half-laugh. Mary hadn't cleaned down here in a while, that was certain. She opened the bottle of whisky and sniffed at it. She wouldn't need it to sleep now. She didn't really *want* to sleep, not down here. She sniffed it again. It smelled sharp and peaty, like she thought heather must smell. Slowly she tipped the bottle back and let a tiny bit onto her tongue, where it burned and spread and warmed.

GWYNN DOZED OFF and on with her head and shoulder against the wall. She jerked awake and nearly tumbled off the stairs in the darkness. She had a sudden attack of vertigo, but she fought it down. She couldn't see; the blackness was a soft pillow that stuffed her eyes and ears and dulled her senses, but she still knew that her feet were firmly planted on the dirt floor of the cellar. If she fell from her seat on the second step, it would not be far.

How long had she been down here now? She listened hard for the sound of the mantle clock, but heard nothing. Long enough for the flashlight batteries, the new ones she'd bought at the shops, but who knew how long they'd been on Leah's shelves?—to weaken and die. Some hours earlier, she had shaken the torch in a panic, and once that had worked; though the beam had been faint it had revived. Now it was dead. She didn't even know where the flashlight had rolled to when she had accidentally knocked it from the stair beside her in the dark.

Mary was coming at eight, she repeated to herself. The mantra had kept her calm through the night. Eight would not—could not—be so far away now. As soon as she heard Mary's footsteps in the kitchen overhead, she'd call out, crawl up the stairs and bang on the door. Mary would unlatch it. Mary would let her out. It would be all right.

The cellar stank of whisky, though. The open bottle, too, had been a casualty in the night, falling from her grip when the flashlight failed, rolling down the last of the stairs, contents splashing out everywhere. Gwynn's mouth felt fuzzy, as though she'd drunk down the remains of the half-empty bottle, but then again, it never took much with her. She felt headachy, too, but that could be the day, the night, not just the whisky.

She dozed again and woke to the measured step she'd waited for all night. Dragging the blanket after her, she climbed the stairs by touch and kicked the door.

"Mary?" she shouted. "Mary?"

"What on earth—?"

There was a metallic scrape and the door opened. Mary peered around cautiously, then frowned. Gwynn, exhausted, tumbled out into the kitchen and was only kept from falling by Mary's strong arms.

"WHAT ON EARTH were you doing down there?"

Mary had not even yet shed her heavy coat, though it was unbuttoned, she being interrupted in mid-doff. Now she flicked on the electric kettle on the way by as she ushered Gwynn into the sitting room and saw her onto the sofa.

The other woman sniffed. Made a face. "Went down for a wee one, did you?"

Gwynn glared. "I dropped the bottle. The whole damn cellar smells like a distillery now."

"And not a very good one." Mary took her coat through to the tree in the entryway, then returned. "How on earth did you manage to get yourself stuck like that?"

Gwynn yawned, stretched, put her pounding head in her hands. Her shoulders and hips ached as well. Sleeping on a staircase was not anything she wanted to do again in a hurry. "I don't know. The door swung shut. The latch must have fallen."

Mary frowned fiercely. "That's never happened to me, not in all the years I've worked here." The kettle clicked off, and she excused herself for a moment. Gwynn could hear her fixing the tea in the pot, and then she heard the sound of the cellar door. Open. She waited for the creak as it swung shut. There was none. Mary said something unintelligible, and then Gwynn heard her close and open the door again.

After a few moments, Mary reappeared, carrying the tea tray, still frowning. She set the tray on the low table and straightened.

"I can't get it to shut by itself," she said peevishly, as though blaming the door for its recalcitrance. "I don't know how you managed it. And what happened to the back door?"

Leaving the blanket, Gwynn pushed past Mary on her way to the kitchen and the cellar. She pulled the door open and released it, it stayed put. Just as it had the previous night, she recalled. It did not swing. It did not close. She looked at Mary, puzzled.

"It shut on me," she protested. "I was at the bottom of the stairs, fetching the bottle. It *shut on me.*"

"And locked," Mary reminded her with a raised eyebrow. "It shut and locked. From this side. All by itself."

They stared at each other.

"Never mind," Gwynn said at last, giving up. "I'm going to take a bath. And then I'm going to bed. In a real bed. Because I don't want to deal with this."

"I'll call Colin about the glass."

Gwynn didn't reply.

34

"COME TO DINNER," she said, when Colin answered his phone. It was Sunday again, and the disappointment had subsided. She didn't think he'd have a gig on Sunday.

There was a long pause.

"Thank God," he said finally. Then, "You're sure?"

"I'm not sure of anything," she said. "But come anyway. Seven."

SHE SCRUBBED EVERY inch of her skin in the tub while the beef was roasting. She dressed carefully in a red dress and heels, choosing sparkling earrings and a pendant that threw fire when she moved. A confidence move. Ex-wives be damned. All of it be damned. She hoped that, by dressing for the evening—by dressing for seduction—she might overcome the last of her confusion and uncertainty of the last week. A headache hung like anxiety behind her eyes, however, and she wished she hadn't opened the bottle of wine so early in the evening.

The cottage was redolent of roast and duxelles. She took one last look in the mirror, hoping her feverish eyes might pass, in Colin's inspection, for excitement. The knock came on the door below, and she drew the curtain aside despite herself, to look down onto the tiny terrace. In the darkness the figure below was impossible to make out. She looked quickly to the street for a glimpse of Colin's work truck, and, seeing it, let the curtain fall in relief.

It took a moment to get the door open, fumbling with the lock as Gwynn did with her nervous hands. She only opened it a crack, just to be sure, and feeling stupid even as she peered out. Colin was back to studying the front of The Stolen Child; he turned slowly, tipping his head to the side. His gaze lingered at her hand on the lock, but he said nothing.

She let him in, then snapped the lock again when she closed the door. Colin watched her, wordless, waiting. Gwynn bit her lip, slowly raising her eyes to meet his clear gray gaze. She couldn't answer the question she saw there; she pretended not to see it at all.

"I'm sorry," she said instead. "Bear with me."

He nodded. "I'm sorry, too."

They stood awkwardly. Gwynn dropped her eyes.

"You're lovely," he said at last.

Gwynn swallowed.

Colin reached out his arms, and after a moment she moved into them, pressing her face into his tweed jacket, breathing the scent of him, listening to the steady sound of his heart. She was surprised to realize how much she had missed the touch, the smell, the sound.

"When you're ready," he said, "*If* you're ready—I'd really like to kiss you hello."

SHE BROUGHT HIM a glass of wine. He stood in the dining room, slowly and carefully looking at the drawings she had laid out for him with some trepidation. Before he could say anything, she returned to the kitchen to plate the dinner.

"Can I help?" he called after her.

"No, no, it's fine," she said quickly.

Colin followed her into the kitchen, pushed the curtain aside, and examined the newly glazed glass in the door. "Did you ever find out what happened here?" he asked, turning to her.

Gwynn looked away. "An—accident. It wasn't any big deal."

He kept his eyes on her face for a long uncomfortable moment.

She willed herself not to spill the whole story to him.

He let the curtain drop. "I wish—" he began, but then shook his head.

35

UPSTAIRS, DINNER EATEN, dishes washed and carefully stacked on the sideboard to dry, it was Gwynn who took the lead. In her red heels, she was closer to Colin's height, and she leaned into him, biting at his lips, sliding her hands beneath his tweed jacket, along the curve of his back to his hips. He let her, opening his mouth against hers, whispering her name as she pulled him to her. She reached up and pushed his jacket from his shoulders, then unbuttoned his shirt and ran her hands through the curling dark hair of his chest.

"I've missed you," he said.

"Welcome," she whispered against his mouth, "to my cottage."

IN THE NIGHT she dreamed. She saw her great-aunt Gwynn from across the room, but this was the nineteen-year-old Gwynn from the photographs in the scrapbook, and the room—she looked around— was the public bar at The Stolen Child. The brickwork and the beams were the same, as was the great fireplace at the far end of the room. The tables were different, the chairs seated with worn red upholstery. Polished brasses hung against the walls. Gwynn was speaking to a stocky man who turned, his eyes blazing darkly. Tommy Chelton.

Don't, she wanted to shout.

Then suddenly she was close to Tommy, so close—and she *was* the nineteen-year-old Gwynn; she *was* her great-aunt. She looked down at her hands, then over at the spotless mirror behind the back-bar at her curling red hair. She turned back to Tommy Chelton, who was eyeing her in a way that made her uncomfortable, but she nodded as he said, "I have some birds. Up back of the house. There's a dovecote. Come up and have a look sometime."

She calculated quickly. Martin's last letter told her he'd be back home on leave come Christmas. "Can we go now? Can I see them? I'd really love to get a bird for Martin. It would mean so much to him. Maybe you can help me choose one—if you'd sell me one?" She stumbled over her words in her excitement.

Something had closed down in Tommy's expression at the mention of Martin's name, but she barely registered it.

"We can go up now," he said. His voice had grown louder cutting across the late afternoon chatter of the pub. He leaned a bit closer. "If that's what you want."

Then he turned away, pushing through the crowds to the door. Gwynn had to hurry to follow him outside into Eyewell Lane; Tommy crossed without looking either way for traffic and started up the path past Dove Cottage. There was a gate in the stone wall, and he left it open for her without even glancing back. Inside was the garden, grass scuffed, flower borders empty save for scraps of dead plants Gwynn didn't recognize. Tommy had passed through the rear gate, but now he waited.

She was breathless, hurrying after him, and now she leaned a hand against the mossy stone, the other to her breast as she steadied her breathing.

"Up there?" she asked.

"They're up here," he said, indicating the wood. She stepped through the gate, and he dragged it shut behind them. Then he turned and led the way up the incline into the trees, as though indifferent: she could follow him or not.

She looked around nervously. She didn't like it, or him. From a distance, though, she could hear the soft cooing of the doves, and she thought of Martin's last letter, where he wrote about racing birds, and she so wanted to find one for him. For a gift. A surprise. He would come home on leave, and she would say *listen—remember that story you wrote to me about you and your brother racing pigeons?* She would hand him the caged bird, and he would set it free: they would both watch it soar into the cloudless blue sky above the estuary.

Gwynn could barely see Tommy's back through the trees: he was not waiting. She threw a glance over her shoulder at the closed gate. She really didn't want to follow him into the wood, but the thought of the bird, the thought of Martin's face when he saw her gift—

Quickly she pushed her uneasiness aside and hurried after him. Her footsteps startled a rabbit from the underbrush, and after freezing for a moment, it fled along a path only it could see. The cooing was growing louder, and she quickened her pace.

The dovecote loomed suddenly in its clearing. Tommy was nowhere in sight. The door was open, though, and she ducked her head to enter the dimness, where she was suddenly surrounded by the sounds and smells of the birds. After a moment her eyes grew accustomed, and she could make out the boxes lining the walls, the bright eyes peering out at her. She didn't see Tommy, though, did not know where he was until he stepped close behind her and slid a hand up the inside of her bare arm.

Gwynn jerked away quickly. "The bird. Martin—"

He grabbed her wrist, pulled her around, held her against his body, twisting her arm behind her back until it hurt. "Not Martin. *Me.*" He pressed his mouth to hers, forcing her lips apart. Gwynn wrenched her head away. She had been wrong, wrong to follow him. She didn't like him, and now she was frightened and angry. With her free hand she slapped him, hard.

"How dare you?" she spat. Then she twisted away from him and dashed toward the door.

Tommy was there before her; he reached past and slammed it shut, his arm over her shoulder, pinning her to the wood when she turned.

"Let me go," she cried, her panic rising.

In the dimness she saw his teeth as he smiled. With his free hand he cupped her breast and squeezed through the cloth of her dress. Then he bent his head and kissed the pulse at the base of her throat.

"Don't, Tommy," she said. She felt the sobs rising, tried frantically to push him away. "Let me go. I won't tell. I won't say anything. I swear I won't say anything."

"Nothing to say," he said against the skin of her neck. "You followed me up here. Everyone saw you. They saw you chase me up here. I was walking away. You followed me, Gwynn. Because it's not Martin you want, and now everyone in the village knows. It's me."

"No," she cried out, pushing at his chest. "No, Tommy. Don't. Please don't do this."

Once again she freed herself, but she hadn't gone far before he grabbed her and threw her to the ground as easily he might a rag doll. Then he was on her, his knee between her legs, his hand under her skirt, scrabbling at her panties. Gwynn screamed out for help.

"No one can hear you up here," Tommy said. Then he thrust inside of her, and she felt a pain and tearing unlike anything she'd ever felt before.

WHEN HE WAS done, he stood, leaving her sobbing at his feet. He took out a handkerchief and wiped himself, then tossed it down to her before buttoning up his trousers.

"Clean yourself up," he said.

Gwynn could not speak. The pain was unendurable. There was dirt in her dress, dirt in her hair, God help her, even dirt in her mouth. The birds had fallen silent.

Tommy opened the door. Light fell across her legs, her torn underwear. He looked down at her with his black pits of eyes.

"Martin will kill you when I tell him," she sobbed.

"You won't tell him. He wouldn't believe you anyway. No one will believe you." And hideously, Tommy Chelton smiled at her. "You're mine now, Gwynn. Mine."

SHE FELT HIS hands first, then his weight.

It was happening again.

Again.

She felt the panic rise. She was blinded by it. She threw up her hands to ward him off, to push him away. Her resistance had been futile before, but she couldn't bear it, she couldn't bear it again, she couldn't bear him again. The scream rose in her throat—she knew no one could hear her—he had told her, he had laughed. But she couldn't hold it in. She felt his lips at her jaw and opened her mouth and the animal sound rushed out.

"Gwynn—"

The voice at her ear was surprised, shocked. The weight on her body shifted, but the arms stayed, the hold tightening.

"Gwynn, hush. Hush. It's all right. *It's all right.*"

But it wasn't all right. She squirmed and twisted, trying desperately to pull away from the arms that held her captive. She cried out again, pushing, scratching. "No—no! Let me go! Let me go!"

Suddenly she was free. She pulled away, leapt from the bed, and found herself cowering in the far corner, baring her teeth like an animal.

"Gwynn—"

Colin sat up now, reached for the light. He blinked several times. In her corner, Gwynn hunched down, one arm across her bare breasts, the other held in front of her to fight off another attack.

"What is it?" Colin asked quickly, climbing from the bed and taking a step toward her.

"Stay away from me," she cried. "Get away from me!"

He took another tentative step. "Gwynn. It's me. *Me.* Colin." The light turned his hair into a nimbus of fire. She could not see his eyes. They might have been black holes.

"No," she screamed out again, shaking uncontrollably. "Go—just go!"

He stopped. Looked down at her. Hurt. Confused. "Gwynn?"

But she couldn't look at him, couldn't listen to him. Her cheek stung where she had hit the wall. Her hips ached; her insides burned and agonized. She felt the bile rise from her gullet and knew she would be sick.

"Go. Just get out. Take your things. Please." She suddenly found herself sobbing. "Go, Tommy. Just go."

A spasm crossed his face. He pulled the duvet from the bed and tossed it to her.

"Cover yourself," he said quietly, each word twisted from some deep wounded place. "It's cold."

Then he bent to the floor to pick up his clothes before slipping through the door to the stairs.

For a long time after she'd heard the front door close, after she'd heard his truck start and move down Eyewell Lane, she huddled against the wall, crying softly. At last, she reached out a shaking hand to pull the duvet to her and around her shoulders. She attempted to stand and was gripped by a pain so intense she cried out and doubled over. There was blood, she saw in horror, on her thighs.

She dashed for the bath, where she threw herself to her knees over the toilet and vomited until there was nothing left.

36

GWYNN COULDN'T FACE the bed again.

As the weak sun began to define the world outside the front windows, she dragged herself down to the sofa in the sitting room and folded herself in the corner. She clutched the duvet around her body like some sort of armor, crying sporadically, until there were no tears left either.

Gwynn, she thought, staring at the wing-backed chair. *Poor woman.*

Moving hurt, so she elected not to move. *Poor Gwynn,* she thought again, and found herself confused as to which Gwynn she felt pity for.

SHE DOZED OFF and was awakened by the sound of Mary's key in the lock. It took her a moment to recognize the sound .She was paralyzed with fear, unable to place herself in time. Then Mary was bustling through on her way to the kitchen, but pulled up short at the sight of Gwynn on the sofa.

"Are you ill?" she demanded, her usual staid demeanor jarred. "You look terrible. What's happened?"

Without waiting for an answer, Mary shed her coat and scarf as she hurried through the kitchen door. Gwynn leaned her aching head against the back of the sofa and listened to the sounds of running water, of the tea things being drawn hurriedly from the cupboards and clunked out on the tray. So typical of Mary, she thought numbly: tea would fix everything. She hoped Mary was right.

She shuddered again, thinking of Tommy Chelton.

She shook harder when she remembered the stricken look on Colin's face when she'd called him *Tommy.*

"Here." Mary held a mug before her, waiting until she took it before settling on the other end of the sofa. She clucked her tongue. "You're not even dressed."

Gwynn had no idea how to answer that observation, and so remained silent.

The tea was so hot it scalded her mouth, but she welcomed the feeling. Some other part of her body hurting, and with a pain she could understand. She blinked her eyes and took another burning sip from the cup.

"I would have broken out the whisky," Mary said, "but there's no open bottle down on Mrs. Chelton's drinks shelf." The words were wry, an attempt at humor, but Gwynn couldn't rise to them. She kept her eyes closed until she'd emptied her teacup.

"Are you ill?" Mary asked again. There were tight frown lines between her eyes, pulling her sharply etched brows downward.

Gwynn shook her head.

Mary waited, but Gwynn didn't answer further. The silence between them was tense. Anxious.

At last Mary sighed deeply. "I am not a stupid woman," she said slowly, her brown gaze level and searching. "I open the refrigerator and find the remainder of what looks like a very special, very celebratory dinner. Is that a beef Wellington you have in there? Obviously someone went to a lot of trouble over last night's meal. And as I just said, I'm not stupid, and I have a pretty good idea what that special celebratory dinner is all about, and for whom it was cooked."

She paused again, offering Gwynn the opportunity to join in the conversation, to agree with or refute her judgment about her intelligence. Gwynn remained steadfastly silent, bending her head only to gaze into her empty teacup. She wanted more tea, or rather, the scalding of more tea on her tongue that would let her think about something other than the pains everywhere else.

"But he's not here. Our young Colin. I have to say I was hoping he would be—that the pair of you had stopped being so stupid. Still, he's not here, and here you are, stark on the downstairs sofa, wrapped in a blanket, looking like death warmed over. It's fairly obvious to me that something very bad has happened, and I rather think"—she coughed, and looked uncomfortable, but plunged forward anyway—"that you ought to tell me about it."

Grasping the duvet more firmly around her bare shoulders, Gwynn leaned forward painfully and set her empty cup on the table. It said something about the situation that Mary did not immediately reach out to set the cup on its saucer, or on a napkin or a coaster. The uncomfortable urgency of Mary's desire to help was sinking in, and Gwynn blinked once, twice, and tried to find her voice. She threw a quick glance to the wing-backed chair, where her great-aunt was sitting, ankles crossed, hands folded tightly in her lap.

Gwynn stared so hard that Mary's own gaze turned toward the chair, and then back again, puzzled.

The older Gwynn shook her head slightly, just once. Gwynn blinked, and her great-aunt disappeared.

"I can't tell you," Gwynn whispered. Her throat felt thick.

"Can't? Or won't?" There was hurt in Mary's voice. She took a long deep breath. "I hope you know," she said stiffly, "that I'm your friend. At least—I'd like to be your friend. I tried my best to be a friend to Mrs. Chelton, and she resisted me all the way. I figured that was her business—if she wanted to stand off, then she wanted to stand off. But I could still be kind. I could still do what I could do for her." She cleared her throat. "I would hope you understood that." She lifted a hand, let it fall back into her lap. It was the most helpless gesture Gwynn had ever seen from Mary, and it tore at something deep in her chest.

"I can't," she said again, miserably. "It's not my secret to tell."

Mary turned sharply to look at her. "Whose secret is it, then? Is it Colin's?"

"No." This time the tearing was huge in her chest, and she nearly cried out. *His face. His expression.* "Colin doesn't know anything about it. He can't know." The words sounded both foreign and familiar to her, in her voice, and in another voice. "I can't tell him what's happened."

Gwynn's words. But to whom had she spoken them, after she'd stumbled away from the dovecote? No one. The answer, the heart-rending, sickening answer—one that Gwynn knew instinctively to be true—was *no one.* Her great-aunt had never told anyone what had happened that afternoon with Tommy Chelton up at the dovecote. Her great-aunt had carried the cancerous secret of her violation to her grave.

"And you can't tell me." There was infinite sadness in the words, but resignation as well, as if this had all happened to Mary before. With another deep breath, she straightened and stood. "Well, then, if I can't be of any help, I guess I'll have to get back to my work."

The disappointment was so thick in the air as to be palpable.

Gwynn couldn't help but feel she had, once again, failed. Somehow.

At the kitchen doorway, Mary turned back. "Is there anyone you *can* tell?"

Gwynn stared at her, the words ringing in her head. Because suddenly she knew the answer, knew what her great-aunt wanted her to do.

"Yes," she whispered. She hoped Mary would not ask who, because she could not tell her the answer. She simply couldn't.

Then Mary slowly nodded. "Then I guess you'd better wash and dress and go tell them, then."

The kitchen door swung closed behind her and slapped in the frame.

37

SHE DRAGGED HERSELF upstairs, but on the landing, turned right into the spare room, which was still torn apart from cleaning and boxing up donations, the bed unmade. Here she lay down on the bare mattress, meaning to catch her breath, but the exhaustion caught her unawares, and she let her eyes close. Just for a moment. Just a moment.

THEY WERE IN the shop, Gwynn trying to fit the coupons to the available goods, and to the things on her mother's list, her younger sister laughing with someone up near the front counter. When Tommy Chelton slipped into the row of tinned goods behind her, at first, frowning at the near-bare shelves, she didn't see him. As he drew closer, the skin at the back of her neck prickled. She whirled. Her eyes fell on him, and she felt the flush of blood rushing to the surface, the nausea building in the pit of her stomach. She tried to step past him, purposefully looking away, but he moved sideways and blocked the aisle.

"You can't avoid me," he said.

"Let me pass."

There was another peal of laughter from Lucy at the front, full of the immeasurable joy of being sixteen. Tommy smiled slyly and tossed a look over his shoulder to where Lucy stood. "You know what I want," he said, his eyes following her younger sister's movements. "You know you're mine." He was smiling when he turned his black eyes upon her. "You know you haven't written to Martin since you followed me up to the dovecote."

He couldn't know that. Her own eyes flickered to his, and his expression told her he knew his shot had hit home. The nausea was rising in her throat. Again she tried to get around him; again he slid to the side and blocked her way. When he stared at her she felt his touch on her skin, the searing pain that tore her in two.

His fingers trailed along her inner arm, and she jerked away violently. "Don't you touch me," she hissed, a cornered animal.

Again Tommy only smiled. "You know," he whispered, leaning in so close she felt his breath on her cheek, "you want it." Then he laughed, perhaps the ugliest, most chilling sound she had ever heard. She quailed before it. "Meanwhile, maybe I'll find someone else who is more accommodating."

Before she could unravel what he might mean, he turned on his heel and made his way out of the aisle. Closing her eyes tightly, she leaned her forehead against the shelf, trying to control her shaking. Then she heard another laugh from Lucy, and her heart constricted. She nearly flew to the end of the row, scanning the front of the shop for her sister. She rounded the corner just in time to see Tommy jostle Lucy at the counter; he swiftly apologized, and then, with a movement that made her nerves scream, he ran a steadying hand down the inside Lucy's arm. Then he tipped his hat, lifting his eyes past Lucy to give Gwynn a black look before leaving the shop.

GWYNN CRIED OUT, huddled under the duvet in the spare room. She barely registered Mary coming upstairs to look in on her, before she tumbled back into troubled sleep.

GWYNN FOUND HER eyes drawn to the calendar tacked to the bedroom wall.

Nearly a week late. She stared in despair.

She turned away just as Lucy bounded up the stairs and into their room, to throw herself across her yellow coverlet. "You know that Tommy Chelton?" she asked, chewing the side of her thumb.

Gwynn pressed her palms into her eyes, her entire body recoiling at the name. There was nothing in Lucy's voice save the richness of silly laughter. "Yes," she managed. Barely. "I know him a bit."

Lucy rolled over and clutched her pillow to her thin chest. "He asked me if I liked doves. This afternoon, when I was at the lending library? I said I did, and he told me he raised them, and maybe I'd like to come see them sometime?" She laughed. "He's ever so much older than I am. More Gareth's age. I can't think why he'd even talk to me."

But Gwynn knew. She stared at her Lucy's downy arm, where Tommy Chelton had run his hand down the pale skin, knowing Gwynn would see, knowing Gwynn would know.

It was a threat.

She thought of his leer. She thought of his hands on her younger sister. Her innocent sister. She put a shaking hand to her belly.

Late.

In the morning she vomited up her breakfast almost as soon as she had eaten. Then she dressed herself carefully and made her way up Eyewell Lane to knock on the blue door of Dove Cottage.

No one answered. With trepidation that nearly overpowered her resolve, she passed around to the gate in the wall and let herself into the garden. It looked, to her eyes, more barren than it had been before. She crossed to the rear gate, which stood open, a maw waiting to swallow her whole. Taking a deep breath and biting her lip to keep back the tears, she left the garden and entered the wood. The sounds of the cooing doves came to her as she drew closer to the clearing and the low building. The door was open. As she paused, staring at its hulking blackness, Tommy appeared in the doorway; he ducked under the lintel and took one step outside. Then he stopped, waiting, his dark eyes fixed on her face. His lips were twisted into a triumphant smile.

Gwynn swallowed and met his eyes and spoke the hardest words she had ever said.

"I will marry you."

His smile widened. His teeth shone wolfishly.

She spun away quickly, fell to her knees, and vomited for the second time that morning. This time, however, nothing came up. There was nothing left inside her.

38

GWYNN WAS AFRAID Martin wouldn't be there when she limped down to the bench at the waterside pathway. He had sounded unsure on the telephone, but that might just have been a function of his age, she thought, or his telephone demeanor. When she spoke her great-aunt's name, however, his voice became stronger, more certain.

"You've found out something," he had said.

"I don't know." Because what did she know? "I think so."

"I'll be there," Martin had said. "I don't have much time. Mary said she'd be by for shopping around four, so I've got to be back before she knows I'm gone."

"Whenever you can," Gwynn said. An unhappy conspirator.

"I'll be there in an hour."

Now she approached the bench to find him seated there in his suit and fedora, staring off toward the horizon. The sound of the murmuring ocean came to her more loudly as she drew closer; it must have disguised her footfalls, for Martin did not look over until she took the seat next to him.

They sat in silence for a few moments. The gray roil of the estuary before them was mesmerizing, an endlessly returning tide. The other Gywnn might have watched it, might have sat on this bench with Martin, all those years ago. Gwynn studied it, unwilling to speak of her great-aunt, now when she was finally here with Martin. He needed to know what she knew; but it would hurt him, the old man, now when it was impossible to fix. She shifted uncomfortably on the green slats.

Martin cleared his throat. He too seemed unwilling to open the conversation, and when he finally spoke, it was not about the elder Gwynn at all. "Young Colin was by this morning to fix a leaky faucet for me."

Gwynn stiffened. She kept her eyes on the gray line between the gray sky and the gray sea.

"He looks like hell."

"I don't want to talk about this," she said.

Martin tapped the back of her hand with a gnarled finger. "He's a good lad. That's all I'll say about that."

"I told you—"

"That's all I'll say about that."

Now Martin sighed, his shoulders slumping. He suddenly seemed older, shrunken, almost fearful. "And the more I think about it, the less I want to talk about what you've discovered." Again he sighed, deeply, and Gwynn was reminded of his tears, fiercely held in, when he'd shown her the photographs of the young Gwynn in his scrapbooks. She glanced at him, and saw him blinking against the wind. "I'm afraid of what you'll tell me."

His voice had grown so soft that she barely heard him over the breeze and the tide.

"Would you rather I not say?" she asked quietly. "She's dead, your Gwynn. There's nothing left to be done for her."

Martin held out his hands. "I could try to understand her. That much I could do." He shook his head again, then pulled a large handkerchief from his pocket and blew his nose loudly. "Sorry."

They fell silent again. A seagull fluttered to a landing a few yards away and took a tentative step toward them, fixing them with its beady eye. Gwynn didn't have the heart to tell it she had nothing for it; it would have to come to the sad realization by itself. It opened its yellow beak as though to squawk, but made no noise.

"And we saw her," Martin broke out suddenly, violently. "Both of us. We've seen her in the cottage. She had a terrible life, and now she isn't allowed to have a peaceful death? That's wrong. Wrong. We have to do something."

"But I don't know what to do," Gwynn protested helplessly. She looked down at her hands, balled in her lap. Useless hands.

"We have to find out what happened. We have to know. She must want us to know."

Gwynn shook her head. "She had all those years, Martin, to tell you. And she didn't."

"Because she couldn't," he said roughly.

She looked at him and could see the tears leaking from the corners of his eyes, openly, and he did nothing to hide them, nothing to wipe them away.

"I married someone else. There was always a part of me that loved Gwynn—there's still a part of me that loves Gwynn. But I had made a vow to Mary's mother, and I had to keep it. Gwynn knew that. She understood me, enough to stay away."

"And now?"

Martin turned on the bench to look fully into her face, his blue eyes blazing with the strength of whatever emotions were wreaking havoc inside his frail body. "You found out what happened, didn't you? That's why you called."

Gwynn nodded slowly. "I think so."

Martin grasped her hand. His grip was remarkably strong. "How did you find out? You said there was nothing in the house. No letters. No pictures. Nothing written down. *How did you find out?*"

Quickly she stood up and limped across the path, to stare down at the roiling tide. It looked like she felt inside, boiling and churning, warning of a storm on its way in. She closed her eyes against it, but felt a sudden wave of vertigo—then the extraordinary pain inside, the one Gwynn had shown her, let her feel.

"She let me know," was the only thing she could think to say.

"Tell me." Martin's words were a command, a throwback to Gwynn's Martin in uniform. "Tell me."

Instead she turned to look on his frail form, hunched against the wind on the park bench. "Did you have a brother, Martin?" She shoved her cold hands deep into the pockets of her coat.

He looked up, surprised. "Vern. He died."

"When?"

Martin stared off again into the distance. He seemed to be waiting for the path of the question to be made clear. "When he was young. I don't remember. Eight? Nine? Meningitis. One day he was fine, then he complained of a headache, and the next day he was dead." For a moment Martin looked stricken at the memory, but the expression faded, the pain that of long ago. "Why?"

"You and he—you had racing birds?"

Slowly Martin got to his feet and took the few steps to her side. He stared into her face, intently. "Yes."

"You wrote to Gwynn about them. When you were off at Bletchley. You told her about them."

His voice was now deadly quiet. "Yes. I wrote her a letter."

"She wanted—" Gwynn broke off, for a moment unable to continue. "She wanted to give you a gift. A racing bird. To show she understood. She wanted to get one to give you when you came home on leave."

"She never told me that. After that letter, she never wrote back again." His eyes bored into hers. "She never wrote back. And when I got home at Christmas, she was married. To Tommy." He put out a pleading hand. "Did you find that letter? You said there were none."

Gwynn shook her head. Looking into the wizened face, she could not speak. Could not say anymore.

"Then how? How could you know this?" That question seemed to lose its importance as the realization broke slowly across his face. "Tommy. The dovecote." His mouth worked, as though he could not bear to think the thought which now bore down on him, a freight train. "Tommy raised birds."

They stared at each other for a minute. The pain again, between her legs, the tearing, the blood. "He raped her, Martin," she whispered, and each word, she saw, hit him like a blow.

39

GWYNN BUTTERED A slice of bread and ate a bite over the sink, fearful of being sick. It felt as though she swallowed a brick. She set the bread aside on the counter and stared down the drain, queasy and dizzy.

Slowly she made her way upstairs, holding onto the sofa back then leaning heavily into the walls to steady her passage. She circled the marshaled boxes of Oxfam donations, then slid under the duvet on the unmade bed, fully clothed, exhausted. There she dozed fitfully, forcing herself awake each time the low-slung shadow of the dovecote appeared in her dreams.

You opened the gate.

She lost track of time, didn't care. Somewhere her phone rang, and rang again every few hours, then stopped when the battery died. Sometimes she heard the clock. At one point she dragged herself into the bathroom, where she undressed and sank into the scalding hot water, then scrubbed herself until her skin burned red. Even as she did, she had the horrified feeling that she had done this all before. She wrapped herself in a towel and crawled under the duvet once more, unwilling to enter the other bedroom to find clean clothes, or even pajamas. She slept more. She was hungry, but she knew that if she ate, she'd only vomit. The house phone rang, and she ignored it.

EARLY WEDNESDAY MORNING she thought of the scrapbook, hidden behind the books on the shelf downstairs. Painfully Gwynn dragged on her clothes, then navigated the stairs, which seemed a long wavering tunnel. She staggered weakly into the sitting room and dropped to her knees. Slowly she pulled the books out, feeling sick— knowing in the way one knows things when one wakes up that she had to pin Tommy Chelton to the page, and then—what? Destroy the photograph? Burn it in the stove, perhaps? She had to get rid of him. She could not let him roam freely through her house, through her mind. Through her dreams.

She had chosen to trap the scrapbook behind the heaviest volumes on the bottom shelf. With them on the floor beside her, she reached a trembling hand into the cavern she had created. And felt nothing. Panicked, she scrabbled around, jerking other books from their places, tumbling them to the floor. Her breathing was fast, shallow, frightened. More books, and more, until the shelf was empty. *The shelf was empty.* Martin's scrapbook wasn't there.

It had to be. She ran a hand over the now-bare shelf, bending low to peer into the empty space. Then she took a deep breath and forced herself to begin methodically examining each book she had removed, stacking them all in a pile. Slowly. Looking at the title of each, stamped on the spine, even though none of them looked right, or felt right in her hand. She sifted them all to no avail. She bent again, her breath faster, more painful, and looked at the empty shelf.

The scrapbook was gone. Hurriedly she ran her hands over the piles she had made, in case she had missed it. She had to have missed it. Yet at the same time she knew she hadn't. The book was gone. Martin's book was gone.

GWYNN HEARD THE key in the lock, and turned as Mary entered. Mary's lips were still pressed together in that tight line, the hurt disapproval that hardened her face, but about which Gwynn knew she could do nothing. *It's not my secret to tell.* She heard her own voice in her head, defensive, climbing the register. Slowly, with her hand atop the book shelf, she hoisted herself to her feet.

Mary's shrewd eyes took in the books on the floor, the empty shelf. "If you want me to clean that—" she began, but Gwynn put up a hand.

"No, no, it's not that." She dusted her hands on her legs, more from nervousness than from necessity. "I was looking for something."

Mary nodded stiffly. "What would it be? I might know where it is."

There was nothing arch in her tone, nothing at all indicating she knew what the missing something might be.

Gwynn licked her lips. "A book." She looked down at her pile, realizing how stupid she sounded. "A scrapbook?" She stumbled over the words, trying to figure out how to hint at what she wanted without giving Martin's secrets away to his daughter, if Mary still had no idea what she was talking about. "I thought I saw one. On this shelf."

Mary only shook her head. "I don't think so, really. Mrs. Chelton didn't keep scrapbooks. No pictures. She didn't want to be reminded of anything. It's like she wanted the past to disappear completely."

That made perfect sense, if you'd had her past. Gwynn nodded. "I guess I was imagining things."

Mary untied her kerchief and slid it from her hair. "That's all right, then. Tea or coffee this morning?" She moved off stiffly toward the kitchen, her back ramrod straight. "Just leave those there. I'll take care of them."

"No, that's all right—" But Mary was already gone, through the kitchen door, allowing it to swing shut behind her. Slowly Gwynn returned to her knees to replace the books on their shelf.

The panic was returning, but she fought it back, trying to reason through it as she set one book next to another. If not Mary, then who? If not here, then where?

She feared she knew the answer to both those questions.

GWYNN PURPOSELY CHOSE the part of the afternoon when she thought The Stolen Child might be less crowded; she wanted to speak to Paul Stokes alone, without a herd of people around when she accused him of theft. The idea appalled her. Well, why should it? He'd let himself in before, without permission, without a key—he'd had to break the kitchen window to undo the latch to the door, but that hadn't stopped him. Wasn't that breaking and entering? And if you were going to commit B & E, why stop at one time? And why not pick up a thing or two while you were at it?

Like the spare key.

Gwynn wondered when she had last looked at the glass dish on her dresser top, really looked at it, and noticed the spare key. The one she had thought she might give to Colin. The one she would never give to Colin now.

Paul Stokes, that afternoon, had gone through her dresser drawers to find the hidden scrapbook; what was to stop him from availing himself of a spare key while he was at it?

She wanted to spit in the street.

Instead, she drew a deep breath and pulled open the door of The Stolen Child. The sudden fear gripped her, the memory of the last time she'd been in here—but she hadn't been in here, it had been the other Gwynn; it hadn't been her, *it hadn't*—she tried to still her breathing, her racing heart. Inside, the public bar was nearly empty, only a woman in a fur-collared coat sitting at a side table, reading a newspaper. It was simply the dingy Child of the present, no crimson upholstery, no gleaming brasses. She wasn't Gwynn Chelton; Tommy was not at the bar.

No, that was her cousin, Paul Stokes, leaning on both arms against the bar itself, gazing down at the book open before him. She did not have to move any closer to know what book he was so carefully examining. He did not look up until she was nearly upon him.

There was that smile again. The one that showed all his teeth. Gwynn bit her lip, but moved resolutely forward until only the bar separated them. Stokes did not straighten, as he might have for a customer. But then, he knew that she was not a customer.

"You've been in my house again," she said without preamble.

"Ownership is in dispute," he countered. "We've been through this before."

"Your case has no merit."

"We'll let the courts decide, shall we?" His voice was cloyingly pleasant. It made her skin crawl—but he knew it would, and that's why he did it.

She tried to force back her anger, because he wanted her to be angry, he wanted her to feel violated—*if he only knew*—he wanted to have the upper hand, and she couldn't give it to him. "Possession," she ground out, quoting her grandmother Lucy, her great-aunt's sister, "is nine-tenths of the law."

Stokes shrugged. "All right, then." He dropped his black gaze to the book on the bar. Slowly, almost offensively, he turned the page with his beefy hand, and Gwynn saw, upside down but oh-so-recognizable, the photograph of her great-aunt at the dance, the photograph where Tommy Chelton looked on the unsuspecting girl with such a frightening *possessive* look. Gwynn shuddered, because she, unlike her great-aunt, knew what was coming, and it was unbearable. Except that Gwynn Chelton had had to bear it.

"You've been through my things again."

"Prove it." Paul Stokes didn't even bother to look up.

She reached out, her stomach churning, and put her hand on the scrapbook.

Slowly, possessively, Paul Stokes pulled the book from beneath her fingers.

"Possession," he parroted in the oily, faux-pleasant voice, "is nine-tenths of the law." He laughed, looking down at the photograph. "At least—that's what I heard somewhere."

"You bastard," she hissed. "You *bastard.* This isn't even mine. It's not our great-aunt's. It wasn't hers. It belongs to someone else."

"Prove it," he said again.

"Just give it back," she said desperately. "He's an old man. These pictures mean something to him. They're important."

"They are important, aren't they?" Again Stokes seemed to be studying the face of Tommy Chelton, almost as though he knew how uncomfortable that made her. "They mean something to me." Slowly he looked up, and the expression on his face made her shiver. "The pictures of my great-aunt. My poor *dead* great-aunt. They mean something to *me.*" He narrowed his dark eyes. "She was unhappy, you know. Sometimes I thought I heard her, late at night. Crying out. Rather like I thought I heard you crying out just the other night."

There was something so ugly in his tone that she could only stare, swallowing hard, before turning and fleeing from the darkened public bar.

SHE COULDN'T HAVE.

He couldn't have.

After all these years?

And the other night?

Once inside the cottage, Gwynn slammed the door and slid the bolt.

He had a key.

She dragged one of the heavy dining chairs into the hallway and wedged it under the knob. Then she leaned heavily against the wall, sobbing in fear, in pain, and in frustration.

40

MARY SEEMED PREOCCUPIED Friday morning. She moved around the sitting room with a duster, her forehead creased deeply; there was no coffee laid out when Gwynn appeared downstairs. Wordlessly, Gwynn went into the kitchen and rooted around for the press, the coffee, a cup. From the other room she heard a small crash, then the sound of Mary swearing. Gwynn froze, hand on the press. She had never heard Mary curse; something was definitely wrong. She reached into the cupboard for a second cup, because Mary was obviously in need of one.

"No," Mary said, as Gwynn brought the tray into the sitting room and lowered it onto the low table. "I can't take the time. I've got to get done here and get over to Dad's."

There was something frightening in her tone. Gwynn straightened quickly, too quickly, and prayed Mary hadn't noticed her gasp.

"What is it, Mary?" she demanded. "What's wrong?"

"I don't want to bother you with this," the housekeeper said stiffly. "It's just a personal problem."

"Mary. Tell me."

At first it seemed she would not budge, but then worry got the best of her, and Mary shook her head. "I don't know. The other day he seemed out of sorts when I took him down to the shops. Wasn't interested. Not like himself at all." She paused for a fraction of a moment in her dusting, lowering her head. "When we got back to the house, all he wanted was to put his pajamas on again and go to bed. No supper. Not even soup. He hardly touched anything yesterday, either."

This, Gwynn understood, was the ultimate in tells for Mary. If someone didn't want food, death might just be imminent. And her father was more than ninety, after all.

Gwynn bit her lip, stricken. Martin wasn't supposed to be out unsupervised; she knew this. Yet she had encouraged him, because she had needed him. She had needed to share the burden of the knowledge of Gwynn's violation, and who else to share it with but the man who loved her? Might still love her? Maybe it had been too much. Gwynn berated herself. He was an old man. He didn't need to bear the weight of this oldest of heartbreaks, for a woman for whom he could do nothing. *I can understand her.* She heard his words again, and knew in her gut that letting him convince her to tell him what she had learned had been wrong. Selfish.

"I haven't seen him like this since Mum passed," Mary continued fretfully. "Sad. To the point of sickness." She shook her head again and returned her attention to the dust. "I've got to get done here and go make sure he's all right this morning. I might need to take him to the GP."

Sad to the point of sickness. Gwynn knew what that meant. She felt it herself, deep within her chest. Deep within her womb. For the woman who had given up her life and her happiness for her younger sister, who had married and moved to the States. For the pregnancy that had ended—*no children*—for the child conceived in rape, and who had never been born.

That was just as well, Gwynn thought in agony as she sank onto the sofa and poured a cup of coffee for herself. A child of rape. Perhaps it had been a false pregnancy; perhaps her great-aunt's system had been so shocked by the violation that she had only been that: late. Or perhaps there had been a miscarriage. Without a further glimpse, allowed to her by her great-aunt, Gwynn had no way of knowing. And perhaps that sort of ignorance was truly bliss.

THUS GWYNN WAS surprised, early Sunday morning, when the telephone awakened her and she answered it to find Martin Scott on the other end.

"I hope it's not too early," he said, without a greeting.

It was, and she yawned, but guilt kept her from saying so.

"I had to call before our Mary got to your house. I need to see you."

"It's Sunday," she protested groggily, listening as the mantle clock rang the hour. Eight chimes. On a Sunday. She felt queasy, dizzy. "Mary is going to church. Doesn't she take you with her?"

He snorted, but it was forced, the ghost of his accustomed good humor. "Not anymore. The beauties of old age. You put your foot down, and even your children have to listen to you."

Gwynn knew he was trying, but his tone was thin, tired. "No, they don't. And your Mary wouldn't listen to you anyway, so don't give me that."

"All right," he returned. "I just don't want to go. And I tell her I'm old."

The laughter was brittle, overlaying something else that moved like a dark river beneath it. They both knew they were skirting the real purpose of the call.

"Tell me," Gwynn said at last. Simply.

"I need to come by," Martin said.

"No," she objected. "Let me come to you."

"I need to come to Gull Cottage. And I might need your help." He sounded uncomfortable, but determined.

"For what?"

"I can't tell you over the telephone," Martin hedged. "Can you be ready for me in about an hour?"

"But why?"

"Just be ready. Can you be?"

Gwynn didn't like the sound of it. But, as guilty as she felt, she couldn't turn him down. "In an hour," she agreed reluctantly.

GWYNN TOOK A quick bath, pulled on her clothes, and was waiting with the tea at the ready when Martin appeared at the door. Again he wore the fedora pulled low over his brow, as though that would disguise him from any prying eyes. He entered the hall, and his glance took note of the dining room chair against the wall, but he said nothing about it. Instead he only moved past into the sitting room.

He had aged even more since she had seen him last, Monday afternoon on the waterfront. He seemed smaller, seemed to have shrunk—instead of a sprightly, spirited older gentleman, Gwynn found herself faced with a stooped old man who moved stiffly, gingerly, in fear of falls and broken bones. He had a stick today, blackthorn, and he leaned heavily on it as he lowered himself painfully onto the sofa.

Gwynn poured him a cup of tea, and turned the tray slightly to bring the milk jug and sugar tongs closer to his hand. Then she too sat, but on the sofa, not in her great-aunt's wing-backed chair. She waited.

"Thank you," he said formally, "for letting me come."

Gwynn nodded in acknowledgment. The words hung between them, and she watched him pour a bit of milk into his coffee, then drop in a lump of sugar. She had done it wrong again. Probably always would. He appeared to take great pains with the stirring.

"I still don't know *why* you've come. What is this about, Martin?"

He lifted the cup to his lips, but didn't take a drink; his eyes skirted her to rest on the chair, moved back to its proper place. The marks it had made scraping uneasily over the carpet had been eradicated by Mary's industrious hoovering, but Gwynn imagined she could still see them. Somehow, too, she could imagine the impression of her cousin's body in the upholstery, claiming ownership of their great-aunt's wing-back.

Suddenly she stood and went to the chair. She crossed her ankles and folded her hands in her lap, trying to channel the other Gwynn. *It's your chair*, she thought, trying to make an impression on it, and on the atmosphere. *It's yours. I'm reclaiming it for you.* But she only felt a confused fear and sadness, and was unable to tell whether it was her great-aunt's, or her own.

She met Martin's eyes. The blue seemed dull, glazed.

"What's happened to you?" Her voice sounded shrill to her own hears. "Martin, what is it?"

He shook his head. Even his fluffy white hair was dull, flat.

"I can't sleep, young Gwynn," he said quietly. "I dream of her."

Gwynn kept her eyes locked on his face. She licked her dry lips.

"I do, too," she whispered.

But again he lowered his head. "No. You don't understand. She comes to me. I hear her screaming. And then I hear her sobbing. And there's nothing I can do."

He was clenching his bony hands in his lap so tightly that his knuckles showed knobby and white.

Then in her mind's eye she could see him as he had been then, a young freckled-faced man in uniform, home on leave, dancing with a beautiful red-haired girl in his arms. Dreaming of his future with her, of their life together, of their children. *He had loved her.* The handsome young face superimposed itself over the lined one before her, and she could read plainly the heartbreak there. *No. He still loved her.* Gwynn dropped to her knees on the carpet beside him, took his clenched hands in her own. The hands that had held her great-aunt all those years ago, the hands that had returned home that December and found themselves empty. Forsaken.

"Tommy Chelton was a monster," she whispered, holding onto his hands as though to give him a lifeline. There was such hatred in her voice that Martin looked up sharply.

"Is that how you knew?" he asked.

She lowered her head and did not answer.

"Tell me, Gwynn," he said, more urgently. "Does she come to you in dreams as well? Do you hear the screaming? Do you hear her sob?"

She shook her head, the tears starting again. She refused to look up.

"But why wouldn't she tell me? Why wouldn't she write to me?"

"She didn't tell anyone. He raped her in the dovecote, and then he gaslighted her—he convinced her no one would believe her—she'd followed him up there of her own accord, so she must have known what would happen. That's what everyone would think. They'd blame her."

Martin was openly crying. They both were.

"And she was afraid of what you would have done."

"I would have gone after the bastard. I would have killed him with my bare hands."

Gwynn took a deep breath. "Part of her knew that. Then you'd have been in trouble, and she didn't want that, either." She wiped her face with the back of her sleeve. "He shamed her. She couldn't tell anyone. I don't think she ever told her own mother."

"But she married him, Gwynn. After what he did to her. She *married* him."

Now Gwynn squeezed her eyes shut, willing the horror away—but it did not go. "She had no choice, Martin." Her voice broke. "She had no choice." Slowly she told him about Tommy Chelton's threats, about the pregnancy which, in the end, was not.

For a long time the only sounds were the ticking of the mantle clock and the labored breathing of the old man on the sofa.

"How can you know this?" he asked again, raggedly.

She couldn't meet his eyes.

Martin freed one of his hands, then she felt his bony finger beneath her chin, tipping her head up.

"Does she come to you?"

She shook her head now, she could feel the tears splash against her skin. "No, Martin," she said, her voice nearly inaudible, even to her own ears. "No, she doesn't come to me." She took a deep breath which tore at her insides, then opened her eyes to look straight into his face. *"She is me."*

Martin looked down on her in horror. "You—are each other," he whispered. "That's how you know what happened to her? Because it happened—"

"To me," she said.

"Oh, Gwynn," he said after a moment, his voice strangled in his throat. He leaned forward until his wrinkled cheek rested against her head. "Oh, my Gwynn."

"WE NEED A drink," Gwynn said, at last.

"I'll get it. Same place?" Martin leaned on his stick all the way out into the kitchen. He returned with the new bottle under his arm and two glasses in one hand. He sank back down onto the sofa and poured out two healthy fingers for each of them.

"To hell with the coffee," he grunted, shoving one glass toward Gwynn, who had returned to the chair. "We both need this straight, and plenty of it." He downed his shot in a single gulp, then leaned back and closed his eyes, his breathing labored.

Gwynn drank hers more slowly. If she had her way, this bottle would see some good use this morning. Drunk before noon—it didn't seem like too bad an idea at all. Martin would help. It might even be worth the hangover.

"Does anyone else know about this?" Martin asked after a pause.

Gwynn took another sip before answering, letting the whisky burn its way down her throat and into her gullet. It was supposed to radiate warmth once drunk, had always done so for her, so she waited, half-hoping. Nothing, though, was getting through this chill.

"No," she admitted at last. "I haven't told anyone."

"No one at all?"

She chose to ignore the implication which lay behind his words. "No one. Mary asked, the morning after it—happened—in the dream. But I couldn't tell her. I knew it wasn't my secret to tell."

"Yet you came to me."

Her glass was suddenly strangely empty, and she leaned forward to pour another two fingers into it. "She wanted me to tell you. My great-aunt." *Don't ask anymore. Just don't.*

Martin nodded, and poured more whisky into his glass as well. "I see." Then he shook his head, half angry, half confused. "No. I don't see. She could have told me. Years ago. Back then."

"Not while your wife was alive."

Martin fell silent again.

The clock on the shelf rang the hour.

Gwynn roused herself, looking down into her glass, which was approaching empty once again. She had to stop, she told herself, because, while on the one hand she would welcome the obliviousness of drunkenness, on the other, she wouldn't welcome the ensuing hangover, which would make everything a hundred times worse. She glanced at Martin, sunken and small on the sofa. He'd made pretty good headway on his own drink: he'd be drunk, too. Then he wouldn't be able to get home, and Mary would find he'd been out, and there'd be hell to pay. Especially if she found out that Gwynn had been the whisky supplier.

"You wanted to come see me about something," she said, trying to bring the bleak morning back into focus. She suddenly hoped he wasn't going to ask for the scrapbook; she didn't want to have to tell him where it was now. Nor how it had come to be there.

Martin leaned forward, elbows on knees, and set his glass down on the table. "It doesn't matter now. I don't think I should bother you with it."

Gwynn too set her glass down. "You'd best just tell me. You said you would need my help. Tell me what it is you need."

Still he evaded her eyes. "It's not important now."

The *now* hung between them like a live thing.

She cleared her throat. "It's *all* important now." She didn't even know what she meant by that. "What did you come for, Martin?"

He pressed his thin lips together, and again clenched his hands between his knees. "I thought—I needed—" He stopped, coughed, drew out a carefully pressed handkerchief from his pocket and wiped his mouth before going on. "I needed to go up there."

The morning had suddenly grown still, and dark.

"Where?" Gwynn asked, but it was only a stall. She knew.

"The dovecote," he said, his voice low. Then he shrugged, and the effort seemed to pain him. "But it doesn't matter now."

Gwynn swallowed hard.

"You need me to take you up there?"

Martin grimaced, lifting a bony hand and letting it fall helplessly. "I thought I needed to go up there. To see if it would help." He looked away, toward the window, where the roofline of The Stolen Child was visible. "I didn't think I could make it up there by myself, not with this stick." He blinked a few times, quickly. "But it really doesn't matter. I don't want to go up now. I don't want you to have to go up there now."

Gwynn hadn't been up there in weeks, save in the dreams. The thought of the dovecote made her cold, dizzy, nauseated. How could her great-aunt have lived in its shadow for the rest of her life? But then, the place where she was didn't affect Gwynn Chelton's feeling shackled to Tommy; in her mind, Gwynn knew, her great-aunt would always have been shackled to Tommy Chelton. Him, or his memory. She would have always lived in the shadow of what he had done to her, that late summer afternoon.

Again she closed her eyes, listened with her entire body, trying to feel any message that her great-aunt might be sending. Martin had had to be told; but did he need to be taken up there? The raw note in his voice made plain that he had made up his mind that the journey was a necessary one; what if he attempted it alone? What if he fell, was injured, was alone?

"I'll go with you," she rasped out.

"No, Gwynn," he said.

"I'll go with you," she repeated, without looking at him. She picked up her tumbler and tossed back the remains of the whisky, feeling the shock in her throat, wishing for the false courage that was supposed to come with it. "Let's go now. I've got a flashlight in the kitchen." She didn't wait for his further objections, but pushed away from the chair and went to the kitchen door. "It'll be dark in the dovecote."

GWYNN REMEMBERED THE dimness so thick it was tangible. She felt it again on her skin, and her resolution faltered. But she took a deep breath and opened the cupboard for the flashlight, heavy and sturdy in her hand. She could hear Martin coming behind her. Though she knew they were brand new, she tested the batteries, and, satisfied, opened the back door.

The brambles still clung to everything, still spread their way across the path she and Colin had cut and uprooted. They clawed at her jeans, at her shirt, at her skin. Gwynn slowed, pushing them aside as best she could for Martin. Behind her, he stopped every few feet and swung his walking stick, attempting to beat his way through. The sky lowered over them, dark and sullen. As they neared the gate, she could see through the opening, that last distance between wood and wall where it refused to be closed. If anything, the world beyond the gate and wall looked darker and more menacing than the day itself.

"Be careful," she said over her shoulder.

Martin only grunted, whacking with his blackthorn. Then he stopped, lifting his head to listen. "Doves," he said, wonder in his voice.

Gwynn paused with her hand on the rusted and broken latch and tilted her own head. The rustling and cooing grew stronger.

"There are still doves?" he asked.

"No."

"Then how?"

"I don't know."

She dragged the gate across the scarred ground until the opening was wide enough for them to pass through. "Watch your head." She ducked under, and Martin followed, his wizened face a play in confusion.

Outside the wall, the air seemed thicker. A miasma. Again Gwynn fought back the urge to flee, back into the house, back to relative safety. *Martin needs this,* she thought, steeling her spine. *Martin needs me.* She bit her lip and pushed on into the trees with their glistening boles, where the sky was scarred by dark branches crisscrossing overhead.

Gwynn needed her. And had needed Martin, had been unable to reach out to him.

It was getting harder to breathe. She slowed, half-turning to wait for Martin. He was laboring along the vague path through the trees, jamming his stick into the ground and pulling himself along with its help. He reached her and stopped, his chest heaving.

"Are you sure?" she whispered, close to his ear, almost afraid someone would overhear. Who? They were alone in the wood, along with the cooing of doves, which no longer existed.

"I've never been more sure of anything." His jaw, unevenly shaven, was hard, his Adam's apple working as he strained to take a full breath. "Take me up there. If you can."

Gwynn took his arm now, and they walked together through the trees along the faint path, which shone oddly in the dimness. It led them to the clearing, and Martin paused again, looking on the wreck of a building, tiles missing from the roof, the piece of burlap flapping loosely in the window beside the sagging door. She saw it through his eyes: the crooked lines, the wood sinking slowly into the earth. Soon it would fall in of its own accord, and that, she knew, would be a good thing. It couldn't happen soon enough. For even as she saw it as Martin was seeing it, it transformed in her sight into the building from which

Tommy Chelton had emerged that afternoon all those years ago and stood waiting, for the words he had been expecting from her great-aunt.

"What's happening, Gwynn?" Martin whispered. "Tell me what's happening."

But she couldn't.

There was no sound. The doves were gone. They had always been gone. She looked down, half-expecting to see the single dead bird at her feet.

There was a single dead bird, its red-rimmed eye staring sightlessly up at her.

Gwynn caught her breath sharply, stopping so abruptly that Martin stumbled against her, and it was all she could do to retain her balance and hold him upright.

"Whoa, there, Gwynn. Easy, now. What's the matter?" Then he peered at her closely, licking his lips. His Adam's apple worked in his throat. "Which Gwynn are you?"

Gwynn swallowed again, her fingers digging into his sleeve. "Both," she said, and realized that it was true.

For a moment Martin stiffened in surprise, but then he covered her hand with his own. "Let's go back."

She looked into his face, and he returned her gaze steadily. "You need this." She dropped her eyes to the dead bird on the leaves before her, expecting it to be gone. There was nothing there. She prodded the ground gently with the toe of her shoe.

"But you don't." Martin cleared his throat. "You've seen it. You've felt it. You've *been* it. You don't need to go through this again."

"She wants me to take you up here." The words both made sense to her and didn't. There was no time to worry about that now. Keeping her hand on Martin's arm, Gwynn took a step forward, around the dead bird which wasn't there, toward the sagging door.

It opened surprisingly easily under her touch.

Inside it was cool and dim, much as she remembered. The smell was of earth and decay, the floor covered in rotted straw, which deadened their footfalls. As her eyes adjusted, Gwynn saw the thick rafter beams overhead, and the empty boxes that lined the walls. No rope. No feet. No circular tracings in the dirt. The ghosts of the birds were silent now, but she could still hear them in her head, imagine their hushed conversation as the other Gwynn stepped forward into the long barn. She didn't want to go too far down into that memory, into that dream;

she clutched at Martin's sleeve now with a shaking hand, trying to remain grounded, trying to remain in the present.

The dovecote, she told herself fiercely, was empty, abandoned, the violator and the violated both dead, the birds gone, the time past. It was over, she told herself. *Over.* Still she held on to Martin's arm, the tweed of his jacket a welcome roughness to her touch.

"Tell me what to do, Gwynn," Martin whispered suddenly.

She sought his face again in the dimness, but he was not looking at her; his words were addressed to the air around them. They did not echo under the beams, but instead swelled to fill the dark space.

They waited.

Then Gwynn felt the faint stir of the air that told her they were not alone. She tightened her grip on Martin's arm, her eyes darting about toward the dark corners, the dim overhead. She could see no one, but her neck prickled, the hair lifting. Slowly she turned back toward the door, where the sliver of dull light fell inside from the narrow opening: no one stood there. *No one she could see.*

He had come up behind her, Tommy Chelton had. He had touched her in that ugly possessive way, running his fingers down the inside of her arm. Gwynn glanced down now, feeling the burning, expecting to see a hand, a furious red scar from the touch—but there was nothing save the pale glow of her arm below her sleeve.

"Who's there?" Martin called out sharply. "Who is it? Gwynn, is it you?" He jerked away from her hand, turning almost drunkenly with the aid of his stick, his eyes wild in his face. "Gwynn, I want to help you. Tell me what to do!" He staggered away, calling frantically into the darkness. "Gwynn, I'm sorry—I'm sorry! Tell me how to help you!"

She didn't feel Gwynn near her, nor in her. The movement on the air was not her great-aunt, but something dark, pulsing. Something angry and evil.

"Martin!" she cried.

He wheeled, and his eyes traveled beyond her, to something over her shoulder. She turned but could see nothing.

"Gwynn," he gasped, and then, dropping his blackthorn stick, he folded to the ground, in slow-motion, his legs giving way and his body sinking without grace, without a sound.

With a strangled cry, she tore herself away from the thickened air which mired her, throwing herself to her knees next to Martin's crumpled form.

HE WAS BREATHING. Under her hand his chest rose and fell, shallow, but steady. She looked around helplessly, desperately. There was no help up here—of course there was no help. She dashed to the door, wrenched it open further, and looked down through the trees toward the cottage, but she could see nothing, no one.

"Hello?" she shouted. "Help! Someone!"

Nothing. She looked back over her shoulder at Martin, where he lay in the straw, his arm thrown out awkwardly, his stick under one leg. She shouted again, even while recognizing its futility. Then she ran back to drop to her knees at Martin's side. Her hand found his chest again, and she leaned over his mouth, trying to feel the movement of air on her cheek. His eyelids fluttered, opened, closed again.

"Martin?" she called to him, her voice thick with panic and tears. "Martin? Can you hear me?" She lowered her forehead to his chest and let out a sob. "Martin. Don't die, Martin, please don't die."

She felt the weak movement of his hand against her hair.

"Gwynn," he said again, his voice barely audible. Then, more strongly, "I'm here."

She grasped his fingers. "Martin. I need to get you help. Can you hear me? I need to run down to the cottage. Can you hang on?"

His knobby fingers moved in hers.

"Yes," he whispered. "Get help."

Gwynn struggled to her feet and ran.

41

"WHATEVER WAS HE doing up there?" Mary asked "It doesn't make sense. Do you know how he got up there?"

The paramedics had found them at the dovecote; Gwynn had left instructions for them to come through the house and garden, and had left the door open. Mary had rushed up through the trees in their wake. Gwynn had returned from phoning for help and discovered Martin at the edge of the clearing. The knees of his suit were muddy and torn; he was leaning against the trunk of a tree, his head cradled in his hands, his breathing shallow and ragged, his face as white as milk. *I couldn't stay in there,* he'd told her.

Now Gwynn huddled in the plastic chair in A and E, her own head in her hands. She couldn't bear to answer the other woman.

"How did he come to be at your cottage in any case?" Mary went on, her voice querulous with worry. "He's not supposed to be out and about without help. He's ninety-four, for God's sake! He knows better."

I know better, Gwynn berated herself. *I knew I shouldn't have let him. I knew I shouldn't have encouraged him.* She tugged at her hair anxiously, guiltily. She could feel the weight of Mary's suspicions around her neck. What if Martin died? He was an old man. The dovecote had been a shock. His heart, these past several days, had been overworked, had suffered more than it had since he'd returned on leave that long-ago December to find his love married to someone else. She should have let him be. Left him alone to his comfortable sofa in his comfortable robe and slippers, to meet his comfortable end. Instead of dragging him out in pursuit of the haunt of his long-dead love. *I knew I shouldn't have taken him up to the dovecote.*

Somewhere far off, she could hear Mary's voice, still puzzled, still angry, still querulous, still frightened. "Why? He's never done anything like this before. Never. Not until you asked him about Mrs. Chelton."

The *you* hung heavy between them.

"Mary," Gwynn said at last, still clutching her head. "I—I'm sorry." She couldn't explain. Mary would never forgive her if anything happened to her father. *Anything else.* Mary would probably never forgive her anyway. "I tried to stop him." *And he tried to stop me.* "I tried to make him go back."

Under the antiseptic lighting, Mary's suspicions and disapproval pulsed, beating at her, exacerbating her pounding headache. Gwynn bent double now, resting her forehead on her knees. The nausea was creeping up again, and she could taste the bile in her throat. *Don't be sick,* she ordered herself, alternating the words with her silent plea to Martin: *don't die.*

She wanted someone to pat her back, to soothe her, to comfort her. *Where are you, Colin?*

There was no answer from Colin, or from anyone else.

MARTIN WAS WHEELED back into the cubicle, and his eyes were closed. An IV monitor clicked fluid into his arm; an oxygen tube snaked up his nose. Turning away from Gwynn, Mary crossed to his side, her displeasure still apparent in the stiffness of her back. She leaned over and took his hand from the top of the sheet and held it between both her capable palms.

"Oh, Dad," she said, and there was sadness and frustration in her voice.

He opened his eyes and looked up at his daughter, his expression softening. "I'm all right, Missy," he said, his voice rough. "Just a bit of a heart thing. Nothing for you to worry about."

"What on earth were you doing up at that ruin, Dad?" Mary demanded.

Gwynn studied her hands, waiting.

Martin shifted on the bed, the mattress crackling beneath him. "Don't blame Gwynn."

Mary leaned closer. "What?"

"I went up there. I've been thinking all this week." He stopped, coughed a small dry cough, then started again. "I wanted to see the place where—where—Tommy Chelton died." Again he shifted, and his eyes searched the cubicle until they fell upon Gwynn, but only for the smallest of moments before he looked back into Mary's worried face. "She didn't want me to go. She followed me up there. She tried to get me to go back, to call you, to go home." He smiled crookedly "But you know how stubborn I am."

Mary nodded, still holding his hand, but her shoulders relaxed a bit.

"I know, Dad," she said quietly. "I know how you get."

The look Mary now cast at Gwynn was as close to an apology as she would be getting, Gwynn knew, even if she deserved one.

"I know exactly what you're like." She pulled a chair closer and sat at the bedside, uncomfortably low, having to look up into his pale face against the pillows. "But I want you to stick around, Dad. I want you around a bit longer."

Martin nodded, and patted her hand. "I'm sorry, Missy. I'll try to be good."

Gwynn chose this moment to slip from the room, leaving them alone together.

42

PAUL STOKES WAS leaning against the stone front of The Stolen Child when she returned from the hospital in a cab. As she paid off the taxi driver, she saw him, out of the corner of her eye, push himself away and start across Eyewell Lane toward her. Without waiting for her change, Gwynn turned her back and hurried toward the blue front door. It was locked, of course, and as she fumbled in her bag for her keys, she heard his steps on the path behind her, then his breath, uncomfortably close.

"You want me to unlock that for you?" he asked.

"Get away from me," she growled.

"Just wanted to make sure you were all right," he protested, holding his hands up to illustrate his harmlessness. "What with the paramedics and the ambulance here and all. Just a little bit of familial concern."

"Yeah, right." Gwynn found the key at last and jammed it into the lock. "More likely you were hoping I was dead or something." She couldn't keep the bitterness from her voice. "So you could inherit."

Stokes shrugged. "That would save time," he agreed. Nastily. "Of course, you'd have to die intestate, or name me in your will."

"Highly unlikely." The key refused to turn. She pulled it out and pushed it in again. "How do you know I wouldn't be leaving the property to some other relative in my will? Husband? Child? You don't know anything about me."

His smile was ugly. "No husband. No child. No time, I guess, since your husband died so—tragically."

Gwynn staggered back as though slapped. She stared at her cousin. Before she could turn thoughts into words, though, he held out his hands once again, palm up. "I just wanted to check on you, that's all. Make sure you're all right. And Martin Scott? Mary's father—that's who that was in the gurney, wasn't it?"

"If you know so much, why the hell are you asking?" The key turned at last, and Gwynn kicked open the door. "Why don't you leave me alone, Mr. Stokes? Just leave me alone." She stepped inside, then turned to slam the door behind her, but not before she heard his laugh.

"Like your lover Colin's left you alone?" he asked. "Looks like everyone's leaving you alone, Gwynn. Leaving you all alone." There was a threat in the words. "It could really depress a woman, I expect. Make her feel desperate."

Now she did slam the door and leaned against it, breathing heavily. After a moment the laughter died away, as did the steps back down to the street.

43

GWYNN PUSHED THE sketch block away peevishly. Scattered on the floor at her feet were several unsatisfactory attempts at pictures of items on Belinda's list, along with line drawings of the cottage door, of the dovecote, of a curtain blowing at a broken window. *I don't care,* Belinda had nearly shouted down the telephone line earlier. *Scan them all. Email them to me. I need* something. *We've got a deadline here.*

The silence in the cottage was mind-numbing.

Gwynn had to do something other than fail at drawing. Anything. She had to move. Shoving her arms into the wool pea coat, she pulled on some gloves and headed out the door. Purposely, she did not spare a glance for The Stolen Child; if her cousin were watching from the front windows, waiting for her to leave so he could let himself in and rifle the place, let him. *Let him.* She'd had enough of him. She'd had enough of all of them. She wasn't even sure who *all of them* encompassed, and she wasn't even sure it mattered at this point.

She turned right and headed uphill, away from the village. Soon her thighs were burning with the effort, and other than slowing her pace a bit, she did nothing but welcome the feeling. Action. She found herself fitting her steps to the cadence of the song in her head; then she realized what the song was: "No Ghosts." *A hell of a lot he knew.* She pushed on, determined to out walk this hopeless feeling. She would leave it behind if she could.

Gwynn turned into a lane, then another. To her right, a footpath. She was tempted, but she had no ordinance map. She was nearly to the end of her endurance anyway, she ached so much. The vista that opened out beyond the hedgerow, however, called to her. She looked to the bleak sky—no sign of a break in the regular clouds, but no more storms on the horizon for a while. Still, she'd heard of people wandering off into the maze of public footpaths and getting turned around. A movement caught her eye, and she looked up to see a red kite soaring away overhead. Taking a deep breath, she turned her steps along the path.

Gwynn didn't want to think. Instead, she looked, slowing her strides. The footpath would be lovely in June and July, with the blazing sun overhead, the bird calls, the scent of the wild roses that would line the way. Now the branches on either side were bare, the leaves fallen or lusterless. It suited her, the November countryside. It suited her bleak mood, the general feeling of anxiety, as though something were on the verge of happening, something just out of sight, something she was powerless to prevent. She touched her finger to a startlingly red rose hip, and moved on.

In the distance she could make out a cluster of buildings: a white-washed stone house surrounded by outbuildings which had been left their natural color, and were nearly faded into the landscape. There was something familiar about them. She rifled her memory with little success, until she saw the spot, midway between the high hill on which she found herself and the cluster of buildings, where a blackened circle marred the brown grass. Trevelyan Court Farm—from a different angle. A rueful smile played about her mouth as she found herself patting her own pockets; but she had left the extra packet of matches in her purse, and she had left that on the kitchen countertop back at the cottage. If she came upon Giles, she would be unable to help him in his never-ending quest to light his pipe. Again. Poor man.

Gwynn thanked what providence had set her feet on this particular track. The Trevelyans. Of course. Giles and Bel and their warm welcoming kitchen. Practical human conversation. Touching her upper arm gingerly—even though the bruising was nearly faded away by now—she headed along the worn track down toward the farmhouse. She hoped that same providence would have them at home; she hoped they wouldn't mind an unexpected visitor.

She heard the frenzied barking as she skirted the curve of the upper field. *Star.* Gwynn felt her mood shift. She trailed her eyes over the surrounding fields, looking for the flock of sheep the dog would be working, but she did not see them. Still, the barking. She shaded her eyes with her hand, searching the high meadows for the flash of black and white, the streak that was Star on a border-collie errand, but could not find her. Her speed on the hillside increased, and the barking grew closer. More frenzied.

"Star?" she called. "Where are you?"

The dog shot up the hillside toward her, from a hollow that still remained hidden from view. Gwynn stopped, held out a hand, but the sheepdog circled her, just out of her reach, still barking, and then streaked back down the hill again.

"What's wrong, Star?"

Again she appeared, circled, ran back down to disappear into the hollow.

Gwynn broke into an awkward run.

GILES TREVELYAN LAY hidden in the tiny hollow as though cupped in a hand. Beside him, standing guard, Star looked up at her and barked one more time. Then she sank to her belly, her head on her paws. She whined gently.

Gwynn's breath caught in her throat. She stumbled the few feet to his side and fell to her knees. Giles lay on his stomach, his legs tangled, his arms thrown wide, as though welcoming the ground as it rushed up to meet him. A few inches from his splayed fingers lay his unlit pipe, a chunk of tobacco, burned around the edges, dislodged next to it. She reached out a shaking hand and touched Giles on the shoulder of his barn coat.

"Giles?" she said. Then, urgently, "*Giles?*"

He did not answer, did not stir. She hadn't expected it, she thought wildly, but she had *hoped.* Beside them, Star whined again.

"Hush, girl," she said distractedly, trying to pull her flyaway thoughts together. Trying to think. "Hush." She touched Giles' cheek, above the bristles of his white beard; his face felt cold, so cold. Frantically, with both hands, she grasped his shoulder and turned him over, gasping. "Giles?"

He was heavy. Gwynn lost her grip, and he rolled over onto his back, his black-current eyes staring sightlessly upward. There was blood on his scalp, blood on his face.

Gwynn scrambled to her feet. Star lifted her head, but did not cease whining. "Stay," she whispered to the dog, holding a hand out—it had blood on it, she noticed, in shock. "Stay." It seemed dreadfully important that someone stay with the old farmer, but she had to go for help. She took off down the track, past the blackened bonfire site, toward the cobbled farmyard.

Bel must have seen her coming through one of the kitchen windows, for she opened the door as Gwynn stumbled into the farmyard. Bel's face paled at the sight of her, and she looked upward, beyond the barns, into the high fields. "Giles?"

"Get help," Gwynn gasped.

Bel just stood, still looking up at the hillside, and began a high keening.

THE FIRST PERSON to show up, even before the police and paramedics, was James Simms. Today he wore his shiny business suit, apparently having just come from the office.

"Bel," he said, letting himself into the kitchen. Bel looked up from her seat in the rocking chair, her face drawn and white. Her lips moved, but she said nothing. He hurried to her side. "Where?"

Bel made no move.

"Up in the pasture," Gwynn said. Her voice was thick, not her own. "Beyond the burn circle." She swallowed. "Star's with him."

Simms looked her up and down, his eyes narrowed behind his wire-rimmed glasses. "Stay here with Bel," he ordered, and disappeared back into the yard. The kettle whistled, and automatically, Gwynn rinsed and filled the teapot, letting the leaves steep while she watched through the window as the solicitor headed up into the pasture. Star would find him. Star would bring him to the place where his master lay, staring into the bruisy November sky.

Gwynn was pouring a cup of tea for Bel when she heard the sirens heading up the long track from the road. Bel did not look up, merely rocked. The chair creaked steadily against the tiles. Gwynn set the cup and saucer on the small table beside Bel and slipped out into the farmyard. "Up there," she shouted to the paramedics, waving a hand toward the tiny dark figure up on the hill. An officer swung himself out of the police car, which then followed the ambulance out of the yard. As the policeman approached, his eyes widened with recognition.

"Mrs. Forest, isn't it?" he asked.

She nodded.

"You found him? You called?"

Gwynn nodded again, and with one last glance up at the procession on the hillside, she led the policeman into the kitchen. Bel Trevelyan still rocked, white-faced, the cup of tea untouched beside her.

"Mrs. Trevelyan?" The officer, Gwynn thought now, looking at him where he bent over Bel, was young, terribly young. Too young for this job. She returned to the teapot and fixed him a cup. "Are you all right? It's me. Evan. Evan Collier?" He took his hat off and set it aside.

Bel looked up at him, her expression uncomprehending. She put a hand on his sleeve. "Giles," she whispered. She dropped her hand to her lap and looked away.

At the sink, Gwynn lowered her head. In her pocket, she fingered the pipe she had picked up from the ground.

BY THE TIME Penny showed up, darkness was falling, and with it, shock had set in. Gwynn couldn't bear to sit in the kitchen with Bel, who was, it seemed, close to catatonic; she had never been invited further into the house, so now she sat on the bench outside the door in the encroaching night. The paramedics had gone away with their burden, the attending doctor having declared Giles dead. Now Star sat at her feet, staring out into the darkness in her silent dog way. Up on the hillside, lights had been set up in a mockery of the bonfire, the hollow cordoned off.

Penny lowered herself slowly to the bench beside her. She touched Star on her grizzled head, once, as though acknowledging the dog's grief. Gwynn held herself stiffly away. There was something odd and awkward sitting here with Colin's ex-wife, Giles' great-niece.

"All right?"

"I bought him matches," she said, bewildered. "At the shop."

Penny sighed, running a hand down the length of her braid before tossing it over her shoulder. She turned toward the lights on the hillside. "He would have liked that."

It didn't matter now, Gwynn thought numbly.

"I didn't know the footpath came here," she said, aware of the non-sequitur, but unable to think of anything else to say.

"You were walking?" This was the same question the young policeman had asked, the same one she had answered.

"I had to get out of the house."

Penny nodded. She seemed to want to say something, but then bit her lower lip and remained silent.

Gwynn too looked up toward the lights. Shadowy figures crossed and recrossed, tiny on the hill. "What will Bel do? Who will stay with her?"

Penny answered the second question first. "She's got Jamie. He'll take care of her."

"Who *is* he? What is he?" Gwynn shook her head. None of it made sense. She remembered back to the night of the bonfire—the morning after, really—and watching Bel Trevelyan pluck a bit of hay from Mr. Simm's thinning hair. There was an intimacy there that she didn't understand, but one which was totally unremarkable to everyone else in the room.

"He's her brother. Youngest of them." Penny leaned forward, looking away from the place where the bonfire had been lit just nights ago, and where the police klieg lights shone now. The place where the fire had been lit for so many years previously. Gwynn wondered inanely who would light the fire now. Whether anyone would. Whether Trevelyan Court would continue as a farm, or whether the stone outbuildings would be converted to holiday homes and sold off to incomers. Incomers such as herself. But what did that matter? What did anything matter, in the face of Giles' death?

"Someone killed him," she said slowly, looking down at her hands. For a moment she could still see the blood, though she had washed it off in the sink hours ago, watched the tainted water swirl away down the drain. "Someone killed him."

Penny gasped, looked at her sharply. "You're sure of that."

"He was—face down. There was blood on his head." She saw again those black-current eyes, blindly staring up at the November sky.

"He could have fallen," Penny offered. "He could have had—I don't know—a heart attack? And fallen."

But Gwynn remembered how Giles' body had lain, his arms thrown wide. "He didn't try to catch himself. He didn't try to break his fall. He wasn't clutching his chest." She tried to convince herself that what she had seen was something else, that what Penny suggested was believable. She couldn't shake her own conviction. "Someone hit him, Penny. I'm sure someone did. Someone killed him."

44

HAVING EMAILED OFF the drawings with a sinking heart, Gwynn found herself pacing through the cottage. From the dining room through the sitting room, into the kitchen, back. Waiting for the disappointed rejection and probable dismissal from the project that was bound to come. It couldn't be helped. No matter how hard she had tried, no whimsical woodland creatures had erupted from her pencil, no fairy princesses. Only brooding broken-down buildings, lonely doorways, fog, drizzle, leafless and lifeless trees.

The car slowing to a halt in the street before the house drew her attention. Gwynn saw two men climbing out of the dark blue Vauxhall. One of them pushed back his tan coat and tucked his hands into his pockets, leaning back on his heels to look up at the cottage appraisingly. The other, in an almost identical raincoat, came around to join him. Gwynn drew back from the window, letting the curtain fall back into place, knowing they'd probably noticed her watching.

She had never believed what she'd read in books, that it was impossible to mistake detectives for anyone else. Now she saw that it was true. She felt her chest constrict. Police detectives. She'd expected them, of course, especially after she'd been warned by Constable Collier, up at Trevelyan Court Farm, that they'd need to speak to her again in the morning.

Two men who had become surprisingly important to her: one hospitalized, one murdered. And police on the terrace. Frantic for a moment, she wondered whether she needed a solicitor. She only knew James Simms. What were the chances that the brother-in-law of the dead man would represent her? *Dead man.* Her breath caught in a small sob which surprised her. Murdered man. She was certain of it. She closed her eyes against the vision of Giles' blank surprised face, but it was no use. She only imagined it more clearly.

Gwynn distracted herself with the small courtesies: what did one offer the police for refreshment when they came calling? The knock was so sharp that, even though she knew it was coming, she jumped. She took a deep breath before unlocking and opening the door.

"Miss Forest?" the man in front asked. He flipped open his ID card; the second policeman did the same. "Detective Inspector Barrows, Detective Sergeant Laundryman. Could we have a word?"

Gwynn stepped back. "It's *Mrs.* Forest, actually."

"Your husband is here?" The voice was neutral, not even curious. His eyes flickered to her hand on the door and up again.

"I'm a widow." She led them into the sitting room and indicated the sofa; she claimed the wing-backed chair for herself with a hand on its high chintz back. "Can I offer you something? Coffee? Tea?"

A glance passed between the policemen, so quickly she might have missed it had she blinked. "Sergeant Laundryman will get it, if you tell him where the things are."

"On the tray, on the counter. There's only one cup. There are others in the cupboard overhead."

Laundryman disappeared into the kitchen, and she could hear him opening and closing doors. Gwynn sat, and in her distraction, noted that Barrows tugged at the knees of his trousers before sitting, just as Martin had.

Detective Inspector Barrows cleared his throat, taking a small notebook from his inside jacket pocket and flipping through the pages, a thin line between his pale brows. He found the page he wanted and looked up. "We need ask you about yesterday. At Trevelyan Court Farm."

Gwynn nodded. "Of course. Though I don't know what I can add to what I told the policemen who were there last night."

"We sometimes find that people remember things later, Mrs. Forest," Barrows said noncommittally. He waited as Laundryman returned with the tea tray. "And I'd like to hear your story firsthand, if you wouldn't mind going over it again with me."

It didn't really sound like a request, but probably she was just being paranoid and melodramatic. Gwynn picked up the teapot and held it aloft. Barrows and Laundryman held their cups out to her, and she filled them wordlessly, then poured the steeped black tea for herself.

"Sorry," she said as she set the pot back on the tray. "I always pour the tea backwards—my friends keep saying I'm doing it the wrong way." She flushed, snapping her mouth shut against her own babbling. She lifted her cup and blew on the steaming tea.

"You were up on the footpath?" Barrows prodded. Laundryman produced his own notebook and pen from an inside pocket and scratched at a page.

Still Gwynn held her cup, but did not sip. She stared down at the steam rising from the surface. "I'd gone out for a walk. I went up that way, toward the top of Eyewell Lane, took a couple of turns, and ended up on that footpath."

"You were going to the farm?"

She shook her head. "Not at first. I really didn't know where I was going. But I didn't think I could get too badly lost, and if I did, I could just walk back the way I'd come."

"Not at first, you said. I'm afraid I don't quite know what you mean by that."

"I finally figured out I was up in the fields above the farm when I came out of the trees. So I thought it might be nice to go down and visit with them." Gwynn fought back another surprise of a sob. "With Giles. And Bel."

"You knew them well?"

Without thinking, she raised the cup now to her lips. The tea was scalding hot. "Yes. Well enough, I suppose. I'd met them before. We'd brought brambles up for the bonfire, and we were up again for Bonfire Night." She raised her eyes to the two impassive faces. "How is she? Bel? Do you know?"

This time she could not mistake the look that passed between the detectives. She had trouble reading it, however. Compassion? Concern? Something else?

"Mrs. Trevelyan," Barrows said, "is doing as well as anyone can, under the circumstances."

"Which isn't well." Gwynn thought of the poor woman's face, the shock, the inability to respond. The untouched cup of tea near her hand. Her brother Jamie kneeling by her chair, trying to coax words out of her which would not come.

"You said 'we,' Mrs. Forest," the inspector said. "Who is 'we'?"

She set her own teacup and saucer on the low table. "Me, and—the handyman. The wood man. Colin Moore." *My lover, the one I threw out of the cottage.* She leaned back in the chair, trying to feel her great-aunt, trying to find courage. "I hired him to help clear out the back garden. It was—is—quite overgrown. We took a load of brambles up to throw on Giles Trevelyan's bonfire up in his field. That's when Giles invited me to the *craic* for Bonfire Night. Colin Moore took me back up to the party when the day came." The detectives shared a look again. "I have no car."

"This Colin Moore is a special friend?"

"He's one of the friends I've made since I've been here," Gwynn answered stiffly. She wished they'd stop looking to each other like that, as though they didn't quite believe her and were telepathically sharing impressions. She felt her face warming. *Special friend.* Everyone knew what that meant. And she'd made more friends since she'd been here? That made her sound like one hell of a promiscuous woman. *I'm not sleeping with him anymore,* she wanted to protest, but knew that would only make things worse.

Worse? Things weren't bad, she admonished herself. She hadn't done anything wrong. Damn these police detectives for making her feel guilty for—for what? "So I thought I'd just walk down to the farm and see them in passing. Giles and Bel." She glared at the detectives defiantly. "They were nice to me, both times I'd been to the farm." That made her think of Bel's ministrations with the bruising on her arm, and she touched the place Paul Stokes had grabbed with his large hand. Paul Stokes, who was *not* one of the friends she had made since she'd been here.

"Something wrong, Mrs. Forest?"

The detectives were watching her intently. She pulled herself together sharply. "No. Upset, that's all."

"Did you notice anything else before you found the body? Anything that struck you as strange or out of place?"

Body. Not Giles Trevelyan. There was no sympathy in Barrows' voice. If he had noticed she was still shocked by Giles' death, he wasn't letting on. All the more reason, she told herself sternly, to get a grip. She took another deep breath, cupping her face in her hands, thinking hard. The dull November light, the brooding clouds. The barking sheepdog. The walking stick under Giles' leg. Dropping to her knees, turning over Giles to find his blank stare. Her fingers, finally, curling over the short stem of the unlit pipe. "Other than Star barking, it was quiet. So quiet. No birds in the thickets. Nothing."

"You didn't see anyone?"

Gwynn shook her head again. "The field was empty. Only me. And the dog Star. I didn't even see Giles until I followed Star over the little hill." Her voice was shaking, her hands, too, and she reached out again for the teacup, to keep those hands occupied. She picked it up, and the cup rattled in the saucer. Tea splashed out over her hand. It was lukewarm now. How quickly it had cooled. She set the cup down.

"You're here on holiday?"

Gwynn was momentarily taken aback by the sudden shift in the questioning. Detective Inspector Barrows, she noticed, had not drunk his tea, either.

"Or are you renting?"

Her neck prickled. In her parallel internal conversation, Gwynn told herself that, as policemen, they had to ask these questions. They probably had to speak to her as a suspect: she had found the body, after all. She was, to use the parlance, in the frame.

She caught herself in that train of thought and looked up sharply. "My great-aunt willed me the property. I'm trying to decide what to do with it." Her lips felt numb now, and she couldn't hold back the question. "It was murder, then? I mean—you're detectives."

The scratching of Laundryman's pen stopped for the smallest of moments, then resumed. Inspector Barrows met her eyes, but his expression was inscrutable. "Early days yet. We're awaiting test results."

The awfulness of the situation, which refused to be held at bay, struck her fully. "Postmortem," she whispered, and the words tasted foul in her mouth. "Autopsy." Again she closed her eyes against the visions the words conjured up. "Poor Giles." But the old farmer was dead, and could suffer no more indignity. "Poor Bel." She looked up. "There was so much blood on his head. On his face. Someone hit him. Do you know—with what?"

"You don't think he fell?" The question was an evasion, but it was more than that at the same time. She felt the probe.

"He didn't look like he fell," she said.

"What do you mean?" The tone was so calm, the man might have been remarking upon the weather.

"His arms spread out like that. Thrown out. He didn't try to catch himself. He would have tried to catch himself if he'd stumbled, don't you think?" Gwynn wasn't having any luck controlling herself. Her voice was rising again; she took a deep breath, and another. "I said this all before. I told Constable Collier up at the farm. One of the policemen took notes." She looked pointedly at Detective Sergeant Laundryman's busy hands. Surely they shared notes. Surely that policeman had reported to his superior officer. Surely this wasn't necessary.

"Yes, and we're sorry to have to make you go through it again." The soothing words sounded like a rote recording. "But it's a necessary evil, as we're sure you'll agree."

"Yes." She sighed after a moment, exhausted. "I know."

There was a knock at the door.

"You're expecting someone?"

"No—no." Gwynn started to rise, but Sergeant Laundryman waved her back down.

For such a heavy man, he moved with a surprising speed and lack of noise. She found herself thinking she should resent the way the two detectives were manipulating the interview, not allowing her to leave the room, vetting her visitor—but she was too tired to worry about it. She listened dully to the voices in the entryway; across from her, Detective Inspector Barrows was listening as well, his eyes half-closed in concentration.

"Good afternoon, Gwynn," Mary said formally from the doorway. "I've come to work on clearing out that upstairs bedroom, as we'd agreed." Her voice was stiff, as though she were reading from a script. Lying did not come easily to her.

Gwynn quickly looked away to hide her surprise. They hadn't agreed. She didn't think they had agreed. Had they?

"Yes," she said, sounding wooden to her own ears. "I'd forgotten." She'd already told the two officers that she wasn't expecting visitors. Perhaps Mary didn't qualify. "Yes. Go on up, why don't you, and I'll join you when I'm done here." She nodded, hoping Mary understood: *I've got this under control.* Hoping she did, actually, have this under control. "Do you know Detective Inspector Barrows? DS Laundryman? This is Mary Tennant."

Mary tipped her head in acknowledgment. "We've met," she said tightly. "When they asked me a few questions earlier." She nodded to each of them in turn.

"Mrs. Tennant," Inspector Barrows greeted. He got slowly to his feet. "It's all right. We've mostly wrapped things up here. Unless there's anything else you need to ask, Sergeant? Anything I've forgotten?"

DS Laundryman held up a hand and shook his head. "No, no, thank you, I think I'm set here." He snapped his notebook shut and pocketed it.

"Right, then. We'll be off. We'll type up a statement, and then perhaps you'll come along to the station and sign it. In the next day or so—we'll let you know."

The detectives thanked her for the tea, the general dogsbody Laundryman carrying the tray through into the kitchen before taking leave. Gwynn shut the door behind them gratefully and returned to the wing-backed chair, where she slumped without grace.

Mary handed her a shot glass which she seemed to have conjured out of thin air, her lips pressed thin.

"Drink this. You look like you need it." She lowered herself to the edge the seat so recently occupied by the inspector, her back straight. Everyone, it seemed, thought Gwynn looked like she needed a stiff drink. "Was it bad?"

"Why did you come?"

"I saw the car. I hope you don't mind."

Checking in on her. Despite being rebuffed. Just as she had all those years for Mrs. Chelton. Gwynn told herself she didn't need anyone to check on her. She sipped the whisky cautiously, tasting sudden irrational anger, and something else—fear?—at the back of her throat. "They were polite. But cagey. Evading my questions. Wanted to know why I thought Giles hadn't fallen. Why I didn't think it was an accident."

"What did you tell them?"

"About the way he was lying on the ground." The whisky, as always, burned on the way down; she would never get used to it. Gwynn realized she was close to tears. She thought of the last time she'd drunk too much and hurriedly put the shot glass down. She tugged at her hair. "I keep thinking of the blood." Her voice was losing strength.

"I'm sure you do."

The kindness in Mary's voice was Gwynn's undoing. She pressed her fingers to her eyes to prevent the tears from falling.

"Blood. It's what happens," Mary said with surprising bitterness, "when you get clubbed in the skull with an enormous rock."

Gwynn met her eyes in shock. Mary's gaze didn't waver.

"Who told you that?" Gwynn's glass still contained most of the two fingers of whisky, but her ears rang almost as if she'd downed the entire bottle. "About a rock? No one said anything to me."

"Evan Collier let it out to me. This morning. At the shops." Mary shook her head. "Foolish lad. Never could keep his mouth closed."

"So they knew." Gwynn wanted to spit. "They knew all along that it wasn't an accident."

Mary leaned forward, almost as if to offer comfort, but thought better of it and sat back again. "I wonder why they wouldn't have said anything to you about it."

"Bastards," Gwynn said darkly. Then the thought struck her. "You don't think that they knew about Paul Stokes?"

"What about him?"

"About me, hitting him with a rock."

Mary's lips thinned once again. "Quite a coincidence, they might think." She wiped a hand at a phantom crumb on the table "But who would tell him? And why would they keep the information about Giles being hit from you?"

"Too much of a coincidence," Gwynn muttered. "Because if they know I hit one man with a rock, it's only a small step to thinking I hit another. That's my *modus operandi.*"

45

"I UNDERSTAND," DETECTIVE Inspector Barrows said as he lowered himself into the chair behind the desk, "that there's some bad blood between you and your cousin, Paul Stokes."

Even though she had prepared herself for it, the baldness of the statement knocked Gwynn back. "Who told you that?"

"I don't think that's important," Barrows said. He leaned back in the chair as though uncomfortable. "Is it true?"

Gwynn studied her hands. "I don't know if bad blood is the right term. He's angry with me because our mutual great-aunt, Gwynn Chelton, who died last spring, left me her cottage. I guess he'd hoped she'd be willing it to him at her death."

"You make it sound rather tame."

She glanced up. Barrows had his fingertips pressed together, a steeple, before his lips, as though concentrating hard on her answer. "I don't know what you mean. I'm sorry he feels that way, I suppose."

"Sorry enough to attack him? Sorry enough to hit him with a rock?"

Gwynn caught her breath. So it *had* come to that. "Did he leave out the part where he threatened me first? Because it sounds like he did." It sounded as though Stokes had tailored the story to make her into some kind of raving lunatic, randomly swinging stones at people.

"So there *is* bad blood." There was a certain satisfaction in Barrows' voice.

"Listen," she blurted angrily. "I didn't attack Paul Stokes. He was leaning over me on a stone wall, threatening me if I didn't sign over the property to him—he had a paper, he had a pen—and he wouldn't let me get up and leave. So I knocked him over—"

"With a rock in your hand—"

"I hit him in the arm. The *arm*. And yes, with a stone from the wall he'd forced me to sit on so he could lean over me and threaten me. I was frightened, and he knew it, and he used that to try to get me to relinquish the cottage to him. So I hit him in the arm to escape from him."

"Who else was there?"

Barrows' bland manner was infuriating. Gwynn wondered if his intention was to make her so angry she said stupid things. If so, it was close to working. But she was experienced, she reminded herself, thinking of Richard, and that way he would anger her, repeatedly, intentionally, in his manic stages. It was years ago, but remaining calm was a learned skill, like riding a bicycle. She would not let Barrows manipulate her.

"No one," she said slowly, measuring her breathing. "I have no witnesses." She looked Barrows straight in the eye over the expanse of his desk. "But that means he has none, either."

Barrows sighed, straightening an already straight piece of paper on the blotter. "It's an interesting story, however, wouldn't you agree? That you hit a man with a rock"—he held up his hand to forestall any protests—"by your own admission, mind you—and just a few days later, another man is killed when his skull is crushed with a rock. In very nearly the same place. And again, with no witnesses."

"I found Giles," she said evenly, her voice low and grating. "I didn't kill Giles. I counted him as a friend."

Barrows nodded. "Yes. Mrs. Trevelyan seems to think so."

Again she looked up. "How is she? This must be so awful for her." She shook her head. "I haven't been up to see her."

"Why not?"

"I didn't know if she was up to visitors."

"So not that good a friend, then?"

He was trying to trap her again. *Richard. Remember Richard.* "I'm not family. Not like her brother. Not like Mr. Simms."

The silence stretched. Barrows was watchful, waiting to see if she had more to add. The paper on the desk—the only paper on the desk—drew his attention after a few moments. He opened the desk drawer, withdrew a pen, made a mark on the sheet. Gwynn strained her eyes to see, but it was too far away.

"Speaking of family," Barrows said at last, tucking the pen back into the drawer as though tucking a baby into bed, "you told me you were a widow?"

"Yes." Gwynn heard the confusion in her own voice and attempted to rein it in before Barrows noticed. "My husband died six years ago."

Now he picked up the sheet of paper and nodded. "By his own hand, it says here."

She swallowed hard. Was the piece of paper a dossier on her? If so, it was rather brief. Then again, up until she'd landed in the village, she'd led a rather tame life. Blameless, even. "Yes. Richard was—Richard committed suicide."

"How did he do that?"

"I think," Gwynn said sharply, her resolve failing her, "you probably know. I think it must tell you that in whatever file you've gathered on me.

Barrows glanced up, unperturbed. "Just checking my facts."

She blew out a breath. *Remain calm.* "Richard hanged himself. In the orchard behind our house. He had been—depressed."

"And you found him."

"I found him." Suddenly she could bear it no longer. "I found him. He was dead. It was the most horrible moment of my life. Until Giles."

"Whom you also found."

"Stop it," she said. "Just stop it. I found them both. You know that. But I didn't kill either of them. What is it that you want from me?"

Barrows stood and walked around his desk so quickly she thought for a moment he was going to strike her. Instead, he continued to the door and opened it. "I'd like you to remain available, Mrs. Forest. In case any more questions come up. That's all. I'd like you to make sure you don't leave the village."

46

THE SCRATCHING AT the front door awakened her.

Gwynn had been dreaming of the strand, of walking along the shoreline with her shoes in her hand, legs of her jeans rolled up, her toes digging into the sand. The sun was warm on her face and bare arms. She heard herself singing. Birds circled overhead, gulls soaring and diving, landing and then leaping up once again into the air.

Her song changed to Pat's, the one about the doves.

Up ahead she saw a stooped figure making his was along the shingle, the stick he used to help himself along basically useless. As she watched, a wave built out on the water, swelling to enormous proportions, balancing at that wave-point just before breaking as it moved toward land. She opened her mouth to shout out a warning, but the man was too far away, the seagulls screaming too loudly. The scene unfolded in slow motion: the wave, the man, certain doom. She broke into a run, shouting words that went unheard, torn from her lips and whirled away into the air.

She was too late. The wave broke, sweeping up the beach, and the old man was swept from view. Still she ran on, shouting, but it made no difference. She looked out into the swirling waters desperately, hoping for a hand, something, anything—but there was nothing. Except, when her eyes fell to her feet, the walking stick. She bent slowly, curling her fingers around the knob.

Now Gwynn flexed her empty hands at her sides as she made her way groggily to the front door. There was an urgency to the scratching in the early morning that demanded her attention. "Who's there?" she called, leaning against the door, her hand on the chair wedged under the knob.

The scratching came again.

Carefully she dislodged the chair, drew the bolt, and opened the door a crack.

Star sat on the doorstep, waiting. She looked up at her and whined softly. Gwynn drew the door back to let her in.

The border collie padded through the entryway and into the sitting room. Gwynn followed her, curious. The dog went to the side of the wing-backed chair and sat, looking up at her expectantly.

"What is it, Star?" she asked softly. She made no answer, not even a whine. Gwynn sat in the chair next to her, and she pushed at her hand with her wet nose. She patted the dog's head, stroked her soft ears. "Are you lonely? Do you miss him?"

Beneath her hand, the dog was still; Gwynn sensed it as an enforced stillness. Star sat at attention, expecting something.

"What do you want? Are you hungry?" She thought about the contents of her kitchen, of her refrigerator. Was there anything out there a dog would eat? That was a silly question. Dogs were eager to please; they'd eat anything. Except perhaps vegetables. Raw vegetables. "Come on then." She stood. The mantle clock struck six, the last ring dying away on the dark morning. "Do you like peanut butter?"

Star did not move.

Yawning, she moved to the kitchen door. Star turned her black head slowly, studying her intently. "Come on," she said, patting her thigh. "Star, come."

Still the sheepdog did not move, other than to watch her every step carefully. After a moment under this intense scrutiny, Gwynn returned to the chair and sank into it slowly.

"Does Bel Trevelyan know you're down here?" As soon as she asked the question, Gwynn felt idiotic. *Do your parents know where you are?* The dog had come down and presented herself for some reason having to do with dog logic, though Gwynn had no clue what that reason might be, and Star was not letting on. At least, she did not understand what the dog was trying to tell her. If she was trying to tell her anything at all. She had not made any noise since Gwynn had let her into the house; she had not moved in several minutes. She simply watched, with her intelligent brown border collie eyes. Gwynn put her hand on the furry head again and rubbed it. "What do you want me to do?"

Outside the window the dawn was breaking, the morning growing slowly lighter. Another gray and cloudy day, but no rain this time. Gwynn sighed. Probably it would be a good idea to dress and walk the dog back up to the farm. She rose and turned to the stairs, Star followed her, claws ticking on the wooden floors. She followed her into the small bedroom, where Gwynn quickly made the bed and then dug out some clean clothes from the laundry basket. Star followed her into the bath, and lay down beside the tub as she climbed in. At least, Gwynn thought as she pulled the curtain closed around her, she did not attempt to leap into the tub, too.

"I DON'T KNOW what to do with her," Bel said, her voice thin and querulous. "She's Giles' dog, she is—she never left that man alone for a minute. Followed him everywhere. Now it seems she's at a loss—goes where Giles went, looking all over the farm for him. And cries. At night she cries, and I'll tell you true, I can't bear it. I can't."

Bel sat in the rocking chair near the fire, still. Or again? She did not rock, but just sat, her blue eyes wide and vague behind her thick glasses. At first, when Gwynn had entered the kitchen with the dog, Bel had frowned, trying to place her. She seemed older and more fragile today, her shoulders hunched, as though the world were pressing down on her. Her hands were clenched defensively in her lap. The kitchen itself looked dingier, as though a light had left it. And perhaps, for Bel Trevelyan, it had.

"She didn't want food, She wanted to follow me around the house. I didn't know why she was there." Gwynn didn't mention her growing conviction, as she followed the lanes toward Trevelyan Court Farm, that she needed to check on Bel—that Star was hinting that something bad, something *else* bad—had happened to her neighbor. So strong had this conviction become, that she had steeled her nerves and taken the footpath through the woods and into the high meadow, knowing she'd get there faster; she'd been careful not to anywhere near the hollow, still cordoned off with yellow police tape. She'd been careful not to go anywhere near the portable incident room, either, though the hour was still a bit early, and the room looked deserted.

Yet Star had been in no rush to get back to the farm, Gwynn realized. Star had stayed to heel, keeping close and silent as they came down the long hill into the farmyard. When Bel had called out in answer to Gwynn's knock, Star had followed her into the kitchen and lain down in front of the door.

What on earth did the dog want? Gwynn wished she knew. She wished she knew how Star had known how to find Gull Cottage.

"Can I make you some tea?" she asked Bel now, helplessly. "Breakfast. Have you had breakfast?"

Bel, apparently out of words, made no answer.

Gwynn busied herself with the tea things, neatly tucked away on the sideboard. She brought Bel a cup, then found a frying pan, some butter, some eggs from the bowl on the counter. She was whisking the eggs when the door opened and James Simms entered on a burst of cold air. Star looked up quickly, but then lay back down, her black head on her white paws.

Mr. Simms cast a curious glance at Gwynn. He unbuttoned the wool coat he wore over his pinstriped suit.

"Star came to the cottage this morning," Gwynn said without preamble. "Early. So I've brought her back."

Mr. Simms nodded, setting his coat over a chair back and going to his sister, listless in the rocking chair. He knelt at her side. "Bel. Have you slept?"

Bel looked at him in despair. She frowned for a moment, then her expression smoothed over, as though someone had run a hand over it. "Here."

"You need to sleep," Simms said quietly.

"Not there," Bel said sadly. "He's not there."

Gwynn turned away from the pair, feeling the tears prickling behind her eyelids. She focused her attention on the scrambled eggs in the pan, stirring them gently with a wooden spoon to break up the curds as they cooked. She found a plate in the cupboard, and, eggs done, she slid them onto it. She cut a slice of bread from a thick loaf, and buttered it. A fork, a napkin—she carried them over to the rocking chair. The little coffee table at the side bore the ring stains of recent cups; she wiped it off before setting the plate on it.

"Breakfast," she said, her voice sticking in her throat.

Bel did not answer.

Mr. Simms looked up, his expression pained. "Thank you." He straightened slowly. "I can take it from here."

Gwynn knew a dismissal when she heard one. She was secretly grateful to be relieved of a duty she had no idea how to perform. The grief in the kitchen was so thick she felt she had to push it away from her face with her hands, in order to breathe.

Mr. Simms saw her to the door. She stepped outside. Star followed, fully alert now.

"Stay, Star," she commanded. Star did not even deign to sit. Gwynn touched Mr. Simms wordlessly on the sleeve, as much of an expression of sympathy as she felt she could give him, and took a few steps into the yard. The dog followed.

"Star," she said again, hardening her tone. "Stay here."

But Mr. Simms shook his head. "Let her go, if she wants." He looked up, his eyes behind his thick lenses suddenly like his sister's. "That is, if you want."

Gwynn looked down into the brown eyes of the dog and wondered about loyalty and allegiance. "How old is she?" she asked. It was the only question she could think of.

Mr. Simms shrugged. "I don't know. There's always been a border collie following Giles around, as long as I can remember—since I was a small boy. Protecting him." He looked up into the gloomy sky. "Maybe Star thinks you need protection now." He cleared his throat. "Maybe Giles does."

On that prophetic note, Mr. Simms let himself back into the farmhouse. Gwynn sighed and turned away, with Star heeling at her side.

47

GWYNN CAME OUT of the shop, carrying the bottle of lamp oil and some canned dog food in her bag. Star still sat at attention by the door. The dog lifted her head and stood, awaiting their next errand. Gwynn shifted the bag to her other hand and touched the black head with growing fondness.

"It's all right, girl," she said, rubbing behind her ears in the way the dog at least put up with from her. "No danger in the shop." Star wagged her tail once, her expression of approval. "Down to market, then, shall we?"

They headed down the hill, Star close at her heel. Gwynn was becoming used to her shadow, though she noticed people doing a double-take when they passed. No doubt they recognized the dog as Giles Trevelyan's, and wondered at her companion. In the past few days, Star had made no move to go home, and neither Bel nor her brother had been by to collect her. Other than vacuuming more frequently on account of the dog hair, which seemed to appear in the corners in little clouds, Mary had made no further comment, either. Star had adopted Gwynn as her charge, watching over her intently during the day, sleeping on the carpet at the foot of her bed at night.

Now they made their way from stall to stall, Gwynn selecting root vegetables and potatoes to go with the chicken she had purchased from the meat truck. She browsed slowly, almost luxuriously, relieved in a small way to be away from the cottage and its sadness, the garden and its anger. Today there were strawberries, fat and hot-house grown, but she didn't really mind, thinking of cream and shortbread, the latter made by Mary, a dozen in a small box back on the kitchen counter.

She was pocketing her change and heard the familiar, unwelcome voice.

"All right, then, cousin?"

Gwynn whirled. Star slipped in front of her protectively, the fur on the back of her neck bristling.

"Fine, thank you, Mr. Stokes," she said. She moved to turn away, dismissing him, but he put up a hand.

"It's just that I haven't seen you since your breakup with Colin Moore. A bad night for you, wasn't it?" His smile was more of a leer, and there was an ugly, knowing light in his black eyes. His voice, his words, carried. As he no doubt knew they would.

"I don't know what you're talking about." She looked back to the vegetable stall, and the vendor dropped his gaze quickly.

"Well, never mind, Gwynn," Stokes said, his voice oily in its fake condolence. "There are plenty of other fish in the sea, if this one didn't work out. He's not worth crying over." He smiled again, wolfishly. "I was just worried about you, see? You've seemed so down lately. Depressed. And to break up with your boyfriend like that—can't have helped, can it?"

That sympathy. Gwynn felt her eyes widen as she looked into the round red face. He was playing some game, the rules of which she didn't understand.

Had he been watching her again? "I'm not depressed. I'm fine."

"In any case, if you need a shoulder to cry on, you can always come on over to the Child. I'll be there." He winked slowly. "And don't you worry. I don't hold a grudge about your attacking me with that rock on Bonfire Night. I know you've been under a lot of stress."

How could his voice carry like that? It seemed as if the entire market had gone silent, listening to him. She looked around; no one met her eyes.

Paul Stokes laughed. "Just make sure the shoulder you cry on when you come on over isn't the one you damn near broke when you hit me with that rock up at Trevelyans'. That one *still hurts*."

Now he'd done it, and he knew he'd done it. The fake sympathy had turned to triumph. By now everyone in the village had to know how Giles Trevelyan had died; and now they knew about her tendency to hit people with rocks when stressed. By now everyone knew about that rift between her and Colin Moore, and everyone here who pretended not to listen knew she was unbalanced.

"Don't worry about it, Gwynn. Things will get better. Don't you worry." Stokes reached out a beefy hand to pat her on the shoulder in consolation and kindness and sympathy, while she stood shocked, frozen in place.

Star snarled.

Stokes jumped back, dropping his hand quickly. "Stupid dog." He peered down at Star, and then back up at her. "That's Giles Trevelyan's dog."

Gwynn set a reassuring hand on Star's head. The low growl faded, but the dog still bared her teeth at Stokes. "It was."

"What the hell are you doing with it?" Stokes took another step back, his fists tightening by his sides.

"Star is a good guard dog." Beneath her hand, she could feel Star's coiled tension. She was ready to strike if need be. "She keeps me safe." The dog growled again, low in her throat.

Stokes took yet another step away, his eyes never leaving the dog. "Well, you keep it away from me, do you hear? If that mangy thing comes after me, I'll kill it, see? And I'll be within my rights. So you'd better keep that animal under control."

"Leave me alone, Stokes," Gwynn retorted sharply, "and you'll have no problem at all. Don't touch me, don't even come near me. Do you understand? *Stay away from me.*"

Shaken, she bent to whisper to Star, rubbing her ears. "Let's go home, okay?" She turned away from Stokes and the stall and the curious eyes, but not before she heard the shout.

"Crazy woman! All I was trying to do was help!"

48

STAR ONLY RAISED herself to a sitting position at the knock, looking up expectantly. No barks, no growls. Gwynn moved the chair and opened the door.

It could have been the first time Colin had appeared; he stood with his back to the door, looking over at The Stolen Child. He turned slowly.

"I've brought the firewood."

Gwynn kept both hands on the door. "I didn't order any firewood. I don't need any firewood."

His hands were in his pockets. "You will before the week is out. You don't want to be cold."

This would have been what it was like for him, bringing wood to Gwynn Chelton. Colin did things for her, even when she didn't ask. Because she was a lonely, frightened, bitter woman. Gwynn felt the blow to the gut.

Star slipped out the door between them.

"Let me get the gloves," Gwynn said, resignedly. "And the money."

Colin cast her one sharp look before turning on his heel and heading back down to the truck, where the barrow was strapped to the top of the load.

HE POCKETED THE notes without looking at them, without a word. Gwynn peeled off the work gloves and then twisted them between her hands, watching Colin heft the barrow easily up onto the remains of the wood in the bed of his truck. He took one more look over her shoulder at the cottage.

"I think," he said at last, "you had better tell me what happened."

She was silent.

Colin moved impatiently. "You owe me that, Gwynn. Just that much."

She put a hand on Star's head, to steady herself. Star moved away from her touch. Gwynn looked down, surprised: Star had never done that. Taking a deep breath, she forced herself to raise her eyes to Colin's face. A good face, she had thought on that day a lifetime ago when she had met him: strong, with determined bones, but kindness around the eyes. She stared. The eyes. The steady gray, honest, eyes. She had forgotten that. She licked her lips nervously. How she had forgotten that.

These were not the eyes of Tommy Chelton.

Colin did not touch her. He was waiting, willing her to make the first approach. But she couldn't. She held back, feeling another touch on her skin, feeling revulsion and disgust. She couldn't help it.

"You called me by his name," Colin said now.

"I—I didn't know what I was saying," she whispered. "I wasn't—myself."

He nodded, as though she were confirming his suspicions. "No. You were—her. Weren't you? The other Gwynn."

The other Gwynn. How awkward. How unbelievable. How strange to hear the words from someone else's lips. "Yes. She was—with me."

"She came to you in a dream."

It sounded ludicrous. Yet it was true. Words failed Gwynn, and she lowered her eyes, twisting the gloves in her hands until her fingers hurt.

"Did she tell you—what had happened?" Colin too seemed to be having trouble speaking the words.

He almost understood. *Almost.* There was still that gap between knowing and *knowing.* Gwynn wondered if it were even possible for anyone to understand. Then she shook her head sharply. Martin understood. Yet Martin had loved her great-aunt, despite everything. Even though he had pushed the feeling aside and had married the woman who was to become Mary's mother, he had loved the other Gwynn. Enough to understand now. Enough to feel her presence through another person.

"It wasn't that," she choked out, still twisting her hands. "She didn't—tell me."

Gwynn could feel Colin's sudden stillness, his shock at finding out the thing he'd known all along, but hadn't want to face.

Because he loved her.

She saw, from the corner of her eye, his hands lift slightly from his sides, and then fall again, helpless. Then ball into tight, furious fists.

"And it was rape."

His word fell like a bomb, making a crater between them, a crater she couldn't pass over. Not now. Not yet. Maybe never. She nodded.

"And you—felt it."

There it was. Gwynn recoiled, expecting his recoil as well. Feeling dirty and shamed and angry and a mix of everything that couldn't be explained to anyone who had never felt anything like it. Feeling like the young Gwynn Chelton had, all the years ago: the shame and the horror that Tommy Chelton had exploited to get his way. The shame she had not been able to envision for Lucy, her younger sister, the girl who had gone blithely off to America with her flyer husband, safe from Tommy, unaware of what had been sacrificed to ensure her safety and her happiness.

The hands were still fists, and she could see, shaking with impotent fury.

"I'm sorry, Gwynn," he choked at last. "I'm sorry. I didn't know. I didn't understand. I never would have made it worse had I known. Please believe that."

She nodded, still watching her hands.

"You poor woman," she heard Colin whisper. "That poor woman."

"COME WITH ME," Colin said, the door to his truck open, his hand on the guitar case.

Star lay on the pavement at her feet, seemingly relaxed, though her brown eyes never left Gwynn.

"Come deliver the wood. Come to the gig," Colin said. Almost pleading, though she knew Colin would not plead; it wasn't his way. "Come back to the flat." He paused. "Come away from this house."

"I can't," Gwynn said.

Her throat felt raw. She pulled her sleeves down over her hands, crossed her arms over her chest. She was cold, though the sun shone weakly now, and there was no wind.

He leveled his eyes on her, the gray the same color as the sky, as the sea the last time she'd sat on a bench overlooking the water. With Martin. Martin lying in the hospital, the monitors ticking away the messages his much-weakened heart was sending out. An even gray. A private gray. Colin waited for her to speak, to explain further. She couldn't. She couldn't let those words out over the rawness in her throat, the soreness in her entire body. If it was her body.

Gwynn wondered, for a panicked second, if this was the way her great-aunt had felt, every time she had looked at the young Martin, when he had returned home from the service. She wondered if the expression on Colin's face was the same one the other Gwynn had seen on Martin's.

Hurt. Uncomprehending.

She felt the dizziness again, the nausea. She reached out a hand and clutched the side of Colin's truck to steady herself. At her feet, Star lifted her black head, brown eyes on her. She whined, once.

"It's all right," Gwynn whispered, as much to herself as to the dog. She closed her eyes.

She opened her eyes, Colin was closer, the gray gaze still on her face, but he still did not touch her. "I will catch you," he said carefully, "if you fall, Gwynn."

"I won't fall."

He waited. Slowly Star lowered herself back to the pavement. The dizziness passed.

"Because," Colin said at last, as though after a great decision, "I love you."

"PLEASE," HE SAID after a time. They still stood on the pavement. Star still lay beside Gwynn's feet, still on high alert. The afternoon was growing cooler, and Gwynn found herself shivering. "Please come away from here. Stay at the flat."

"No," she answered.

"I'll sleep on the floor. Hell, I'll sleep in the truck, or at one of the guys' places. Just come away, Gwynn. Look what's happened to you here. This place is bad for you." Colin took a deep, agonized breath. "This place is *evil.*"

Now, at last, she raised her head and looked at him. Willed him to understand the urgency. "I've got to stay. I've got to see this through."

Colin stared at her for the longest time. At last his shoulders slumped and he turned to look down Eyewell Lane, defeated. "But what is *this?*"

Gwynn could only shake her head. "I don't know. I don't *know.* Gwynn Chelton needed something from me. *Needs* something from me. That's why she left me the cottage. There's something I'm supposed to do here, Colin."

"But *what?*" His voice was rife with frustration.

"I don't know," she could only repeat. The conviction was growing, had been growing for some time now. "I don't understand yet. But I think I'll understand soon. Whatever it is—it's coming soon."

"Let me help, then."

Gwynn shrugged. "I don't know how you can. I don't know *if* you can."

Colin turned back to her, opened his mouth as though to speak, but no words came. He took one deep ragged breath, then another. His eyes—those eyes, the steely color of the November skies—studied her face; he might have been memorizing her features, her expression. It would be so easy, she thought despairingly, so easy. Just to throw it all up, to hurl herself into his arms and take the protection he was offering. To give up, to give in. She knew, though, that she couldn't. She owed something to her great-aunt, who had trusted her to figure out what she was supposed to do. She steeled her spine and the expression on her face.

Finally, he nodded. Once. "Well, there it is, then."

He took one last deep breath, then leaned forward to kiss her cheek. Then he climbed into the cab of the truck, started it, and drove off up Eyewell Lane. She watched the taillights until they disappeared over the rise and he was lost to her sight.

"Come on, then, Star," she said, fighting back tears. Star got to her feet and followed her up the steps and into the cottage.

49

IN THE DREAM that night she found the note on the kitchen counter.

Gwynn. Dovecote. T.

. . . the T incised into the paper by the pressure of the pen and the writer.

It was not the kind of note her father had sometimes left for her mother, letting her know where he was; it was not the kind of note her mother left when she'd gone down to the shops, to let the three of them, her children, know not to worry because they did not find her bustling in the kitchen.

It was a command. Gwynn recognized it as such. As always, she told herself she would not jump to his bidding, would not go, just because he ordered her to. And always, her mind veered immediately to the consequences, and immediately away again. Of course she would go. Tommy knew she would go. He counted on the power he still held over her. Counted on it, and relished it. Silently—for who was there to talk to, anyway?—she slipped the note into the pocket of her dress and went out into the back garden.

The roses were dead, the flower heads torn from their thorny branches and crushed underfoot. For a moment she stared, dumbstruck. Every single flower, every single bud. The varietals she had planted and tended so carefully over the past seven years, the bushes she had planted in place of the child she had lost. Petals—pink, red, white—torn apart and flung to the ground, and then ground into the mud, with enough anger to destroy any semblance of beauty. The work of burning fury, burning hatred.

She wanted to run, to flee out the side gate and down onto Eyewell Lane, back down into the village to her parents' house; but she knew what her father would say, what he had said the only other time she had gone home, crying, unable to bear life with her husband anymore. *You chose him. You made your bed.* And now Lucy was gone, off to the States with her American flyer husband, safe. It was the sacrifice she had made, to spare her little sister, who would never know. That one time, she had squared her shoulders against her father, stiffened her spine. She would not go back to her father again, would not abase herself.

Instead, she would go up into the wood. She passed through the gate, which stood open for her as if party to the invitation—the command. Gwynn wiped her sweaty hands on her dress as she made her way uphill through the trees to the clearing, where the dovecote hunched close to the ground, dark and menacing. There was something wrong, she thought; there was something missing. It took her several moments to realize: the doves. They were silent. She had never come up here when they had been silent. Always there had been that underlying muted conversation between the birds, the ruffling of feathers as light as a breath of air in the trees. There had never been silence. Something was wrong.

She forced herself to go on.

She nearly stumbled over the first bird.

It lay in the path, soft silver wings spread awkwardly, its beady red eye open and staring, its neck bent in an impossible way. A few steps further, two more, their necks broken, their small bodies tossed to the ground as so much trash. Near the closed door, another.

The silence was terrifying.

SHE COULDN'T OPEN the door. But she had to open the door.

She lifted a shaking hand and pushed, gently at first, and then more firmly. As the door slid inward across the dirt floor, the light traced a path on the rotted straw. She took a hesitant step into the dovecote, her eyes blind at first, but then slowly growing accustomed to the darkness.

"Tommy?" she called.

Her voice didn't echo, but seemed to reach out into the dark barn until it was swallowed whole.

No birds. Not even a rustle. She licked her lips nervously. "Tommy?" Her voice cracked.

She dared not step outside the pale box of light that fell from the door behind her; her shadow stretched forward into the darkness. The birds were dead. She knew that. All the birds were dead, all with their necks broken. To tread into the dark barn was to tread on their small, cooling bodies. She found herself shaking. Cold.

"Tommy?" This time her voice was a whisper.

Slowly she became aware of the slow creaking noise from the depths of the darkened barn. Steady, as though something were being moved gently by the wind. She closed her eyes, took a step forward, beyond the safe square of pale light on the floor. Her foot touched something soft—a dead dove—she stopped for only a moment, then slowly brushed the carcass aside with her shoe and took another step into the dim interior.

Slowly, slowly, her eyes grew used to the darkness. She saw the movement first, before her brain understood the shape. The dark form turned gently in the stillness, assuming a human outline, and she froze, paralyzed, watching the pale moon of a face turn to her. The eyes were dark holes, but it was the distended neck, the ligature biting into the flesh, the knot beneath the ear, the stretched rope leading up into the invisibility of the rafters overhead that told her everything she needed to know.

As the moment stretched, she registered it all: the overturned chair a few feet away from the place where his toes just barely scraped the ground, leaving trails in the straw and dirt below. And the creak, the slow even creak of the rope as Tommy's body turned away from her, and then slowly back.

GWYNN HAD NO idea how long she stood there in the dream. No idea how long she stood there in life. *No idea.* But she knew that Tommy, alive and now dead, would be with her forever. And that, perhaps, had been his intention.

She fingered the note in her pocket. *Gwynn. Dovecote. T.*

When she woke, she was still cold. She understood now that she'd never be warm.

50

IN THE MORNING Gwynn let Star out after she'd eaten. Star didn't mind the rear garden, but navigated her way through the brambles as through a maze, to do her business along the stone wall. Gwynn shut the door after her, knowing she'd come back when she was done, and would scratch gently at the door until let in again.

Gwynn was tired. The dreams had exhausted her; she had awakened in the small bedroom to find the duvet tangled around her legs and her skin clammy with sweat, her heart pounding as though she'd been running, as she had been, away from the dovecote, away from Gwynn Chelton's dead husband.

Just as she'd done, six years previous. How she'd run away from Richard's blood-suffused face, his distended neck, the noose that held him suspended just above the grass beneath the apple tree. Back to the house she had shared unhappily with him, to the telephone, to dial 911. *He's dead*, she had cried into the receiver, *I think he's dead. Please come.* The police had arrived, and the rescue, and Richard had indeed been dead. Except in her dreams, where he reappeared nightly for months. Hanging. Those months when she had described the dreams and the reality to a counselor who had done nothing for her except recommend tranquilizers, until she'd finally quit going.

Gwynn Chelton, she knew, had not had the benefit of counseling, nor of tranquilizers. Gwynn Chelton had probably braved her dreams alone for all those years. No wonder she had ended her days as an unhappy, unfriendly woman. Tommy Chelton could not have capped their bitter relationship any more effectively.

THE TELEPHONE RANG in the sitting room, and, somewhat unwillingly, she went out to answer it. Mary.

"Dad's missing," Mary said without greeting. Her voice shook, but then she controlled it. "Have you seen him?"

Martin. He wasn't supposed to be exerting himself. He wasn't supposed to be out. Mary had been, this week, looking into care homes, despite her father's objections. The visiting nurse was no longer security enough.

"I haven't," Gwynn said quickly, checking the time on the mantle clock. She had overslept again, and it was nearly ten. "How long has he been gone?"

"I don't know. Oh, I don't know!" For the first time in their acquaintance, Gwynn heard real fear in Mary Tennant's voice, coming to her plainly down the telephone line. "I told him I'd collect him this morning to take him to church—"

Church. Oh, Martin wouldn't enjoy that.

"—and I've just got here, but he's gone. There's no sign of him. The flat's empty."

"His bed?"

Mary sniffed. "It was slept in—it's not made." There was the sound of Mary blowing her nose. "His hat's gone. His stick, too. Oh, I knew I should have stayed last night. I knew it. He can't be trusted. He said he'd stay put, and he had the newspaper, and he'd be fine."

Martin's first night alone since coming home from the hospital. He'd been doing so well, Mary kept saying all last week. Gwynn suspected that that was because he knew what Mary had in store for him: a move out of his long-time home. He had been trying to avert it. *He's just not getting any younger,* Mary had said matter-of-factly. *He needs watching if we're going to keep him around.* Gwynn had wondered sadly whether he'd want to stay around much longer once he'd lost his independence, his home; but she'd said nothing. Martin was Mary's father, and, as much as Gwynn had come to love him, this was a family matter.

"Have you called anyone? Aside from me?"

Again the sniff. Could she be crying? Gwynn felt the slow fingers of fright: if Mary cried, the world must be coming to an end.

"Colin, and the police."

"What do the police have to say?" Somehow, with her knowledge of the police over the recent weeks, Gwynn had little faith in them.

"I had to remind them that Dad is past ninety, and that another old man had been attacked and killed outside the village recently. They weren't very helpful at first, but then I played the senility card."

"Your father's not senile!" Gwynn exclaimed, horrified. "Oh, Mary, no!"

"Of course he's not, but do you think they're going to stir themselves very quickly to find a man who's in his right mind? Better they think he's losing his faculties than think they're just talking to a hysterical woman." The anger helped Mary get back on track. "Look, can you go out and search along Eyewell Lane? He's come to you before—he might be headed in that direction again. And if you find him, call me on my mobile, will you?"

"Of course," Gwynn said. "I'll go now."

She hung up the phone and got her coat. It was then she remembered Star, doing her duty to dog and country, out in the brambles of the back garden. She went to the kitchen door, surprised she had not heard her scratching. But then, she'd been distracted.

Star wasn't on the stoop. Gwynn called for her, and whistled, but it didn't look as though the dog were in the garden at all, nowhere finding a path among the brambles. She must have got tired of waiting, Gwynn guessed, and taken herself out through the gate. Probably she'd meet Star prowling in the street. Perhaps this was the day Star finally decided to return to the farm? Gwynn really didn't have time to wait around. She closed the door, the urgency of finding Martin Scott overriding her feeling of unease at the missing dog.

No sign of Star out front, either. She *must* have headed off to the farm, Gwynn reasoned, and maybe it was about time. Still early on Sunday morning; Eyewell Lane was empty, The Stolen Child still buttoned up tight. Just as well—she couldn't bear the thought of Paul Stokes watching her, making up stories about her to spread in the village. Still, she wished Star were with her to act as bodyguard.

The sun was noncommittal, and the day had a sorry grayness to it that Gwynn had come to expect in this November, neither summer nor winter, but turning toward the colder end of the year. She buttoned her coat as she turned down toward the village, trying to think logically. If Martin Scott were walking from his house to hers, he'd have to be somewhere in between, and as he was ninety-odd, he didn't move quickly. But then again, when had he left his own house? She wished she'd thought to ask Mary if there had been signs he'd eaten breakfast, for that might have given a clue. Or if not that, what time Mary had left him the previous evening, safely tucked into his bed for the night.

Was that movement behind the curtain in The Stolen Child? Gwynn refused to look, but walked on resolutely, turning at the foot of the hill away from the harbor, toward Clear Street, the road that would take her north, in the direction of the head of the estuary and Martin Scott's house. How being housebound must have chafed at the old man—someone who valued his independence, someone who had slipped in and out behind his daughter's cautious back, justifying the deception by saying he *didn't want to worry her.* Now to be threatened with the care home, somewhere he'd be locked down tight. Of course he'd bust out of the joint just as soon as Mary wasn't looking. He'd had a scare, up there at the dovecote—hell, *Gwynn* had had a scare when he'd collapsed—and the doctor had said he could go at any time. But Martin Scott was not a man, she didn't think, who was willing to wait around for the Grim Reaper to come calling. He'd want to be out there, challenging death on his own terms.

She sighed, scanning the road ahead. Poor Mary. Gwynn so admired Martin, but surely he led his daughter the proverbial merry dance. It must be exhausting, loving her father so much Mary had to keep him alive at all costs—when the costs were not really any that her father cared to pay. Gwynn could sympathize with Mary's desperate attempts to keep her father in line, but even more, she could sympathize with Martin, who wanted to live while he was still alive. Fighting off the Reaper's scythe with his blackthorn stick.

While she was waiting for a Peugeot to pass, so that she could cross the road at the end of Eyewell Lane, she thought she heard a bark. One sharp bark. She whirled quickly, looking back up the road, but there was no sign of Star. Or of any dog. Gwynn frowned fiercely. She'd probably imagined it in her worry. Star was probably making her business-like dog way up to Trevelyan Court Farm by now. She'd be back to Gull Cottage whenever she felt like it. If ever she felt like it. Gwynn felt a sudden stab of loneliness at Star's desertion. She turned toward the estuary.

HAVING SEARCHED ALONG the green, passing the park bench where she had, such a short time before, strategized with Martin, Gwynn made it up to the little semi-detached house without seeing much but a passing Panda car. She knocked on the door, but no one answered. Looking over her shoulder furtively, she rattled the doorknob. Locked.

"Mary?" she called, knocking again. Pounding.

The police car slid into the drive. Gwynn ran to the door, where the police officer was rolling down the window.

"Are you family?" he asked. Constable Collier.

"Have you found him?" she demanded. "Martin. Have you found him yet?"

Collier peered at her. "Mrs. Forest, is it?"

"Yes, yes, but—Martin?"

Collier shook his head. "Not yet. Mrs. Tennant has gone to collect a recent photograph for us, so we can put the word out."

Gwynn's chest constricted. "I'll keep looking, then."

But where? Leaving Collier in the drive, she set off, back down the road this time, rather than by the estuary, her hands in her pockets, her shoulders hunched. The sky was gray, as it had been for as long as she could remember, and she found herself praying that it wouldn't rain. The thought of Martin out, perhaps collapsed, was bad enough, but the thought of a cold rain on his wrinkled skin, and he unable to get out of it, was unbearable.

51

GWYNN STOPPED IN at the shop, where Leah hadn't seen Martin, but where she was keeping an eye on the street. She hurried up Eyewell Lane to Gull Cottage, where she'd left the blue door unlocked in the hope that an exhausted Martin might take shelter there. On the way, she met a Rover which slowed to a stop. Mr. Simms leaned out the window.

"No sign of Martin Scott yet, then?" he called to her.

Gwynn took a step toward his car. "I've been from here to his cottage, both on the street and the estuary path. Nothing."

Mr. Simms pursed his lips. "I've seen the police patrols." He gestured over his shoulder. "I've been up to the farm. Bel's not seen anything up there."

The dog. Gwynn looked up sharply—in her searching, she'd forgotten all about the missing border collie. "Is Star up there with her?"

Simms frowned. "No. Isn't she with you?" His pale eyes raked the street. "We haven't seen her up there since you brought her up."

Where was she, then? Gwynn looked up the street, then down. Where was Martin? She chewed her lip anxiously. Perhaps dog and man were together? Star seemed to have a predilection for protecting people; maybe, in her inscrutable dog way, she had found Martin and was staying with him? It was a long shot, but it was something to hold on to. Something to hope for. Gwynn thought of the one short bark she had heard earlier. Star. Star trying to alert her?

But if Star knew Gwynn were close by, and if she needed her— Gwynn thought of the way she'd led her to Giles Trevelyan and caught her breath abruptly—surely Star would have come for her. Surely. She glanced up and down the street once again, her ears straining. She heard nothing save the smooth hum of the Rover's engine.

"I'll be heading down to the office, then," Mr. Simms said. "If you find out anything, let me know." He coughed slightly. "Martin Scott is a good man."

With that cryptic pronouncement, he released the handbrake and set off down toward the intersection.

THERE WAS NO sign that Martin had made it to Gull Cottage. Gwynn pushed open the front door and called his name. No answer, and her heart sank. She peered into the dining room, called up the stairs. Nothing. Then she became aware of the movement of cold air through the house, much as if it were breathing. She stopped, listening, her blood pulsing unnaturally loudly through her ears. She had felt this before.

Slowly she stepped into the sitting room. "Martin?" No sign of anyone here, but in the kitchen the door creaked as it swung gently.

Gwynn swallowed, staring at the door. "Martin?" she whispered, but she knew it wasn't Martin. She knew. She forced herself to move forward, one step, another step, another, until she paused with a palm pressed to the door. A breeze from the other side pushed the wood against her hand. She closed her eyes for a second, willing courage into her veins.

The door to the garden stood open, but the kitchen was empty.

Gwynn pushed into the narrow kitchen and reached a hand to close the door, but then stopped abruptly. Martin could be out there. In the garden, or—beyond.

Fumbling, she pulled open the cupboard door and reached the flashlight. Not there. She wrenched open the next door, and the next. No flashlight. And no time. The storm lantern, newly filled just the other day, stood on the counter. Next to it, the scrap of paper, yellowed with age, anchored to the countertop with the sugar bowl.

Gwynn. Dovecote. T.

52

HEEDLESS OF THE brambles, Gwynn ran through the garden. They'd grown up again, and it was as though hands reached for her, tried to hold her back. Ahead, the rotted gate. She grabbed it with her free hand and dragged it back so fiercely it broke from the top hinge and hung drunkenly.

On the ground just outside lay Martin's blackthorn. Gwynn tripped over it and nearly fell. The cry caught in her throat, and, checking the lantern flame, she bent quickly to retrieve the stick. He was here. Somewhere. Out here.

Not somewhere. She knew exactly where he had gone.

Then she heard the bark. Again, a single sharp yelp, just as it had been earlier.

Please, Star, she prayed. *Please be with him.*

But the note. The note on the counter, just as it had been in her dream. Just as it had been in Gwynn Chelton's reality. How had it come to be there? She had left it in the drawer of the bedside table, unwilling to touch it again, unwilling to unfold it and look at the incised command. Pieces of paper did not transport themselves from closed drawers in upstairs bedrooms to kitchen countertops. There had to be human agency involved. But what human agency? *Please,* she prayed again, incoherently. Why would Martin have brought it down? How would Martin have known it was there?

Again the bark. Seized with a sudden panic, she brandished the walking stick in front of her, the best weapon she was likely to find, and rushed up the hill into the wood.

THE CLEARING WAS deserted. Silent. Instinctively she looked for dead doves, birds with their necks twisted and broken, but there were none.

"Martin?" she called. Her voice wavered. "Star?"

No answer.

She paused, looking at the door, the way it hung crookedly. Was it closed more than it had been the last time she'd been up? She couldn't tell. She threw a glance over her shoulder: she should have brought someone. She should have called someone. She cursed herself now for not calling for help, cursed her flagging courage. It wasn't too late. If she ran back down to the cottage, called the police, called Mary—but no. What if Martin was in there, collapsed again, his life ticking away with the labored beating of his heart? And Star had barked. Star was here. Somewhere.

Swallowing, she moved toward the sagging building. The lantern was in one hand, the walking stick in the other. She shoved open the door with her shoulder. The blackthorn she held aloft, just in case.

"Martin?" she called again, stumbling into the soft thick air of the dovecote. In the wavering circle of light from the lantern, she could barely make out the empty boxes, the rotten hay on the floor. "Martin, it's me. Gwynn. Are you here?"

She sensed the movement first, and spun. When she saw the rope suspended from the overhead beam, she let out a small scream and dropped the blackthorn stick.

The door slammed shut behind her with the sound she recognized from her dreams.

"MARTIN'S NOT HERE."

Gwynn whirled. She lifted the lantern and saw, leaning against the door, Paul Stokes.

"Thought you'd come for that note." He had his arms crossed over his chest, his cigarette tucked in the corner of his mouth. He held a flashlight, the flashlight from the kitchen. He withdrew a packet of matches from a pocket. He lit his cigarette, shook out the match, and dropped it, then ground it into the dirt floor with the sole of his shoe. "Can't have that starting a fire." He blew smoke up toward the rafters.

Gwynn could not speak. She bent quickly to gather the walking stick, but, his foot flashing out like a snake, Stokes kicked it away.

"No, you don't. No weapons for you, cousin." He picked up the stick, hefted it in his beefy hand. "You could do someone an injury with this—even if it isn't a rock." His laugh was unpleasant. He moved closer, so close Gwynn took a step back. "And I'll have that, too." He wrested the wire handle of the lantern from her surprised hand.

"Where's Star?" she demanded. "Where's my dog?"

Now Stokes raised the light to her face, and she blinked, blinded.

"Least of your worries, I think. Here you are, feeling lonely and depressed, and all you can do is ask about a dumb animal?" Another laugh. "It's run off, Gwynn. Run off and left you. Like everyone leaves you."

Gwynn ignored this. "Star was up here. I heard her."

Stokes shrugged. "I dragged that damned dog up here. I knew you'd come looking for it. But it ran off when I needed the rope for—something else."

The noose. Hanging from the rafters behind her. Gwynn felt her neck prickle. She blinked against the blinding lantern light.

"You're crazy. If you wanted to frighten me, you've succeeded. But I'm done with your game." She made a move for the door, which she knew was somewhere behind him.

He thrust the blackthorn stick out at her knees, and she tripped and fell.

For one hysterical moment, she felt his weight on her—but that was Gwynn Chelton, that wasn't her; that was Tommy Chelton, not Stokes. That was then, this was now. Gwynn drew a deep breath, full of dust and the must of rotten straw. She coughed as she dragged herself to her hands and knees. "What do you want? I'll sign the damned paper, but it won't do you any good. No witnesses. Under duress."

The tip of the stick was under her chin, forcing her head up. "I want what's mine. I want the cottage."

Follow the money, Giles Trevelyan had said.

Stokes might not have simply waited for Gwynn Chelton to die, Giles Trevelyan had said.

Suddenly Gwynn was very afraid.

It was hard to breathe, and the blood was pounding in her ears again.

Be practical, she told herself. *Keep him talking. Stall for time.* Because, she realized, Star was out there. Everyone was looking for Martin, and someone would come across Star, and she would bring someone up here. If Gwynn could stall for enough time.

Slowly she got to her feet, the tip of the stick poking uncomfortably into the skin under her chin. She wiped the straw from her hands on her jeans, concentrating on tiny details. "How much money do you need?" she asked, trying to sound conversational. "I have plenty of money. I can help you."

His hand was rough on her arm, the same arm he had bruised on Bonfire Night, and she winced more in memory than fact. "Sit here and don't move."

Gwynn hadn't seen the rickety chair beneath the noose. Stokes forced her down onto it; the chair rocked, and the seat cracked, but it held. She gripped the sides with both hands to keep from shaking.

Stokes tucked the walking stick under his arm. He lifted the oil lantern and raised the wick; the light brightened and the lantern began to smoke. He glanced over at her and smiled. "Have to set the stage, as it were."

"Money," she replied quickly. "You need money, I have money. Let's talk."

Stokes shook his head. The lantern cast a larger circle of light, wavering in the dimness of the dovecote. He was not wearing the red windcheater today; probably, Gwynn thought nonsensically, that coat was far too easily recognizable.

"Too far along for that." He straightened. "You're too far along for that. Too depressed. Alone in a village where you know no one, can't talk to anyone about your split with your boyfriend."

"How much do you need?" she persisted desperately.

"Thinking too much on your husband, you have been," Stokes continued, sighting along the blackthorn as though along a gun barrel. "And the coincidence of your great-aunt's husband. How they both hanged themselves." He turned slowly to face her, still sighting along the stick. "Suicides run in families, you know. Something about suggestibility. How the impossible becomes possible if people near and dear to us do it first." His sudden jerking upward of the stick suggested the kick of a gun, but now he was pointing the stick at the noose, which swayed above Gwynn's head.

IN A MOMENT of screaming clarity she saw it. She saw the young Gwynn cast one last look at the swaying shadow that was Tommy Chelton, then, without checking for life, turn and walk out of the dovecote, careful to leave the door open.

Saw her walk slowly back to the cottage and seat herself in the wing-backed chair.

Saw her watch the hands of the clock on the bookcase move slowly: a quarter hour, a half, one hour, two.

Only then did she stand, go to the back garden, smudge some dirt on her hands and knees—and rush through the side gate and down to the road, crying for help. Gwynn Chelton's tears came easily. They were tears of relief.

"NO," SHE OBJECTED sharply.

"You know," Stokes kept on, "I felt so sorry for you, Gwynn. I offered to help you, to keep you company, to listen if you wanted to talk, but you kept pushing me away. I told people in the village how worried I was about you. I told people in the pub how depressed you seemed, and how you wouldn't let me help."

"No." She gripped the seat harder, measuring the distance between the chair and the door. She could make out the vague outline of light, where the door fit imperfectly, even closed.

"And the more you repeat something to people, the more they believe the truth of it."

"It won't do you any good," she protested, her voice rising. "My will—"

"You have no other relatives, Gwynn. I'm the only one left." Now he approached, leaned forward to look into her eyes. "And even if you've left everything you own to charity, the fact that you're a suicide supports my arguments about the balance of mind."

Stokes' eyes were black holes in his face. In her fear, she watched him fade into Tommy Chelton and then back to himself again.

"I'm not," she ground out, "a suicide."

Again he shrugged. He tapped the shaft of the stick against his other palm. "You will be." He glanced up at the rope swinging from the rafter, and smiled that sickly smile once more.

Gwynn's eyes flickered to the door and back. *Keep him talking*, she repeated to herself. *Stall for time. Star will come.* She desperately hoped that was true. Suddenly she started to her feet, but just as quickly, Stokes shoved her back onto the seat roughly.

"No, you don't," he said.

"You're crazy," she repeated. "I'm not depressed. I'm not suggestible. I'm not going to hang myself."

"It's not a problem." Stokes tapped the stick against his palm a few more times, measuring its heft; then he took a few steps to his left, looking up at the rope. "A little rap on the head, and I help you up." He turned, paced the other way, always keeping between her and the door. He frowned. "I don't think you'd be that heavy."

"No," she said again, more shrilly. She could not keep her voice under control. She ran her eyes over him, looking at his legs, wondering if she could trip him, knock him down, get past him. She had to take him by surprise. There had to be a way. "Even if you did that, an autopsy"—she blinked, took a breath—"an autopsy would show bruising. It would be investigated. And any investigation would lead right back to you."

Follow the money, Giles had said.

She froze.

"A rap on the head," she whispered.

"Like the one I—I mean, you—gave Trevelyan, who asked one question too many." He nodded. "You're a smart one, you are. But of course, remorse at your killing the old man is also weighing on your conscience. Adding to your depression. I tried to cover for you as best I could with the police, but they were too clever for me, and I had to tell them all about your violent tendencies. Sad." He sucked gently on the stub of his cigarette, and the end glowed red. "And if, when you kicked over the chair you stood on to reach the noose, it tipped your lantern into the hay—well, there wouldn't be much left of you to autopsy once the fire brigade put out the blaze. A devil of a time getting up here to put it out, they'll have."

Stokes had it all planned. He had thought about this for a long time. That was obvious. And she—she hadn't considered the possibility at all; who would? Gwynn closed her eyes. She knew who had: Giles Trevelyan. And then Colin. They had both warned her, and she'd disregarded them.

"Don't." She gripped the seat of the chair tighter, watching Stokes pace. The rope above her head swung gently in the movement of air beneath the bowed roof. How many feet to the door? Could she make it? She would have to dodge him and wrest open the latch—and then what? Outrun him, back through the wood to the cottage, back into the street. Her mind clicked over to that familiar clarity beyond panic. She was in better shape than he. She'd be faster, through the trees. Could she lock herself inside the cottage? Could she phone the police? *It's my cousin. He's trying to kill me. He's already killed our great-aunt.* It sounded far-fetched—would they believe her? Would they come?

She took a deep breath, waiting as he passed before her in his pacing, then leapt up and ran for it.

Stokes whirled and lurched, swinging the blackthorn. It caught her above the ear. The dimness exploded in shards of glitter, streaks of fire. For the second time, Gwynn found herself face down in the dirt, this time with a mouthful of blood. She lay there, winded, defeated.

Then she heard the dog bark.

Gwynn scrambled to her feet dizzily. Stokes' arm went around her throat, and he dragged her backward. She heard the stick clatter as he threw it aside. She couldn't see, and there was a roaring in her ears, growing louder. Louder. Desperately she grabbed his arm with both hands and twisted, then bit his wrist. He hit her again, and she staggered but remained on her feet. His arm tightened around her throat, and she kicked backward, as hard as she could. She felt her foot connect with the chair, and there was a sudden sharp smell of oil. Shards of glass crushed under her shoes.

She twisted again, but his grip was strong, and she felt the dizziness moving from her head along into her arms, her legs. No air. She coughed. Smoke? She couldn't tell. Behind her ear Stokes coughed sharply and swore, but he sounded far away and he was receding and it was getting warmer and smokier and she couldn't stand up much longer—

"Gwynn! Go—run!" The voice was high and reedy. Martin. She couldn't see him.

But she could smell the smoke more clearly now, the mustiness of it as it burned the moldy straw on the floor, creeping toward the empty wooden cages that lined the walls. One last effort: she thrust both elbows backward, then slammed her head back into Stokes' face. The arm around her throat loosened, and she fell away from him, toward the floor where flames rushed up at her face.

"Martin!" she croaked frantically, back into the whirling smoke.

"Go!" Martin shouted again. "I'm right behind you—go!"

Coughing, she crawled across the burning floor toward the door. She couldn't see it—with her head throbbing and her eyes streaming, she was confused, disoriented. Something tore at her ankle, and she fell sideways, rolling through the licking flames, and she felt her hair catch fire. She threw her hands up, beating at her scalp. She heard Stokes shout something—his grip tightened on her ankle and he was pulling her back where the flames grew higher, the sound of their ravenousness growing to a roar. She twisted, but could not break his grip.

"Martin!" she screamed.

Then there he was, Martin, encircled by flames, his white hair haloed in a rage of red and orange, his arms lifting the chair over his head and bringing it down again over Stokes' back. There was a grunt, and Gwynn was free, scrabbling away from Stokes and the flames, but not before she saw Martin Scott tumble back with the force of his swing, backward into the roar of the engulfing inferno.

53

HER HANDS WERE bandaged tightly, looking like nothing more than two large Q-tips at the ends of her arms. Gwynn held them up before her and examined them; she couldn't quite understand how they were attached. Her throat was raw and burning when she tried to speak; when she turned her head on the pillow, it made an odd scratchy sound. And the pain. Her head hurt. Her hands hurt. Her eyes hurt. Her lungs hurt, and she couldn't take a deep-enough breath.

A sound escaped her. It might have been a sob, had she been able to manage that much—but she couldn't. Not now. Not yet.

"Hospital," she heard someone say. "You're fine now. Safe."

She knew the voice from somewhere. She couldn't remember where.

"Trust me," the voice said, and then she knew who it was.

She closed her eyes again.

HE WAS STILL there when she opened them later—she had no idea how much later. Only a single light burned in the room, but low, away from her eyes, and she was grateful. He sat still and silent in a chair off to one side, his hands folded in his lap, his gray eyes steady on her. He looked worn, lines etched into his brow; his hair looked grayer than before, but it could have just been the effect of the low light.

He looks like hell, Martin had said that day beside the estuary.

Martin. She had a sudden vision of the old man in a nimbus of fire.

"Colin," she tried to say, but her voice only came out of her raw throat as a rasp. She tried again, forcing the sound so it hurt. "Colin."

Wordlessly he stood to pour her a small cup of water; this he held to her lips, and she took a gulp, surprised to realize that this was the thing she really needed.

"Slow," he said quietly. "Slow."

He set the cup on the bedside table and resumed his seat. Too far to reach. Almost too far to see.

"Martin," she ground out.

Colin looked away, off to the side, as though trying to conjure a vision. Of the old man? Then he lowered his eyes. "Gone."

Her eyes filled, and the tears burned. "He saved me." The chair, held over his head in his frail arms. His precarious balance. His falling away, into the blaze.

Colin shook his head. "You tried to save him. Star had to pull you away from the fire. You kept screaming, trying to get back in to him."

"Stokes," she said through the agonizing tears, which she couldn't stop. "He—"

"Dead, too." Colin cut her off, his voice steely.

The sobbing now wracked her, and only added to the pain in her chest, in her throat, in her head. But she couldn't control it. "He tried to kill me, Colin. He tried—" The rope was swinging over her head, the rope that recalled her husband's blood-suffused face, six years ago. "He wanted it to look like suicide. He wanted it to look like Richard's."

Colin's throat was working. She could see the movement of his Adam's apple in the dim light. "But Martin—"

"How did he even get there? How?" The old man, his stick left behind in the garden.

"No one knows, Gwynn."

"He hit Stokes with a chair. He knocked him away from me, told me to run. If it hadn't been for Martin, I'd be dead." Her hands useless, she covered her eyes with her arm, crying into the crook of her elbow. "Martin saved me. He couldn't save Gwynn Chelton, so he saved me."

"Did he?" Colin asked roughly. "Are you saved now, Gwynn?"

But she couldn't answer him, she was crying so hard.

HER DRUGGED NIGHT was filled with nightmares. She saw Martin engulfed in a ball of fire. She felt herself tumbling across the rough ground of the clearing in which the dovecote had stood, as the roof of the old building collapsed into flames behind her. Star was pulling at her jeans, claws dug into the ground. She heard herself screaming, and was shaken awake by a nurse.

"Hush, now," the woman soothed, adjusting the IV. "Hush. No need to scream like that, love. You're safe now. Safe."

Gwynn didn't feel safe. Not yet.

In the night, the one person who did not visit her was her great-aunt.

Epilogue
December

"IT'S COLD," GWYNN said, wrapping her arms around her chest and stomping her feet in her boots. Beside her, Star drew herself to attention and sat, her black nose in the air.

"Yes," Colin said. He stood nearby, at the edge of the clearing, but not close enough to touch. His own hands were shoved into his pockets. His gray eyes roved over the charred remains of the dovecote, fallen in on itself in a blackened heap. Then he lifted his gaze to the skeletal arms of the trees. The air was still acrid with the ghost of smoke.

Gwynn held the pale pink rose between her stiff scarred fingers, having stripped the thorns from its stem as she'd made her way along the woods path to the clearing. She lifted the flower to her nose now and breathed deep its delicate scent. Just the one rose, a surprise bloom in early December, amongst the brambles which no longer protected the cottage. Perhaps one rose was enough.

"I miss him," she whispered.

This time Colin did not speak, but only nodded.

"And her."

There was nothing here now, nothing of the fear and anger she'd felt on the first day, and on the last. No sound of cooing birds, no sobbing in the distance.

Slowly Gwynn stepped forward, knelt in the damp leaves, and laid the rose among them. As she knelt, her head bent, she felt the first snowflake touch her cheek. A second caught itself on her lashes and melted there.

Colin took a step nearer, reached out a hand. After a moment, she took it and rose stiffly from the ground. The pink bloom at her feet was a tiny blaze of color against the winter browns, a kind of reminder. She looked on it for a moment longer, then lifted her eyes.

Overhead, a single dove flew across the clearing under the gray sky and disappeared into the trees.

Star stood.

"Let's go back," Colin said. Gwynn nodded.

Anne Britting Oleson lives in the mountains of central Maine with her family. She is the author of two poetry chapbooks, *The Church of St. Materiana* (Moon Pie Press, 2007) and *The Beauty of It* (Sheltering Pines Press, 2010). She is a founding member of Simply Not Done, a women's reading, writing, and teaching cooperative.